Song Of The Snowman

Rhonda Tibbs

ISBN-10: 0982944101
ISBN-13: 978-0-9829441-0-3
See all of our books at:www.rtibbs.net

My deepest thanks to:

God, with whom all things are possible.

My husband, Michael, my hero, my champion, my best friend, for filling my world full of love and enriching my life in all ways possible, I couldn't have done any of this without you.

Thanks to my son, Doug, for saving my very first manuscript from being destroyed. You believed in my dream even when I gave up. You are a wonderful, loving son and a beautiful spirit.

Thanks to my sweet girls, Wendy and Georgie, for all your support and encouragement, for reading the roughest of drafts and making me feel like a real writer and being the daughters I always dreamed of.

Thanks to Bunsi, you magical little person! The world has never seen a better sister.

To my grandbabies—Adam, Ariana, Brooke, Auston, Kierston and baby Karlee. Pure joy!

chapter 1

BRIAN KNEW THAT the evening rush hour was the best time to shop for food. At six, the stores bustled with activity and a quiet, twelve-year-old boy walking the aisles drew little attention. Unlike him, most patrons paid cash for what they took away.

He was a proficient thief by age nine and had played the odds for three years now. He figured due punishment was just a matter of time. Living hand-to-mouth was tough, but the threat of being caught terrified him. Unfortunately, he was hungry and out of options.

He entered the corner grocery and immediately began to perspire. He shut off the voice of fear and his deft hands went to work one more time. The selected items quickly disappeared into the large Army jacket one of his mother's lovers had left behind.

In less than three minutes, he exited the store and spotted his young neighbor watching from across the street. She had witnessed his thievery through the big plate-glass window.

He swore softly and turned in the opposite direction. She hurried across the street and ran four blocks to catch up with his much longer strides. She was out of breath and in tears when she grabbed the back of his coat.

Brian shook her off and continued walking. "I told you to stay home, Stacy."

"I'm sorry," she said.

The sound of her voice breaking was more than he could tolerate. Brian turned to face the thin, delicate eight-year-old. She was tiny for her age — the top of her head barely reached his elbow. She looked up at him, her big brown eyes full of hurt and desperation. Her silky blonde, almost white hair shone under the streetlight, like a halo around her small head.

Everything in him wanted to scoop her up and hold her, but he couldn't give in right now. He had to be hard about this.

He sucked in a deep breath and spoke with as much conviction as he could muster. "Don't ever follow me again, understand?"

Stacy looked down at her feet and he knew his harsh words hurt her feelings, but she had to understand she couldn't come with him. If they caught him shoplifting, she would go to jail too.

"I'm sorry," she said.

"I don't want to hear that. You've got to promise not to do it again."

"I promise."

Brian reached down and took her little hand in his. Stacy smiled up at him and he knew he was forgiven.

They turned into the alley behind the apartment building they called home and climbed to the fourth floor. Five months ago, his mother's restless lifestyle brought them to this rundown suburb of Cleveland. He met Stacy the day he moved into the apartment opposite hers five months ago.

Since the death of her mother earlier that year, Stacy had been on her own. Her father went to work and sat in front of the television with a six-pack of beer every evening until shuffling off to bed. Until Brian came along, this routine left eight-year-old Stacy to make her way through the world alone.

Usually, Brian chose to be a loner — the shame of his life was easier to bear if he didn't have friends whose opinions mattered. He understood that getting involved with Stacy meant taking care of her, but one look in those big brown eyes left him no choice.

From the outside, it might appear that he gave more than he received, but Stacy's presence added new dimensions to his lonely existence. Sometimes, life didn't hurt so much. Loving her meant he was no longer rootless or expendable, but a beloved person with a real sense of purpose.

Brian followed Stacy into the apartment and saw her father staring at a game show on television with his dark, vacant eyes. Stacy approached her father, her small body a silhouette in front of the TV.

"I'm home, Daddy. Brian got something for supper. Are you hungry?"

"You're blocking the TV," her father said in a flat tone, never taking his eyes off the television.

Anger flashed in Brian and he turned to the kitchen before he did the wrong thing. Stacy followed him, watching eagerly as he pulled two cans of Spaghetti-O's, one can of tuna, a package of Ding-Dongs, and two cans of soda from the pockets of the jacket.

Stacy's stomach rumbled loudly and he grinned at her, "I guess we'd better hurry."

Stacy giggled. "You got orange soda this time."

"It was your turn."

He emptied both cans of the Spaghetti-O's into a pan then lit a burner on the small stove.

Stacy pulled a chair to the cabinets and climbed to reach the plates. "What's the tuna for?"

"Insurance," he said.

Stacy frowned. "What's that?"

"In case we need it later." Brian explained.

They devoured the meal in silence, relaxing as the canned food soothed their empty stomachs. Stacy's school provided a meager breakfast and lunch for disadvantaged students, but Brian hadn't eaten since yesterday.

After washing the dishes, he helped Stacy with her homework then did his own while she bathed. Once she was in bed, Brian usually read or sang to her. Tonight, he attempted to read Cinderella, but she interrupted with so many questions about the wicked stepmother he grew frustrated and stopped.

"If Daddy meets a woman like that can I come and live with you?"

"Stacy, I live with a woman like that." Brian closed the book and tossed it on the dresser. "I'm tired. Do you think you can go to sleep now?"

"Stay just a little while longer. I promise not to talk about mothers anymore."

He slumped down in the chair, propping his feet on the metal frame of her bed, and closed his eyes. "All right, just a little while."

"Sing Broken Wings for me."

"Why do you like that song so much? Let me sing something else for a change."

"You want me to keep asking questions or go to sleep?"

"Hey, you can do what you want. I'm staying until nine-thirty and that's it."

"Okay, Mr. Mean, sing My Girl then."

"Worse yet," he grumbled.

Stacy lowered her head and shrugged. "Go on home if you're tired of me."

Giving in, Brian began singing softly.

Brian left the warmth of Stacy's apartment and crossed the hall to his own. His mother was behind in the rent and the landlord turned off the steam heat last week. The rooms were nearly as cold as the January night. The electric company refused to provide service until she gave them a deposit and she hadn't gotten around to that before the latest binge took her away. Except for the light shining through bare windows from a streetlight, the nearly empty rooms were dark.

His mother hadn't been home in over two weeks, but that didn't concern him. She always returned. She would be worn out and disagreeable after her drunken bender, but he preferred her disappearances to the times she stayed home and drank herself stupid. She was an obnoxious drunk and usually made a spectacle of herself. Sometimes, she flew into a rage over something trivial and beat him with whatever was handy. The worst times were when she recounted her tales of hardship. Jean Burnette was someone who had many woes and the self-pity was endless. The list of people she blamed was long, but Brian suspected most of the pain was self-inflicted.

He had a father out there somewhere, but the only parent he knew well was her and she was a pathetic waste. Brian didn't try to love her anymore and stopped fighting the more dominant feelings of loathing and shame. He simply bided his time, waiting until he could legally be on his own.

He moved through the dark apartment to the bathroom and removed the previous day's laundry from the shower rod then turned on the hot water. Other than a roof over his head, hot water was the single luxury the apartment provided him. He stripped and bathed then washed the clothes worn that day and hung them on the shower rod to freeze-dry. He pulled on an old sweatshirt, worn jeans with a broken zipper, and the heavy socks stolen from Sears a few months ago as a birthday present to himself.

The frigid air immediately chilled him and he pulled a mound of old blankets from the living room closet and placed them in a corner of inside walls. He unrolled the blankets and crawled between their protective layers.

Lying there, waiting for warmth and sleep, Brian thought of Stacy yearning for the mother she lost. Her mother's sudden death had stolen her father's spirit and left Stacy a virtual orphan. There were a few pictures in her apartment that reflected better times. Stacy's mother looked like someone you could miss. Her misty brown eyes were just like Stacy's and she had a genuine smile that made him feel warm. He didn't understand why God would take a woman like that and allow his mother to continue living.

He was sleeping deeply when Stacy jumped on him the next morning.

"Wake up! It's snowing!"

He grunted and pushed her away, "Too early. Go home."

"No. Get up. I want to build a snowman before we go to school."

"Nobody's stopping you. Go ahead. I'll see it later."

"Please?"

She stuck a small hand under the blankets and her icy fingers landed on his warm neck.

"Quit!"

"C'mon. Please?"

"All right, go back to your house before you freeze. I'll be there as soon as I get dressed."

One hour later, Brian watched as she placed two blue rhinestone buttons on the snowman's face.

"Now, he has eyes like yours," she said. She picked up a red hat and held out her arms.

"Lift me, so I can put this on his head."

They stood back to admire their work and she cocked her head to one side, frowning.

"He still needs ears."

Brian looked down at her and grinned, "Ears?"

"My mom always put ears on." Stacy scooped up a handful of snow. "She said if you put ears on your snowman, he'll hear the music of the angels and sing songs to you."

"Hey, Burnette! Are you playing with little girls?"

Brian looked across the street and recognized a boy from gym class.

"I heard they might call school off," the boy said as he approached, "at least I hope so, don't you?"

Brian shrugged nonchalantly, thinking of the warmth the school provided. "We might as well get it over with."

They watched Stacy shape the second ear.

"This your sister?"

He shook his head and stuck his cold hands into the front pockets of his jeans.

Stacy stood back from her work and looked to him for approval. Brian nodded and smiled.

"I like it."

Stacy smiled proudly and he filed the image of her sweet face in the section of his heart that he shared with no one else. Whenever he needed a shot of encouragement, he would carefully reach in and lift the image to the light of day.

. The boy from gym class laughed, drawing Brian's attention and ending the moment. "I never saw ears on a snowman. It looks weird."

Brian looked to him. "Did somebody ask your opinion?"

The boy seemed surprised at the sharp question then grew angry and stepped toward him. Brian tensed, waiting for him to make the first move. He had no interest in fighting, but if it came to that, he wouldn't bother being fair. Clashes with his mother's boyfriends taught him the benefits of toughness a long time ago.

The other boy eyed him for a minute then backed off. "I'd better go — I don't want to be late."

Brian hurried to the doorstep for their books. If they didn't hurry, Stacy would miss the free breakfast. Stacy took her books from his hand and looked back to their creation.

"I wish Mom was here."

Brian patted her shoulder. "Let's go."

Brian walked her to school then started toward his own. His thoughts wandered until he reached a pawnshop and paused to stare through the window. In the back of the cluttered display, was one hope he allowed himself to keep.

Last summer, one of Jean's boyfriends taught him a few chords on a battered six-string. While this boyfriend and Jean entertained themselves in the next room, Brian played that old box guitar and fell in love with music. The only problem was he didn't know how to earn forty-five dollars to pay for the acoustic guitar at the back of the display window.

Brian found Stacy waiting in front of his apartment door after school. The red hat from the snowman was in her hand and her face gleamed with tears.

"What's wrong?"

She sniffed and wiped her nose on her sleeve. "Daddy made me take it off."

"Why?"

"It's Mommy's. He's really mad at me. He told me to get out."

"Selfish asshole," Brian muttered. He opened his apartment door and turned back to her.

"I didn't mean to do it," she said. "I don't even know this stupid hat."

He put his books on the windowsill inside the living room and looked back, surprised to find her still in the doorway, wiping new tears from her face. She looked incredibly small and vulnerable standing there. It hurt to know she didn't have anyone that cared about her. He walked back, knelt in front of her, and put his arms around her.

"You didn't do anything wrong."

She began to cry and he lifted her in his arms, carrying her to a spot beneath the bare windows where a patch of sunlight warmed the floor. He didn't know any soothing words or phrases. He didn't believe in the tooth fairy, Santa Claus, or the Easter Bunny and he certainly didn't believe things were going to get better for this girl anytime soon. So, he held her and sang.

"I think your voice is as great as the song of the snowman, Brian," she said. "God must talk through you too."

He sighed and leaned against the cold wall. "God doesn't know where to find me — I move too much."

Stacy cuddled closer and he began another song. She laid her head on his chest and closed her eyes.

Brian sang three songs and she fell asleep in his arms. While he laid her carefully on his bed of blankets, Mrs. Clifford — the apartment manager — stepped inside the flat and looked around at the bareness. Her relaxed expression changed to a scowl and Brian stood straight, his face a mask of fear. Mrs. Clifford was a giant African-American woman with a tough exterior and a reputation for strict rules. His mother had probably broken every rule there was several times over.

She looked at him and her expression softened. "Was that you singing?"

"Yes, Ma'am. I'm sorry if I was too loud."

She waved a hand in the air. "No need to apologize. I enjoyed listening to you." She stepped closer, glanced down at Stacy, and placed one of her big hands on his shoulder. "Would you like to make some money?"

"Yes, Ma'am," he said quickly. It was a relief to know she wasn't there to throw him out on the street. He turned to cover Stacy with the top blankets.

"If you shovel the sidewalks and driveway for me, I'll pay you fifteen dollars. You'll find the shovel in the basement."

Brian worked for three hours, driven by the return of fierce, demanding hunger. While he worked, he made plans for the fifteen dollars. Stacy came out several times, but the temperature had dropped below twenty and he chased her back inside. His bare hands were past numb and each step sent pain shooting up his legs.

He was putting away the snow shovel when he saw a guitar case standing at one corner of the workbench. Careful to be quiet, he lay the case down, and opened it slowly. The polished wood of a six-string guitar gleamed in the fluorescent light. Brian ran red fingertips over the strings and started to pull it from the case. Hearing footsteps on the stairs behind him, he hurried to close the top, but wasn't quick enough. Mrs. Clifford saw him.

"That guitar belonged to my son," she said quietly. "He doesn't want it anymore, but I've put off selling it."

"Would you consider letting me work for it, Mrs. Clifford? I promise to work hard."

A smile lit her dark brown face and she stepped closer, touching his cheek tenderly. "You can have it. I don't want your money though."

Brian's untrusting nature set off a dozen alarms in his brain. Still, he wanted that guitar and was willing to barter. "What?"

"Come to church with me. Come sing in our choir."

Relieved, Brian's face spread into a broad smile. "Can I bring Stacy?"

"Of course. Come on now, I've got a nice supper fixed for you kids."

Like her, the congregation at Mrs. Clifford's Baptist church was of African-American descent, but they embraced the two white children with a warm, generous spirit. Brian learned the joy of gospel music and believed he actually felt the presence of God's love for the first time. For them, he sang from the heart.

For a few months, Mrs. Clifford taught him music on her small upright piano, but decided his talents exceeded her knowledge and convinced another member of the congregation, a music teacher at the community college, to take Brian as a student. Within six months, Brian was a church phenomenon, both as a budding musician and singer.

Stacy attended church with him every Sunday and was his biggest fan. Brian received an abundance of odd jobs from people in the church. Between the money he made and Mrs. Clifford's kindness, he and Stacy never went hungry anymore. He bought a few clothes for them at the Salvation Army store. He continued to do odd jobs for Mrs. Clifford, but refused to accept any money from her.

His mother rarely paid any attention to the events in his life and he was certain she knew nothing about his association with Mrs. Clifford and the church. In truth, his mother never bothered with him unless she wanted something. If she spoke to him at all, she generally screamed, occasionally coupling the outburst with physical assault.

Brian learned years ago that the way to cope with her was to stay out of sight as much as possible. Though he yearned to scream back, his options weren't the best so he usually listened to her rant in steely silence, promising himself that some day he would never listen to her again.

One cold Saturday night in late November, just after his thirteenth birthday, the resolve to keep his feelings under control shattered. When Jean came home, he was sitting in the only chair in the living room, a chair he had found in the alley and dragged up the three flights of stairs by himself, playing the guitar. She staggered across the room to where he sat playing the guitar.

"Get up."

Brian was lost in the music and didn't automatically comply with the demand. Jean yanked the guitar from his hands and hammered it against the plaster wall. The wooden box shattered and a thousand pieces rained down on the bare floor. Without thinking first, Brian sprang forward and knocked her flat on her back. He watched her drunken struggle to rise and his heart pounded hard against his ribs. He clenched and unclenched his fists, wanting to strike back, hating her. She managed to gain her feet and glared at him.

"I'm going to beat the hell out of you!"

"No, you won't," he said.

Jean's eyes narrowed to slits as she examined him. "Well, well junior, when did you get such big balls? Has the righteous Mrs. Clifford been sharing more than the light of God with you?"

"You're disgusting." He didn't bother to keep the contempt from his voice.

"You rotten little son-of-a-bitch. You've been nothing but misery for me since the day you were conceived. Get out of my sight!"

Brian grabbed his coat and slammed the door behind him. He ran down three flights of stairs and punched the front door open. He ran down the street until he reached the high school track where he continued to run. He was too angry to count laps and his lungs filled with fire. Still, he ran. He developed cramps in his calves and thighs and had to limp along. The only solution that ever worked on these occasions was to run until he dropped.

He returned to the apartment building a little after nine. He had no desire to go upstairs, so he settled for the now familiar work area in the basement. He pulled an old paperback from his coat pocket, hoping to stay up long enough to find his mother asleep when he went back upstairs. If he found her awake, he would return here and sleep in one of the old musty chairs.

He settled into a chair and opened the book, but didn't get past the first paragraph when he heard a woman scream. He ran up to the first floor and Mrs. Clifford streaked by with a blanket in her hands. She went out the front door, screaming for someone to call an ambulance.

Brian followed and saw the source of her panic immediately. Stacy's father lay on the sidewalk in front of the apartment building. Dark red blood oozed from his mouth, ears, and nose. Brian stepped closer and peered into his open eyes. Oddly, they looked the same in death as they did staring at the television night after night.

"Daddy!" Stacy screamed from an open fourth floor window — the one her father leapt from only minutes before. Brian immediately went to his friend.

Neighbors came out to stare at the scene. An ambulance arrived and they loaded the lifeless body onto a stretcher. Stacy clung desperately to Brian while the police determined there was no relative to take her.

A kind-faced officer tried to take her hand and Stacy locked her arms around Brian's neck. He wrapped his arms around her and hugged her quickly before two policemen pried her grip from him.

She screamed his name repeatedly as one man carried her to the police car. He followed helplessly, watching the officer struggle to get the petite girl in the car.

Brian shoved his useless hands into the front pockets of his jeans as the car pulled away. Stacy lunged at the back window and screamed his name one last time before they turned the corner.

He wanted to run after that car and pull her out, but knew there were no choices for them.

Mrs. Clifford put her arm around his shoulder. "Come on inside. I'll make you some hot cocoa."

"Thanks, Mrs. Clifford, maybe some other time." He couldn't be with anyone right now. He climbed to the fourth floor, refusing to look at Stacy's apartment door. He quickly stepped inside his own apartment and found he lacked the strength to go another step. He pressed his back against the inside of the door and slid to the floor, drawing his knees to his chest.

Although his throat ached and his eyes burned, he had lost the ability to cry a long time ago. Stacy had been the only person to ever love him and he let her down when she needed him most. He should have taken her hand one last time and ran, deep into the shadows of the night, before they had the opportunity to take her away. He owed her that much for loving him.

Fifteen feet away, Jean snorted and rolled over in bed. Brian peered through the darkness at the sleeping lump in the bed and understood, more than at any other time in his life, how alone he was.

chapter 2

BRIAN DIDN'T PAY particular attention to the unfamiliar car parked in front of the apartment building. It was late afternoon and he was tired from mowing lawns all day in the hot sun. His mind was on a cool shower and food. As he topped the stairs, he heard voices coming from inside the apartment and his spirits sank. The voices meant his mother had returned after nearly a month's absence. Worse, she wasn't alone.

He opened the door and immediately recognized the signs of his mother packing. Her things were tossed all over the bedroom floor and her bed. A man sitting on the windowsill took a deep drag from a cigarette. He flicked the ashes on the floor then examined Brian with yellow tinted eyes. Jean threw more clothes from her closet to the bed and saw him standing there.

"Pack your stuff, Brian. We're going to Pittsburgh."

Brian ignored her and went to the refrigerator for a soda. He could feel the man's jaundiced eyes watching him and anger stirred in him.

Jean stepped out of the closet and looked into the living room. "Did you hear me?"

"Yeah, Mom."

"Do it now."

"Hey, if he wants to stay let him," Yellow-eyes said. "He looks old enough to fend for himself."

"Look, I told you, he's only fourteen. He's just tall for his age. I don't want the law looking for me because I abandoned my kid."

Brian grunted and popped the top on a soda.

Jean pointed a finger at him. "Shut-up and pack."

Brian didn't want to go. At first after Stacy's father took that fatal leap a year and a half ago, living here had been the hardest challenge of his life. Every time he stepped from his apartment, the door across the hall reminded him that she was gone. It felt like her father took her out the window with him. But he had never stayed anywhere this long before. He had built a life here and was thriving. There were people who cared about him here, especially Mrs. Clifford.

Mrs. Clifford had inquired about Stacy, but the answer wasn't much comfort. Stacy was in a foster home somewhere in Ohio and Mrs. Clifford was still trying to locate her. If he left now, he would probably never see her again.

"I want to stay here," he said.

Jean whirled on him. "Get packed."

"No, I'm staying."

Jean crossed to him, leaned close to his face. "You are fourteen, a minor, either you pack your things and get in the car with me or I will turn you over to the juvenile authorities."

He laughed shortly. "Juvenile authorities?"

She slapped him across the mouth. "Shut up and do what I say."

Stunned, he took a step backward. "I hate you."

"So what's new? Get...packed...now."

Brian took a shower, tossed his few belongings in a trash bag, and placed his new guitar in its case. His mother and her new friend were entwined in the pile of clothes on her bed, moaning and grunting their way through a sexual encounter.

Brian had seen and heard it all before, each time it sickened him more. He hurried to the front door. "I'll be downstairs when you're ready."

Mrs. Clifford her eyes widened in alarm when she saw his face and what he carried.

"My mother says we're leaving. I wanted to tell you good-bye and thank you for everything."

"She ready to go right now?"

"No, Ma'am. She's not finished packing."

"Then come inside, Brian. I know you worked hard all day. You must be starving."

Brian knew better than to argue with her about the subject of food. For two years, he had fought Mrs. Clifford's efforts to mother him. In the end, she was stronger. He placed his things by the door and followed her to the spotlessly clean kitchen.

She placed a plate of cold ham, potato salad, sliced tomatoes, and a tall glass of milk in front of him. For dessert, there was moist chocolate cake. While he ate, she instructed him.

"Find yourself a church right away. There are good hearts to be found wherever you go, trust me. Write to me when you are settled and give me your address. I'll keep looking for little Stacy and as soon as I know anything, I'll let you know. Now, let me address some envelopes for you to take along."

Brian just swallowed his last bite of cake when he heard his mother shout his name from the street below. He rose and glanced outside then back to Mrs. Clifford, who was suddenly teary eyed.

"I guess I'd better go."

He hurried to the living room and picked up his bag of clothes and guitar.

"You're more than welcome to stay with me, Brian," she said.

Brian knew his mother too well. She might leave him a thousand times, but he didn't dare leave her. However distorted, even Jean Burnette had rules.

He smiled sadly. "Thank you for offering, but she'd never let me do that."

Mrs. Clifford wrapped her big arms around him and hugged him tenderly. The sensation hurt so much he thought something was wrong inside his body.

His mother appeared in the doorway behind them and rapped on the door. "Get your ass in the car, Brian."

He paused at the door, looking back to Mrs. Clifford. Tears streaked down her sweet face, salting the wound her hug had created.

He climbed in the backseat of yellow-eyes' old Buick and made a space for himself among the debris. The car smelled like old booze, cigarettes, and other less attractive odors. He rolled the window down for fresh air and swallowed the lump in his throat one more time as they pulled away from the curb. Mrs. Clifford stood on the porch waving goodbye and his heart developed a new lesion.

Somewhere down the road, rain fell from the sky in thick bursts and Brian willed himself to sleep. To stay awake meant listening as his mother recited her sorrow one more time. Tonight she was telling yellow-eyes how cruel Brian's father had been. This was her favorite subject and each time she found new twists to add to the description of his father's sinister nature.

Brian didn't remember much about his father, Max Burnette. He'd only been five the last time they saw each other. Over the years, he had gleaned a little information from the Tales of Woe, by Jean Burnette, but the pieces made a rough sketch. His father never loved her — who could? His father cared only about raising his child — in these tales, Brian was always referred to as the son, child, or baby. Brian's father was tall, handsome, and she loved him passionately, but her love was never enough. He was a cold-hearted, selfish man who ignored her passion.

Around two the next morning, Yellow-eyes discovered Jean had finished the bottle of cheap booze and a fierce, drunken argument ensued. He jerked the car to the side of the road and ordered them out.

Still half asleep, Brian found himself standing at the side of the road in a freezing rain with a mother so intoxicated she couldn't walk. She cursed and fought him as he half-carried, half-dragged her away from the road. He dropped her under a tree and sank to his knees to catch his breath. She dug her hands into the mud and grass then flung it at him.

Brian gasped as it hit him. "Stop it!"

"I hated you the moment you were conceived and every day I have to look at your damned face I hate you even more."

Brian grabbed a fistful of mud and flung it back at her. The muck landed in her face and mouth, momentarily silencing her.

She spit the muck out and threw some more, "You selfish son-of-a-bitch. You never loved me, Michael," she cried.

Brian stared hard and didn't feel the cold rain pelting him. "Who's Michael?"

She rolled up into a ball and began to scream and cry, pounding the sloppy ground with a fist. "I hate you. I hate you."

Brian walked back to the roadside, picked up her suitcase, his trash bag, and guitar case. He settled in to wait for daylight and his mother's charming, semi-sober personality, wondering who Michael was.

If Jean remembered the incident the next morning, she kept it to herself and Brian knew better than to ask. They got a ride in the back of a pick-up to a truck stop and Jean surprised him by calling her parents for help. She bought a cup of coffee and a pack of cigarettes with her last three dollars. Brian paid for his own breakfast.

Monday, 18th 2017

Dear Margaret:

Hope this finds you well and enjoying your new home.

Rose and I are being blessed this year by having all the kids and most of the grandkids here over the holidays.

Don and his daughter are here now and Friday she goes home and his son comes. Then he and the boy go home on the 28th.

Margie comes in from Washington DC on the 20th, thinh she leaves On Jan 6.

John comes on the 23rd, his 2 girls come on the 24th and Dawn comes in on the 30th. Not sure when the girls go back but John and Dawn will be here until Jan 6.

Don and Mary were here about a month agofor a week.

I always say, my most faverot part of the holliday is the lights——————————————————

The tail lights on the cars as all of them go home.

OF course you know that is not true but I say it anyway.

Don't think this package is going to be a tridition, but we thought you may enjoy my attempt at making *TWABACKEN* (Spelling)

I know they are not as good a *You and Mom* use to make but they are as close as I can come.

Merry Christmas & Happy New Years.

Les & Rose

He knew little about her relatives. Jean had nothing good to say about any of them. Until they pulled into the parking lot of the truck stop, he didn't even know what state they lived in. The plates on their late model New Yorker said Connecticut.

Part of him tried to hope they would be loving, kindhearted grandparents. As usual, reality was a pain in the neck. He should have known any parent capable of raising a woman like his mother probably wouldn't have much going for them.

Grandmother Davies popped out of the passenger seat. She looked perfect for the part of a grandmother — until she came close and he saw the frost in her eyes. She looked them over quickly and recoiled in disgust.

"Where in the world have you two been? Rolling in the mud?"

"It's a long story, Mother," Jean said.

"Well, get inside and clean up or you're not getting in the New Yorker," said her father.

Brian caught the tall man's eye and he was certain he was looking directly at a shark reincarnated. He remembered reading that sharks had dull eyes. Everything about this old man looked hard and bitter. Jean headed inside the truck stop, but Brian hesitated.

Grandma breathed out loudly and threw up her hands. "What are you waiting for?"

"My clothes got wet in the rain last night. I don't have anything dry to put on."

"Oh, for heaven's sake, go on and change. I don't care if it is wet."

The drive to their home took most of the day and the morning after this heartfelt rescue, Brian came down with a cold and was in bed with a fever when he heard his mother announce she needed a pack of cigarettes. Earlier in the day, he had witnessed the hungry look in her eyes and knew what was coming. He tossed the blankets aside and followed her out the front door.

"Don't follow me, Brian."

"Don't leave me here."

"I'm not leaving. I'm just going out for a pack of cigarettes."

"Mom, please, don't do this to me."

Jean glanced his way and for once they connected on equal ground.

"It won't be for long."

She turned quickly and hurried down the street. He was standing there in his bare feet with only jeans and a T-shirt on or he would have tagged right behind her.

He sat on the lowest step of his grandparent's home and contemplated his fate until chills had his teeth rattling. He went to the small bedroom that had once belonged to Jean's brother and closed the door. His guitar rested in a corner and he cradled it in his arms for a while, but the smooth wood yielded little comfort until he began to play.

The next morning Brian was still in bed, stalling about getting up for the day, when his grandmother's voice seeped through the thin walls. He'd been awake for half an hour and needed to pee, but this meant starting another day in this hateful house, where minutes felt like hours. His room was close to the kitchen and he heard every word his grandmother said on the phone to his aunt.

"Well, I knew this was coming. All she wanted was someplace to dump the boy. He's getting in her way now that he's so big and all. What am I going to do Caroline? He's like a wild animal — who knows what he's capable of." Grandma paused for a dramatic sigh. "I can't believe she'd just leave the little mongrel here."

Brian covered his head with a pillow and screamed.

Living with Jean was always difficult, but at least she was gone most of the time. Her family's brand of cold and cruel was modified for his personal discomfort and there was no escape. Twenty-four hours a day, every day was hell.

Jean's older brother, Matthew, was a successful tax lawyer with a wife named Caroline and two strapping boys close to Brian's age. Aunt Caroline was his Grandmother's confidant and fed the old lady's meanness with relish. Together they had enough venom to stun him at least ten times a day. The worst day of the week was Sunday, when Uncle Matt, Aunt Caroline and their three children came for dinner.

"Any word from Jean this week?" Aunt Caroline asked.

Grandma Davies rolled her eyes. "Of course not. She's not about to jeopardize her freedom."

Brian shifted in his seat and caught his cousin, Matt junior eyeing him smugly. His first instinct was to punch junior's face, but he reined in the impulse and swallowed a wad of anger the size of his fist.

"Freedom?" Caroline sneered. "Do you think that's what she calls it, Mother? Goodness, when I was a girl they called her kind something else."

Brian's face flushed crimson and he rose, drawing Uncle Matt's attention. "You're not excused, Brian."

"I'm not hungry," he mumbled, hurrying to his room.

"Honestly, how rude," Grandma muttered. "What in the world am I going to do with that?"

"Turn him over to the authorities, Mother," Uncle Matt said.

"I can't. Father Reagan expects me to at least try my best. I am the boy's grandmother after all."

"Yes, but Mother, he's not exactly the kind of grandchild you're used to."

Brian closed the door to his bedroom and stretched out on the bed. His instincts screamed for him to get off the bed, open the front door and run.

He moved to the floor, in a corner of the room farthest from their voices, and covered his ears with his hands to help suppress the urge. He never hated his mother more.

"I don't know what you're going on about, Marie." This was his grandfather's voice now and the deeper sound suspended Brian's plummet to depression. "She will return for the little bastard then disappear for another ten years. By the time she feels like coming around again you'll be dead."

His grandmother fled the dining table and streaked down the hall shrieking. The day was ruined and Brian was to blame.

Grandmother Davies and Caroline loved to discuss the life they imagined his mother led — usually in front of him. They discussed her life of squalor and disorder created by drugs, alcohol, and whoring. Brian didn't argue. There was a lot of truth to what they said. Still, he hated hearing them discuss it in their holier-than-thou manner.

He was under constant supervision. They expected him to steal alcohol from the liquor cabinet or help himself to his grandparents' prescription medications. If anyone missed any money, Brian was suspect. If there was an unusual call registered on the phone bill, he was immediately questioned. Grandfather Davies kept a record of the mileage on the car. Brian didn't know how to drive and wasn't about to try. He was certain they were looking for a way to get rid of him and breaking the law would feed into their plans.

Grandmother Davies took him to her doctor for a thorough check-up. She accompanied Brian into the room to consult with the doctor.

"Poor child, he's been through so much. We're not sure what his mother may have allowed him to do or what's been done to him, if you know what I mean."

The doctor and Grandma looked to him and Brian's stomach twisted into a knot.

The doctor nodded. "I can examine him thoroughly if you're concerned about molestation."

Brian shook his head. "You're not doing that to me."

Grandma raised a clutched fist to her mouth and appeared to lose her balance. The doctor took her arm and guided her to a chair.

"This is so hard," she murmured.

The doctor patted her shoulder and looked at Brian. "I understand."

"Just a virtual stranger, dumped on our doorstep," the old fake continued.

Brian watched as she fed on the attention like a parasite. In the end, the doctor led her into another room and she received most of the attention.

Aunt Caroline took him shopping for "decent" clothes and directed a barber to cut his thick, dark hair to a respectable length. In the end, Brian looked like a neater, more handsome, imitation of his male cousins.

He didn't go to the glorified academy his cousins attended. His uncle enrolled him in a Catholic high school known for strict guidelines and punishments, in Uncle Matt's words, "The best place for a wild boy with no moral background."

Though Brian tried to ignore their malice, the considerable rage his mother had created intensified each day he survived in the Connecticut prison with her hateful family. When he wasn't at school, he stayed in his room, either reading or playing the guitar, dreaming of the day he could walk away from the madness dealt him in lieu of a childhood.

He considered running away but his commitment to survival ran deep. He refused to forsake his future to escape the affliction of being born to Jean Burnette. He would do his time until the day he was old enough to tell them all to kiss his ass.

In early November, he was in his usual place on his bed, practicing the guitar when he heard loud voices in the living room. He opened the bedroom door and found his mother coming down the hall.

"Get your stuff, Brian."

He wasted no time. In fifteen minutes, Jean commuted his sentence and they were leaving Connecticut behind. He never thought he would be glad to see her, but today he could have hugged his mother in joy and he might have, if for one moment he believed she wouldn't turn on him.

She was in possession of a clean, late model car and though there was alcohol on her breath she seemed relatively sober. She cracked a window and lit a cigarette then turned the radio down. Brian knew all the signals — she was preparing for a serious talk. He silently prayed it wouldn't be another long dissertation on her miserable life.

"Brian, I know I always told you I wouldn't get married again after what I went through with your father, but I did. His name is Harlan Oakes and he's got this little place about seventy miles west of Philly. You can't imagine how good it feels to find someone who really cares about me."

At many points in his life, Brian might have laughed at her oversight. Tonight, he just didn't care. He was too overjoyed at leaving Connecticut to pay much attention to his mother's selfish patter. He fell asleep as she talked and slept deeply until she shook him awake.

"Wake up. We've got to talk."

Brian sat up and looked around at the dawning of a new day. She had pulled the car over to the side of the road at the top of a hill. The sleepy valley below them slumbered in blanket of fog. He rubbed the sleep from his eyes and Jean shook him.

"Wake up, damn it. This is important."

"Quit! I'm awake."

"You have to promise to keep your mouth shut around Harlan. I don't want you mouthing off about the mistakes you think I've made."

Brian ran a hand through his hair and sighed. "I won't talk to him any-more than I did any of the rest."

Jean slapped him hard and his head bounced off the window.

"That's just the kind of sarcasm I don't need from you. This is important. You can do one thing for me, can't you?"

Brian gritted his teeth and took a deep breath. "Sure."

The small town of Benton Hills, Pennsylvania looked just fine. He saw clean streets and neat homes. Jean pulled into the driveway of a small, white frame house with black shutters and cut the engine. A short, stocky man opened the door and offered a big smile.

"That's Harlan. I mean it Brian, be nice or I'll kick your ass from here to kingdom come."

Brian opened his door slowly and while his mother hugged Harlan he took the opportunity to look around the neighborhood. The little house sat on a small rise with a neat lawn, a row of hedges and there were neighbors on either side. Across the street a boy close to his age emerged, jumped on a bike and waved cheerfully.

"Brian," his mother called. "Come meet your stepfather."

Harlan Oakes had a thousand-watt smile. He beamed at Brian and wouldn't accept just a handshake. He hugged Brian with enthusiasm.

"What a pleasure to finally meet you. You're mom can't stop talking about you. She's so proud."

Brian looked over Harlan's shoulder at his mother who lit a cigarette and ignored him.

"Well, let's go on in the house," Harlan said. "We can bring your stuff in later. I've got a big surprise ready."

He followed Harlan and his mother inside and it took a minute for his eyes to adjust to the interior light.

His mother laughed. "Oh hell, Harlan, don't you think you over did it a bit?"

"What do you mean?"

"Brian doesn't like a big fuss. We usually spend his birthdays quietly."

They turned and watched him, but the reason didn't register. He stared at the room full of balloons, streamers, and Happy Birthday banner with a blank expression.

Harlan patted him on the back and laughed heartily. "Guess you're not awake yet, huh? When your mom told me this was your fifteenth birthday I insisted we bring you home where you belong — no matter how much your Grandma wanted to keep you."

Jean yawned and walked toward the kitchen. "I hope you made some coffee."

Not once, in fifteen years, had he received so much as a birthday card from his mother. Until Harlan mentioned his birthday, he didn't know the decorations were for him.

"So, Brian, what do you want to eat? I love to cook up a big breakfast on Sunday morning, just ask your Mom."

Brian wanted to believe in miracles. He ached to let go of the need to guard against his mother's madness. For a little while that day, Harlan Oakes came close to making that miracle a reality. Fifteen was a fine birthday.

chapter 3

BRIAN SWUNG HIS old Volkswagen into the driveway and parked behind a late model Cadillac and shook his head. "This must be a mistake."

He had lived with his mother and Harlan for nearly two years now and knew the streets of Benton well. The residents of the finer homes on the better side of town — referred to as Snob Hill by the lowlier residents — never ordered pizza. He flicked a lighter and verified this was the correct address. After slipping on his work hat — a baseball cap with a slice of rubber pizza glued to the bill — he headed for the door.

He pushed the doorbell and heard the sounds of a party, but no one came, so he knocked loudly. Finally, the door swung open and one of the cheerleaders from school eyed him coolly.

"Someone ordered pizza," he said.

She turned and shouted, "Pizza boy!"

Amanda Cutler came to the door with her wallet and a group of friends. While the others took the boxes, she pulled a strand of blond hair over one shoulder and smiled coyly.

"How much do I owe you, Brian?"

The use of his name surprised him. They had several classes together last year as sophomores, but never spoke. Pretty, popular, and rich Amanda Cutler of the Snob Hill Cutlers was someone he never gave any thought to. He figured it was an even exchange, since they had so little in common.

"How much?" She snapped her fingers in his face, drawing the attention of the other girls. Their burst of giggling embarrassed him.

"Thirty-eight seventy-four," he said.

Amanda handed over two twenties and he started to make change. Amanda slipped a hand over his and squeezed gently.

"Keep it," she said.

He considered handing the dollar and twenty-six cents back, but didn't feel like talking to this girl anymore than he had to, so he turned and started down the walk.

"Wait," Amanda said.

He turned and she bumped into him. The odor of sweet perfume and alcohol drifted on the night air. She giggled and her loose fitting shirt fell open, providing an unimpeded view of her naked breasts. She didn't bother to pull the shirt tighter and smiled at him.

"Would you like to come inside for a while, Brian?"

Recovering, he pointed to the stupid hat on his head. "I'm working."

"Why don't you come by after you finish?" She reached out, brushing his face with cool fingertips, and smiled. "All my friends will be gone then."

He backed up a step, shaking his head. "I can't."

She laughed and closed the gap between them, her body nearly touching his now.

"Why not? Do you have a date with that Jo Fields?"

"Yeah, and thanks to your generous tip, I can afford to take her somewhere really special."

He hurried away and left her standing in the driveway of her privileged, safe house on the hill, with her flirtatious "I can have anything I want" smile fading.

He finished working at eleven and immediately tossed the detested hat and work shirt into the back of the car. His best friend, Mark, was already seated inside and smoking a cigarette. Brian pulled on a sweatshirt and slid into the driver's seat.

"Give me one," he said.

Mark handed over a Marlboro. "I thought you quit."

"I'm starting again," he responded shortly.

Mark fiddled with the stereo, trying to tune in his favorite station, "Rough night?"

Brian shrugged and took a deep drag on the cigarette. He rolled the window down, put the car into gear, and the little car sped out of the parking lot.

"I saw Jo around seven," Mark said. "She was on her way to the movies with Sherri and Barb. She said her mom went to her grandmas for the night and Kenny's having a party. She wants you to meet her at the house when you get off work."

"Is his band going to be there?"

"Who cares, Brian? It's not like they're in your league."

"I've never heard them play. They might be better than me."

Mark found the radio station he wanted and sat back, "Yeah, right, they can dream."

Since getting his car, Brian spent every Thursday after school driving seventy miles to Philadelphia where he explored the blues clubs he could get into and hanging around after closing to witness the private sessions. Most of the musicians were a minimum of twenty to thirty years older than he and their style didn't appeal to most of the kids his age, but he couldn't get enough.

One slow night, the bass player at a bar on the south side struck up a conversation and they talked music for the next few Thursdays. Eventually, the bass player asked him to play. He ran to the car and brought back his box guitar and played a Willy Dixon tune garnering praise and was invited to sit in on an impromptu session with the band.

Each week he drove to Philadelphia and waited until the wee hours for the opportunity to sit in with the talented group. He had taken Mark along a few times, but preferred to go alone. The education the musicians passed on was priceless.

There were about thirty cars parked in the yard of his girlfriend, Jo Fields', house on the outskirts of town. Inside the detached garage, a noisy band struggled to stay in time together and Mark grimaced.

"How can anybody call that music?"

Brian found space to park and they made their way through the crowd, talking to people they knew from school, until his girlfriend's brother, Kenny, spotted them.

"Hey, Brian, did you bring your guitar?"

"No, I just got off work. I'm looking for Jo."

Kenny held out an electric guitar. "Take mine,"

He held up his hands. "Honest, I'm just looking for Jo."

"Just play one song. Show these guys what you can do. I've been bragging forever." He grinned. "Trust me, when Jo hears real music, she'll find you."

Brian slipped the guitar strap over his shoulder, strummed a little, flexed his fingers then tuned all six strings. After playing a few bars, he turned to the waiting members of the band and asked what they wanted to play. They settled on a popular tune and he turned around to face the crowd.

He recognized most of the faces staring back, but didn't really know them. He attended school with them, competed in sports with them, but he had few friends in this room and most of them didn't know about his passion for music.

He stepped up to the battered microphone and closed his eyes. After the second bar, the crowd of rowdy teenagers fell silent. The only sounds came from his voice and the guitar in his hands. He stopped abruptly and looked at the band then the other kids. His heart pounded and his face flushed a deep crimson.

"Damn," said a voice at the back of the room.

"I'm sorry," he murmured, lifting the guitar strap over his head.

The captain of the football team stepped forward and stopped him. "Hey, don't quit, Burnette."

There was a chorus of agreement, so he shrugged and whipped out the introduction to a song just as his girlfriend, Jo, came through a side door and caught his eye. She smiled proudly and the love in her light gray eyes caressed his soul.

The rest of the band never joined in and when he finished everyone patted him on the back and told him how wonderful he was. Jo waited impatiently on the sidelines, but not for long. Finally, she grabbed his hand and led him outside, behind the old garage, where he locked his arms around her slender body and they kissed passionately. They hadn't seen much of each other in two weeks. Jo's mother had grounded her for coming in twenty minutes late after their last date.

"Let's go," Jo said, breathlessly.

"Go where? There are people all over the place."

"Tree house." She giggled and started running. "I know nobody's up there. I locked the door earlier."

He didn't get home until three in the morning. He parked in the drive and saw the kitchen light was on and he groaned knowing Harlan was in there, waiting with yet another lecture. This had been a long day and Jo had nearly finished him off up in the tree house. All he wanted was sleep.

Brian sat at the kitchen table and listened for over half an hour to Harlan's long-winded speech about coming in at a decent time, getting enough rest, etc. He attempted to appear alert and respectful because he knew Harlan meant well.

Of all the men in his mother's life, Harlan took first prize for most complete denial of her true nature. When she disappeared for days at a time, Harlan actually believed she went to see her mother or any of the other assorted lies she came up with. He also believed her drinking problem was under control, but Brian didn't judge him too harshly for that. After all, she was never completely sober, so Harlan probably didn't know the difference.

Jean had finally learned the value of some discretion when it came to affairs with other men — until she was on a binge, then she didn't care. Brian heard rumors about his mother's behavior around town. He knew Harlan probably heard the same rumors, but the man chose to pretend ignorance — for reasons Brian couldn't fathom. To him, she was worthless and Harlan Oakes deserved better.

Harlan's lecture wound down and Brian apologized. He promised to come home earlier in the future, knowing he probably couldn't keep his word since he had agreed to join Kenny's band. He descended the basement stairs to his bedroom and was sleeping moments after his head hit the pillow.

Brian didn't mention the encounter with Amanda Cutler to Jo. Jo had a fiery, jealous nature and if she heard about Amanda, it would be unpleasant at best. On Monday morning, while he rooted through his school locker for books Jo stood next to him, talking about one of her friends who might be pregnant, Amanda dropped by to stir up a hornet's nest.

"Brian, I'm so glad I ran into you." She laid a pretty, well-manicured hand on his arm. "It was nice seeing you Saturday night. I wish you could have stayed longer."

She winked at him and walked the other way. Jo turned on him with fire in her eyes, a look he knew well. Jo's greatest fault was a very jealous and possessive nature when it came to him.

"Don't make mountains out of molehills," he said, closing his locker. "I just delivered pizza."

"Next time she orders a pizza, you better call me. I'll deliver it for you — no charge."

The garage band was so out of tune, offbeat, and completely undisciplined, Brian found it nearly impossible to play with them. Finally, he discussed the problems with Kenny which ended in a heated debate and Brian walked out. The band took a vote and Kenny agreed to step aside to let Brian guide them.

They practiced until they could come in together and stay in time then practiced some more. He worked hardest with Kenny, trying to help him achieve the dream of being lead guitar, but soon realized Kenny would never rise above the level of mediocrity. Kenny got them play dates and at first the events were torture. Brian's only release was to make the drive into Philadelphia every Thursday and play with real musicians.

On the Sunday before Thanksgiving, after four hours of sleep, Brian stumbled up the basement stairs for breakfast. He wasn't hungry, or entirely awake, but he was present for Harlan's sake. He poured a cup of coffee and sat opposite his mother.

"How nice of you to grace us with your presence," his mother said.

He rubbed his tired eyes and reached for the sugar. Jean lit a cigarette and inhaled deeply, eyeing him.

"Your grandmother called yesterday and invited us to Connecticut for Thanksgiving," she said.

Harlan placed a plate of bacon on the table and Brian picked up a piece of toast, sensing the axe was about to fall.

"We're leaving Wednesday morning, so don't plan on going to school," she said.

He stared at her in disbelief — toast poised halfway between the plate and his mouth.

Her eyebrows arched in surprise. "What?"

"You expect me to go?"

A mean smile played at her lips. "Of course, we're family."

Brian tossed the piece of toast on his plate and sat back. Jean sighed and crushed out her cigarette. Harlan refilled her cup with steaming coffee and took a seat at the end of the rectangular table.

"Your grandmother specifically asked that you come, Brian," Harlan said, "She hasn't seen you in so long."

Brian shot a glance at Harlan then looked right back at his mother and folded his arms over his chest. "I want to spend Thanksgiving with Jo."

"Well, that's all right." Harlan patted his arm. "Bring her along. We have plenty of room."

Jean yawned and opened the entertainment section of the Sunday paper. Brian got the hint — what they said, or did, was of little consequence to her.

"I'll ask," he said, turning back to his food. "If she can't go, I'm staying here."

"You're going. I don't want to hear anymore about it," Jean said.

"We don't get to do much as a family," Harlan said. "Just this one time, Brian, let's give it our all."

Brian looked at his stepfather in unqualified disbelief. They never, ever, did anything as a family, other than eat together on Sunday morning, argue and pretend. They weren't a family. They lived under the same roof, anything beyond that was in Harlan's imagination.

He turned back to his mother. "Would you put the paper down and talk to me?"

"Don't push me this morning, Junior. I'm not in the mood."

"Fine," he snapped, reacting to her favorite slur. He got to his feet and shoved the chair under the table. "Junior won't push you. Junior wouldn't want to make Mommy mad. Junior will just keep pretending he gives a damn about what you think."

Jean dropped the paper and looked up, her eyes narrowing. "Shut up."

"I hate this bullshit! Your family doesn't give a damn whether they see me anymore than you do. I'm not going, damn it!"

"Go to your room!"

Brian laughed at the absurdity and turned away just as Jean threw her coffee cup at him. The hot liquid scalded his neck, upper chest and arm. Without thinking, he overturned the kitchen table and it landed on Harlan.

"Stop! Both of you stop!" Harlan cried, struggling to get out from under dishes, food, and wet newspaper.

Jean jumped to her feet and raised her hand. Brian stepped close and she froze. He recognized the startled look in her eyes. He had seen it plenty of times. He might as well be a ghost.

The resounding crack of her hand made his ears ring and his head snapped to the right.

"Get out of my sight!"

After driving in a blind rage for nearly an hour, he stopped at a payphone to call Jo. He postponed their afternoon movie date and drove to a park on the outskirts of town. He knew he wouldn't run into anyone there. The day was cold and rainy, so he could wait in peace for the welt on his face to diminish, while he thought of an explanation for Jo. The burns from the scalding coffee were primarily on his arm and chest and hidden by clothing. Unfortunately, the mark left by his mother's hand was going to be obvious. Jo would take one look at him and ask questions.

He sat on a damp picnic table in the pavilion and watched the rain pelt the lake. It had been a while since Jean last hit him. He closed his eyes and took a deep breath then exhaled slowly. He came so close to punching her this morning and that was the last thing he needed to do. One more year and he would be free.

"Brian?" Jo called softly.

He cringed and refused to turn. "Why are you here, Jo? I said I'd be over later."

She moved around the picnic table, edging closer. "I was worried. You sounded weird on the phone."

"I told you — I had an argument with my mother. I needed some time to think." He said quietly, keeping his gaze on the lake. Right now, he didn't want to see her loving eyes.

Jo eyed the darkening bruise on his face and the burns on his neck. "Do you have any cigarettes?"

Brian pulled out a pack, removed two cigarettes and lit hers first. Jo sat down next to him on the picnic table, placing her hand on his thigh. They smoked in silence for awhile, watching the rain dance across the choppy water.

"I called your house. Harlan said you and your Mom got in an argument about Thanksgiving. He said you don't want to go with them to see your mother's family."

"That's right," he said tightly. "I want to stay here with you."

"I can't spend Thanksgiving with you."

"Why not?"

"I have to go to my father's. It's his turn. I have to go or he'll get weird about the child support again."

"Damn it."

"I know, I know. You might as well go with your Mom and Harlan."

"I'd rather sit in my room and hit myself in the forehead with a hammer all weekend." He paused and kicked at the bench with his heel. "We're talking hours in a car with my Mother and Harlan, think about it."

"So, sleep all the way. That's what I do when I'm locked in the car with my family."

"It's more than being locked in the car," he began then stopped, sighing heavily.

Jo reached up and gently pushed a lock of hair from his forehead. His thick hair seemed to have a mind of its own. Despite the best efforts, that particular lock often fell down on his forehead.

"You're so handsome," she said.

He looked at her and grinned. "You're so blind."

Jo smiled and touched his cheek. "There are the dimples I love."

"I wish I could get rid of them. They're just like my mother's."

"Well, the only way to get rid of them is to never smile and that would be a sin."

He laughed shortly, "Sin?"

Jo gave him a little shove. "Your smile lights up your whole face. The world sees what a great soul you have."

Brian wrapped an arm around her and they sat in silence for a while.

"I don't want you to spend the holiday alone," she said finally.

He grunted and pulled his arm from her shoulder, "Wouldn't be the first time."

Jo was quiet for a moment then sighed. "I know you hate it when I ask questions, so I'd really appreciate it if you didn't make comments like that."

He glanced at her then reached into his pocket and pulled out another cigarette.

"Okay, Brian, I guess we'll just sit here and talk about everything except your black eye, the burns on your neck and God forbid the past." She leaned close, kissing his cheek. "I love you," she said.

When he finally came home late that evening, Jean was in bed and Harlan was watching television in the living room. Brian sat nearby, popping the top on a soda can.

"Harlan, I'm sorry about this morning."

Harlan smiled tiredly. "It's all right. You got the worst of that mess son."

Brian wondered what it would take for this man to get angry and how much Harlan forfeited in order to justify his mother's behavior. He forced his eyes to the television, but couldn't concentrate. He decided to take a shower and spend the rest of the evening in his room.

Jo talked him into going to Connecticut for the Thanksgiving he knew he would hate. Harlan couldn't have been happier and Jean still wasn't speaking, which was fine with Brian. At four-thirty Wednesday morning, Harlan woke Brian and his mother and kept them moving until they were in the car, off on their Thanksgiving sojourn.

They pulled into his grandparents' driveway and Jean's mother opened the front door, waving and smiling gaily at them. She hugged her daughter briefly and smiled appropriately when introduced to Harlan. Brian stood back, watching his white-haired grandmother pretend. When she hugged him, the pretense of affection made him nauseous.

"Look at you, Brian, so tall and handsome, my goodness," the white-haired fake, cooed, using her most phony voice.

Jean's younger sister and her family arrived the day before, taking over their mother's house. The remaining bedroom was for Jean and Harlan. Brian was to stay the night across town with Uncle Matthew and Aunt Caroline.

His grandfather had died earlier that year from a heart attack, but Brian still expected to see the bitter old man sitting in his chair, giving him that icy stare.

Placing himself in this pretense of family made no sense. He shouldn't have given in to Jo. The reason he kept his mouth shut right now was Harlan. The man was too gentle for his own good.

Everyone went to his uncle's home for dinner Wednesday evening. After dinner, Matt Jr. eased him away to show off his 1965 Mustang. Matt told Brian to hop in for a short drive, assuring him they would return immediately.

Matt took him to a clearing in the woods, behind the high school, where a group of kids were gathered. He introduced Brian to his girlfriend and school friends. Someone offered a beer to Brian, but he declined since he never touched alcohol. He sat on the bumper of the car, smoking cigarettes, making small talk with strangers, while Matt and his girlfriend rocked the Mustang from the back seat.

All those staying at Grandma Davies were gone when he and Matt returned. Aunt Caroline waited impatiently at the front door. Though Aunt Caroline chastised her son for leaving without telling anyone, she slid enough nasty looks at Brian to tell him how she really felt — he was a bad influence. Matt listened politely then told Brian to follow him upstairs and he would show him where he would be sleeping. Aunt Caroline stopped them.

"Wait, Brian. I have something of your mother's. I meant to give it to her when she was here, but it completely slipped my mind. I'm going to give it to you right now, before I forget again."

She opened a small cabinet door in the entrance hallway, pulled out an old shoebox and offered it to him with a smile. "She left this here years ago — back when she first left your father. I'm sure it's important to her."

Brian took the box and followed Matt upstairs. Matt showed him the guestroom and bath then left him alone. Brian closed the door, turned on the bedside lamp, slipped off his shoes and sat on the bed with the box in his lap. He debated whether to look inside, even put the box down a few times only to pick it up again.

This was just a shoebox. There couldn't be anything too important inside. On the other hand, this was not his property. In the end, he snooped.

Inside he found old photographs, a few letters, torn halves of concert tickets, and the marriage license of his mother and Maximilian Burnette.

One of the photographs was of his mother and two males. Her long, sunny blond hair was parted down the middle and she wore short-shorts, halter-top, and a pretty smile. He examined the faces of the males and recognized neither. One was a big man with dark eyes, hair, and full beard. The other looked like a teenager. Turning it over he saw the year was 1967 — the year he was born. Two names were listed — Max and Michael. Max was the father he hadn't seen in twelve years. He vaguely remembered sitting on Max's lap and laying his head against Max's big chest. He turned the photo over again to examine the face of the bigger man again when something caught his eye.

He stood quickly and turned on the overhead light, scrutinizing the face of the younger guy — the one with bright blue eyes — and his breath caught in his throat. It wasn't difficult to recognize the familiar face. He turned the photo over and reread the names — "Max and Michael."

Brian laid the photograph on the bed and went back to the box. He found a few more photographs of this Michael from 1967. On the back of one picture, he finally got a last name — O'Mara.

At the bottom of the box was a letter from an attorney, informing Jean that Max Burnette was seeking complete custody of their child, Brian Michael Burnette. This was the first time Brian knew he had a middle name.

Brian folded the letter carefully and placed it in his pocket along with the group photo. He wasn't sure what he was going to do yet, but he wasn't handing all evidence of the truth over to his mother, some of it belonged to him.

He lay awake, long into the night, staring at the ceiling and thinking. All those years he wondered why no one cared for him were finished. Max hadn't abandoned him after all. He had attempted to keep him safe, away from the pain of Jean's company and failed, but his mother's selfish nature ruled that he belonged to her — not out of love for her child, but to keep her rights intact.

So many things suddenly made sense, but none more than the moments Jean stared at him, as if seeing a ghost and anger filled her eyes. More important was that time in the freezing rain when she called him Michael.

His resemblance to the bright-eyed teenager was uncanny and he finally knew why she resented him so much. Michael O'Mara was the cold-hearted lover she spoke of when she recounted her tales of woe. This guy was the source of all her misery, not Max Burnette.

He fell asleep with one last, bitter thought on his mind. Michael O'Mara was his father — a father who never cared the way Max had.

Jean took the box from his hands and immediately turned on her sister-in-law.

"You bitch! You knew exactly what you were doing when you gave that to him. She turned to Harlan. "We're leaving."

There was an ugly scene between Jean, her mother, and Aunt Caroline at the door, continuing down the driveway, and to the car. Brian jumped in the back seat, grateful to be leaving again. He looked back and saw Aunt Caroline smile as they pulled away.

Jean turned in the front seat and faced him. "So, did you get a good look through my personal things?"

"Yes," he said, still looking out the window.

"I suppose that was Caroline's goal — for you to pry into my private pain."

Brian met her eyes directly. "Why didn't you tell me about my father?"

"Tell you what?"

He sighed loudly and turned back to the window. "I'm not going to let you turn this into one of your games."

"You better tell me what you think you know right now."

He turned to face her. "Let's just say I finally understand why you call me Junior."

Jean laughed shortly. "I suppose you have illusions of looking him up. It would be best to forget that idea. He could care less. It was over between us the day he found out about you. He never loved anyone but himself."

Brian glared hard and this time Jean turned away and poured a cup of coffee. The scent of whiskey drifted through the car and Brian cracked a window. Harlan said nothing, but Brian could see his knuckles were white from gripping the steering wheel too tightly.

Jean leafed through the old shoebox. Suddenly, she turned in the seat and swatted Brian on the head with the lid waking him from sleep.

"Give that picture back you bastard. It's my property!"

Brian sat up and squinted at her. Still half asleep, he didn't comprehend what his mother was saying.

"I should've given you away when my family wanted me to. Having you was the worst mistake of my life. At best, you should've been an abortion."

She climbed to her knees and took a swing at his head with her fist, catching the left temple. Harlan grabbed her blouse and tossed her back in the seat.

"Sit down!"

The unprecedented action stunned Jean into submission.

"I want you to stop talking to him that way, right now. I won't listen to it anymore. You should be grateful you have such a decent kid. From what I've seen and heard these past two days, I know you didn't do anything to deserve it."

"Harlan, you don't know what my life's been like."

"Trust me, I'm beginning to get the picture."

Once they were home, Brian went to his room in the basement and listened to them argue for hours. If Harlan threw them out, he wasn't going with his mother. Even if it meant sleeping in his car until he could do better, he wasn't leaving Jo.

When he came upstairs the next morning, he saw a suitcase by the back door and thought it meant they were out on the street, but Harlan had given Jean an ultimatum — "get help or get out" and for once in her life, Jean was about to do the right thing.

chapter 4

BRIAN KNOCKED ON the front door of Jo's home just after lunch. Her mother and Kenny were working and her younger siblings were at her father's. No one was around. They would have a rare afternoon of privacy.

She didn't answer right away so he sat on the wrought iron railing and studied his tennis shoes patiently. He thought he heard soft footsteps inside and peered through the screen into the darkness of the house.

"Jo?"

There was still no sound and he lifted his head, exposing his face to the warmth of an unusually warm day. It was a perfect day, clear sky, the smell of wood burning in someone's fireplace, an unseasonably warm breeze.

"Hi, handsome," Jo said.

Brian smiled. "It took you long enough."

"You were early." She pushed the screen door open. "Come inside."

"I thought you wanted me to take you somewhere."

She smiled and took his hand. "Come on, we'll take each other."

Jo loved touching him and exploring the level of his need without remorse. She guided his shy hands to the most intimate places and taught him the secrets of her own body, but had always insisted they stop short of actual intercourse.

He usually left those sessions swearing he wouldn't do it again, but she could always coax him into returning without much effort. Sometimes she apologized for teasing him to the point of pain, but most of the time his discomfort seemed to give her a sense of power. He was in love with her and that love meant more than anything to him. He waited patiently for her.

Plenty of girls seemed willing to relieve the ache for him, but he never took the bait. He focused his attention on Jo. Most of their friends were sexually active and everyone, including Jo's mother, figured he and Jo were too.

Brian followed her up the ladder to the tree house and watched silently as she unbuttoned her blouse. She took his hands and placed one on each of her breasts. He was breathing a little harder when she tossed the shirt aside and smiled.

"What are we doing, Jo?"

"You know exactly what we're doing."

"I don't have anything for protection," he said.

"We don't need anything. I've been on the pill for six weeks."

He blinked a few times and stepped back. "Why didn't you tell me?"

She smiled and moved closer. "We can make love and not worry, Brian."

Brian leaned forward and kissed her soft, full mouth. He helped her finish undressing then she watched as he stripped in a hurry. This was the first time either of them saw the other completely naked. Brian wrapped his arms around her and she ran her hands over his arms and back, making him shiver.

She gently pulled him down to an open sleeping bag and straddled his stomach. Brian looked up at her in obvious anticipation and she smiled sweetly and pushed at a lock of hair on his forehead then carefully brushed his eyelashes with a fingertip.

"Your eyes and the sky are the same color," she said. "I can't believe your mine."

Brian watched her, struggling with the desire to take charge and risk going home frustrated again.

"You know, there are lots of girls in school who would love to be your girlfriend. Little do they know you're probably the only boy in the twelfth grade who's still a virgin."

He couldn't concentrate on what she was saying and ran his hands up her thighs, sliding up her buttocks to her back then forward to her breasts. Jo sat back and let him caress her with abandon for a while. Suddenly, she pushed his hands away, looked him in the eye and lowered herself onto him.

Brian tilted his head back, taking in a quick sudden breath. He gripped her waist and pushed deeper. Jo moaned softly and rocked harder, taking him over the edge. A moment later, she followed him to a shared rapture.

chapter 5

THE ALARM RANG for the third time. Brian punched the button then stumbled to the bathroom after only a few hours of sleep. He and Jo had driven to Philadelphia last night and spent a few hours in a motel on the way back. Since that day in the tree house, her sexual appetite seemed insatiable.

A quick shower woke him up a bit. He wiped the fog from the mirror and squinted at his appearance, then grimaced at the sight of his beard. He had to shave much too often for an eighteen-year old.

Harlan's heavy footsteps passed overhead and he opened the basement door.

"Brian? You up?"

"I just got out of the shower."

"Well, come on. I made a special breakfast for your birthday."

He smiled. He had so much to be grateful for and a great deal stemmed from the faithful character of his stepfather.

"Thanks, Harlan. I'll be there in a minute."

Harlan's commitment to his marriage had allowed Brian the freedom to explore what was left of his childhood and during the past three years a sense of security had slipped in and relaxed his tightly wound defenses. The need for self-preservation was still intact, but anger and fear took a backseat to the more age-appropriate processes.

Though his mother was sober, her personality hadn't improved. Sometimes, the ghost-look clouded her eyes and the sharpness of her words still cut him. He no longer believed he would outgrow the impact of her cruelty. He was in the home stretch now, but when he left he would carry the scars with him.

He played in Kenny's band at least three nights a week now and didn't deliver pizzas anymore. The guitar was so familiar to his hands that without it, he felt half-dressed. The same deft fingers that served him well as a young thief now picked out notes with perfection. His voice had deepened, but otherwise the gift was intact and he reached an extended range with confidence.

Sometimes, he saw people watching from the audience. They sat or stood perfectly still and unblinking while a song vibrated up his throat, out his mouth, and into the microphone. At first, the affect was so disconcerting he lost his place. Mistakes like that taught him not to connect too closely with any one person in the audience. He concentrated on the song and kept a general eye on the crowd.

Music might be his first love, but Jo Fields was on equal ground. The love radiating from her light gray eyes had a profound impact on him. The sweet promise of her embrace cured the loneliness in him. Like little Stacy so long ago, he was lovable in Jo's eyes. In her arms, he was whole. Music and Jo brought him complete contentment.

chapter 6

EVERY NIGHT OF spring break, the band played a local bar that catered to a young crowd. On Friday, in the middle of the second set, Amanda Cutler entered and approached the stage. Kenny was singing in his nasal offbeat voice and Brian stood to the side, playing lead, and letting his mind wander. This was one of the bands most requested songs, but he was restless and bored with the cover tune. The play list at most clubs was so familiar he could play their sets in a coma.

Amanda came close to the stage and smiled broadly at Brian. He acknowledged her with an automatic stage smile. Jo jumped to her feet, stretching to see on whom he bestowed this sudden smile and he looked away, before she brought jealous eyes back to him.

At break, he headed straight for Jo. She hadn't stopped staring holes through him. Amanda appeared out of nowhere, with her date by her side, and blocked his path.

"Brian, I wanted to introduce you to Todd Cahill, my fiancé."

Todd offered his hand and smiled benignly. "Amanda's been raving about your talent for months."

"Is that right?" Brian asked, looking around for Jo.

"I might have an offer for you — if you think you might be interested in leaving this band," Todd said.

Brian forced his attention back to Todd. "What kind of offer?"

"I know some people who are putting a band together and if Amanda is right, you'd be perfect to round things out. Can you get to New York for an audition?"

Brian frowned. "New York City?"

Jo came from behind and pinched his side so hard he jumped.

"Ow! Damn it, Jo."

"Kenny wants to talk to you," she said.

"I'll be there in a minute," he said, rubbing his side.

Jo turned quickly and disappeared into the crowd, angrier than ever.

"I'm sorry, I know you're on a break." Todd reached into his pocket for a piece of paper and handed it to Brian. "Here's my number at Penn State. Call me when you've given it some thought or if you have questions. I'll be staying with Amanda's family until Sunday afternoon."

"Thanks. I'll think about it. ."

Amanda leaned in closer, laying a hand on Brian's arm. "Show off a little in the next set. I'm not sure Todd was convinced by that old standard stuff."

Brian removed his arm from her grip and shook his head. "I can't ask the rest of the band to let me show off."

"If you're going to make it Brian, you've got to cut some throats and step on a few toes. Your talent will only take you so far. You can't afford to let the riffraff in this town to drag you down to their level."

"If Todd wants to hear what I can do, I'll show him privately, Amanda."

He found Jo outside smoking a cigarette with Mark and his girlfriend.

"So, what did the princess of Snob Hill want?" Mark asked.

"Her boyfriend wants me to audition for a band."

Jo had daggers in her eyes. "That's not what Amanda wants you for."

"Is the band local?" Mark asked.

"No. I'd have to go to New York."

"Yeah, right, like you have that kind of money," Jo said. "How are you supposed to get there? Is Amanda going to give you a free ride?"

Brian wrapped an arm around her, and whispered in her ear. "Jo, please quit. Amanda doesn't think of me like that."

"She's always wanted you, Brian." She pinched him again, this time on the upper arm, getting a chunk of skin between her nails.

Brian backed away a step, rubbing his arm. "Damn it, Jo. Don't do that again."

She frowned at him. "You're so naive sometimes."

"You don't know what you're talking about. She's engaged to that guy she's with."

"Oh, big deal. I know what I'm talking about, Brian. Amanda has only one thing on her mind. Everybody in school knows she's been infatuated with you since tenth grade. This is not a simple crush."

"That's just stupid talk, Jo. You know there has never been anything between us."

"Maybe in your mind, but Amanda's not all there. She's been seeing shrinks since she was eleven."

Brian groaned, "So, what?"

"So stay away from her."

Brian talked to Todd, made a demo tape, and mailed it to Stan Young, the manager for the band in New York City. Two weeks later, he received a request to audition in person. The day after Brian graduated high school, he and Jo left for New York. They had enough money to stay one week and enough plans for two weeks.

Brian brought his guitar and a small amplifier borrowed from Kenny because his own wouldn't fit in the Volkswagen. He also took the letter from Max Burnette's lawyer and the photograph of Max Burnette, his mother, and Michael O'Mara.

The first goal was to find Max Burnette's lawyer to hopefully get an address for Max. The lawyer's office was on Manhattan's west side and he was with a client when they arrived. They took a seat in the posh waiting room and Jo tugged on the sleeve of Brian's dark blue T-shirt.

"If Max doesn't want you to have his address, promise me you won't take it personal."

He flipped the page of a magazine and frowned. "That will be hard to do."

"He doesn't know you. The rejection will be because of your mother."

The lawyer ushered them inside his office and Brian showed him the letter, explaining that he needed a current address for his father. The lawyer asked his secretary to pull the case file and studied it for a moment before shaking his head.

"I'm sorry, but I can't give you that information."

Jo scooted to the edge of her chair. "He was looking for Brian ten years ago, maybe he still wants to see him. You were his lawyer, right?"

He offered her a thin smile. "I'm still his lawyer."

Brian got to his feet. He wasn't about to beg this upper class jerk for anything. "Let's go."

Jo glanced at him nervously, then stood and walked closer to the lawyer's desk.

"Would it hurt to call and ask?"

The man looked at Brian, long and hard then reached for the phone. "Wait outside."

Five minutes later, the lawyer opened the door. "Come inside, I'll give you the address."

With Jo acting as navigator, they eventually found Brooklyn, and after an additional hour of searching, located the old brownstone belonging to Max Burnette.

Brian stared up at the apartment building where he had lived until he was age five and disappointment rolled over him. He didn't remember anything of his life here. Jo stood beside him, wrapping an arm around his waist.

"Ready?"

"Ready as I'll ever be, I guess."

He knocked tentatively and tried to still his racing heart. The door to the apartment swung open and Max Burnette stared down at them. He was tall, maybe six-three or so, and probably tipped the scale around two-fifty. Recognition registered in his dark eyes and he placed a hand over his heart, taking two steps backward.

Brian followed him inside. "Are you all right?"

Max laughed and threw his arms around Brian, giving him a crushing hug. "It's so good to see you."

Brian had imagined all sorts of reactions, but this one took him completely by surprise. Max laughed and wiped tears from his eyes as Brian quietly introduced Jo.

Max shook Jo's hand with much gentler enthusiasm. "Please, come in."

Brian didn't remember anything about the apartment. He wouldn't have remembered Max's face if he hadn't stared at that old photograph for two years. Somewhere, in the back of his brain, all the bitter memories shifted restlessly. Disappointment filled him until he pushed the useless emotion aside.

Max had never remarried and lived a quiet, lonely life in this apartment. A framed eight-by-ten picture of Brian at five rested on top an old console television.

Jo stood before the picture for a few minutes before speaking. "Is this Brian?"

Max smiled widely. "Yes."

She picked up the picture and examined it closely, then looked over her shoulder at Brian with tears in her eyes. "I've never seen a picture of you as a little boy. You were adorable."

Brian rolled his eyes and she replaced the picture.

Max offered them sodas and headed for the kitchen.

Jo immediately wrapped her arms around Brian. "I never realized how cold your mother is until I saw that picture of you. Does she even own a picture of you as a little boy?"

"Please don't start."

She pulled away and looked up at him for a long minute. Finally, she smiled. "I really love you."

Max came to the doorway of the kitchen. "Are you two hungry?"

Afternoon turned into evening and Brian abandoned his plan to broach the subject of Michael O'Mara. He couldn't dampen the spirits of this lonely man. He would have to find Michael another way.

Max insisted they spend the night with him. Since Jo seemed to be enjoying herself, Brian agreed. While Max dealt with a tenant at the front door, Jo leaned closer to Brian on the couch.

"Are you going to ask him about Michael?"

He kept his eyes on the door. "I can't."

"Are you okay with staying here?"

"Sure, if it's all right with you. We could spend the money sightseeing instead of on a hotel."

She smiled and her wide gray eyes were clear and bright, caressing him. Brian smiled slowly, languishing in the comfort. "I love you, Jo."

"I love you back." She kissed his lips quickly as Max closed the door.

"So, how long were you kids planning on staying in New York?

"I'm here for an audition with a band," Brian said.

Max's eyes widened. "You're a musician?"

He nodded. "I play the guitar."

Max went to the coat closet and produced a twelve-string guitar. He held it out to Brian.

"It hasn't been out of the case for a long time so it's got to be in good shape. You can have it if you want it. A neighborhood kid I used to know left it here a long time ago. I guess after all these years it's mine to do with as I please."

Brian removed the guitar from the case and ran his fingertips lightly over the smooth polished wood. He began to strum slowly, keeping his eyes on the strings. He never played a twelve-string before and the guitar was sorely out of tune. A soft, even resonance told him this was a well-made instrument.

"Was the neighborhood kid named Michael?" Jo asked.

Brian stopped playing and looked at her then to Max who seemed incapable of speech.

"There's a name in the top." Jo pointed to the guitar case and they followed her direction. Indeed, there was a name.

Happy Birthday, Michael — June 2, 1967

The message was hand-printed on the red lining of the case. Brian looked over at Max whose eyes remained fixed on the words in the case. Jo smiled sweetly, trying to look innocent, but Brian knew she was proud of herself.

He looked back to the guitar resting on his lap and wondered why anyone would leave such a special guitar behind. He traced the course of one string, and an odd need arose, as if there might be a trace of this Michael, some clue that awaited his touch.

"What did your mother tell you about her life here?" Max asked softly.

Although Jean was sober now, she still refused to discuss her past or anything else with Brian. All he knew were her tales of woe and Max didn't need to hear those.

"Nothing," he said finally.

Max sighed. "Then I guess it's up to me. I have to tell you, I really don't want to do this. My life's been so empty and, well, when you showed up at my door, I wanted to keep you to myself."

Brian took a moment to digest the statement. The lawyer had called someone for permission to divulge the address, obviously that someone had not been Max.

"I know who my father is," Brian said gently.

Max raised his head in surprise. "Then why are you here?"

"You're the only father I ever knew and you tried to get custody of me. That means a lot. It was certainly more than he ever did."

"Don't be so hard on Mike. He tried to help me find you and fight for custody when you were about ten."

"Mom said he didn't want anything to do with me."

Max shook his head. "It was her. He didn't want anything to do with her."

"That...I understand."

"He was only sixteen years old when they met, but he was a whole lot smarter than I ever was when it came to her."

Jo's jaw dropped. "Sixteen?"

Max seemed a little surprised by her reaction. "Almost seventeen," he corrected, as if that made it more acceptable, then continued his explanation. "Mike had a mountain of problems and she just threw fuel on the pile. Just before she discovered she was pregnant, he told her it was over between them so your Mom decided he didn't have any rights when it came to you."

Max shifted his considerable size in the recliner. "She went home to Connecticut for a while, but came knocking on my door when you were only a few days old. She knew I was crazy about her all along. We got married two weeks later and I found out she put my name on the birth certificate. I think you know the rest of that story."

"Why did he wait so long to try and find me?"

"Well, it's kind of complicated. Mike's life was kind of a mess about that time. Right after your mom took off, things sort of hit the fan for him so he ran away and it took him years to get his life back together. He didn't know your mom came back here and we got married. He certainly didn't know my name was on the birth certificate until eight years ago. When he found out, he came to me and we tried to find you, but your Mom kept on the move and didn't work much so it was impossible to find you."

"Where is he now?"

"He lives on a ranch in Wyoming."

Jo gasped. "Wyoming?"

"Horses, cattle, fresh air, all that cowboy stuff. He loves it there."

Brian realized he had pictured Michael much differently. "He's a cowboy?"

Max grinned, "Not exactly. Mike's got enough money to do just about anything his heart desires. This ranch is home — not income."

"He's rich?"

"Does that shock you, Brian?"

Brian shrugged nonchalantly, but this bit of news didn't settle well with a boy who had once stolen just to keep from starving.

"Hey, if you want, we could call him. Would you like that?"

Brian panicked. "I don't think I'm ready."

Max smiled, but sadness etched his face. "He's a nice man. It will be okay. Just pretend you're talking to yourself in the mirror."

Max picked up an address book near the phone and found the number he needed before punching in a series of numbers into the handset. Jo lifted Brian's hand and held it tight.

"Hi. My name's Max Burnette. I'm calling for Michael O'Mara. Is he available?"

Max listened, then smiled at Brian. "He's home."

"Hey Mike, this is Max Burnette. Listen, I'm calling because I have good news. Brian just came up and knocked on my door this afternoon..." Max frowned as he listened, "Oh, I didn't know they had called you..."

Max listened again, nodding. "Well he knows about you now, but this whole thing is a lot for him to handle, you know?"

He listened for a few minutes then nodded. "Okay, let me ask him."

Max covered the receiver with his hand and held it out to Brian. "He said to tell you he'd appreciate it if you would let him talk to you for a minute. You don't have to say anything if you don't want to. Just give him a minute of your time."

Brian's heart pounded hard as he took the receiver. After waiting for this moment for almost two years, it now seemed too soon. He managed a feeble hello and waited.

"Hello, Brian." Michael O'Mara had a soft baritone voice that rolled over him like a warm bath. "I wanted you to know I'd like to meet you and when, or if, you want the same thing I'd be happy to meet you wherever you are comfortable."

"I guess I might as well get it over with," Brian said.

He immediately regretted the cruel words. There was no sound from the other end for a minute. Brian tried to think of something to say that might soften the sting of his words, but Michael spoke first, in a more restrained tone now.

"How long will you be in New York?"

"For a week."

"I'm flying in on Thursday. Would that be pushing you?"

Two days and he would meet the source of his misery. Wait, that wasn't fair. Michael was the source of his mother's misery. He, Brian, was merely the beneficiary of their mess.

"No, I, Jo and I…Jo's my girlfriend, we don't plan, ugh…" he stopped talking to take a deep breath, embarrassed by his nervousness. "Excuse me. We don't have any plans for Thursday. That would be great."

"Good. I'd better check with Max to see if this is all right with him. Thanks for talking to me."

After Brian handed the phone back to Max and released a shaky breath, Jo kissed his cheek.

Max concluded the call and replaced the receiver. "All set. He's flying in around eleven in the morning."

"I can't believe he's coming. I mean, just like that, he says he'll be here. All the way from Wyoming," Brian's voice trailed away. He looked over at Max. "Are you okay with all of this Max? I mean, my coming here, and now, this?"

Max smiled slowly and winked. "Just make sure to say hello to your mother for me when you go back to Pennsylvania."

chapter 7

A YELLOW CAB pulled to the curb in front of Max's brownstone and Brian watched as a tall man with dark, shoulder-length hair emerged. He couldn't see the man's face, but knew instinctively that this was Michael O'Mara.

He walked to the kitchen where Jo and Max were playing cards. "He's here."

There was a knock on the door and Max got to his feet. Brian inhaled deeply and Jo slipped an arm around his waist as Max opened the door.

"Hey, you got here quicker than I expected," Max said.

"I had luck getting a cab. You look good, Max."

"Thanks. I could say the same about you."

Max stepped back and Michael looked past him. He took a few steps inside and held out his hand, smiling slowly.

"Hello, Brian."

Brian looked up slightly and met the most remarkable blue-violet eyes. In fact, everything about this man seemed unusual. Fine, silver strands mingled with the dark waves of thick shoulder-length hair. There were a few lines at the outer corners of the mesmerizing eyes and a gentle, white smile contrasted his tanned face.

He wore ordinary blue jeans, a white long-sleeved shirt, and cowboy boots. Still, an innate refinement about him raised this basic style to a different plane. He looked as if he belonged on the cover of GQ — not on a ranch somewhere in Wyoming.

Brian accepted the outstretched hand, but couldn't speak. All the prepared speeches were beyond his grasp at that moment. Michael released his hand and turned his attention to Jo.

"You must be Jo."

"It's a pleasure to meet you, Mr. O'Mara."

"Please, call me Michael."

"All right, Michael," she said, then giggled.

The telephone interrupted this with the loudest ring Brian ever heard. Max picked up the receiver and informed Michael the call was for him.

Michael grimaced. "I forgot to call home when we landed. Please, excuse me."

Jo and Brian followed Max into the kitchen. While Max poured everyone iced tea, Jo wrapped her arms around Brian and held on until Michael joined them a few minutes later.

"I'm sorry for the interruption. Today was my first cross-country flight. They were worried I'd wreck the plane."

"You have your own plane? You fly?" Max asked.

He nodded. "If you saw where I live, you'd understand."

Max herded them back to the living room and Jo sat close to Brian on the couch. Brian glanced across the space between he and Michael and the room suddenly seemed much smaller than half an hour ago.

"So," Max said. "How's life out west?"

"We just finished our busiest time of year with the cattle."

"Do you ride a horse or use helicopters to keep an eye on things?"

"We use ATV's or horses. It depends on what we're doing." Michael turned from Max and zeroed in on Brian. "Where are you living now?"

"Pennsylvania."

Michael frowned just a little, "With your mother?"

"I just finished high school and plan to get my own place."

"If they hire him after that audition on Friday, he'll have to stay in New York," Jo said.

"You kids are welcome to stay here," Max said.

Brian shook his head. "Jo can't stay. She has to finish her last year of school."

Michael listened to them banter, watching each person patiently then smiled at Brian. "What are you auditioning for?"

"A band — I'm a musician."

"What instrument do you play?"

"The guitar."

"I gave him your old twelve-string." Max nodded in the direction of the guitar, still resting near the couch.

"You can have it back, if you want it," Brian said.

He really didn't want to talk about music or guitars. Suddenly, he wished they were alone. He deserved some private time to ask the questions his mother would never answer.

Michael picked up the guitar and strummed a little. "It's not in tune."

He tuned the strings in pairs and played a bit with obvious expertise. Brian watched his slender, capable fingers and understood Michael wasn't trying to impress them. He played the song to be sure the guitar was tuned correctly. He was a perfectionist.

"Guess we know where you got your talent, don't we?" Jo whispered.

Michael handed the guitar back. "Why don't you try it now?"

Brian had no desire to play. Not now, maybe never, in front of this man.

"Thanks for tuning it, but I don't feel like playing right now." He put the guitar aside and watched Michael's face. "Did you want to be a musician?"

Though barely perceptible, Michael's eyes darkened a shade. "I wanted to be a classical pianist."

"What changed your mind?"

Michael offered a tiny smile, "Life."

Obviously, he didn't share himself easily. Brian thought of his own secrets and wondered if the habit could be an inherited trait.

After more small talk, Max invited Jo to join him on a trip to the grocery store for dinner supplies. One hour earlier, Brian might have panicked to be alone with Michael. Now, it was a relief to see the door close behind Jo and Max.

Michael stared at the closed door and Brian used the moment to study his handsome, young profile. He couldn't imagine what this man could have ever had in common with someone like his mother.

"Did your mother..." Michael stopped, his eyes flicked over Brian then away. "How was life with your mother?"

The careful demeanor told Brian all he needed to know. Michael indeed knew her well.

Brian drew in a deep breath and chose a middle-of-the-road answer. "It could have been better."

Michael digested that for a moment then shifted his position in the over-stuffed chair. "How did you find out about me?"

"I found a picture of you." He smiled shyly, deciding against a longer explanation. "I just knew."

"I wish things had worked out differently, Brian," Michael said. "I'm sorry."

Brian shifted under the weight of the apology and chose to ignore the responsibility of a response. "Are you married?"

Michael watched him carefully for a minute before answering. His words came slowly, as if he were thinking one thing and saying another. "I've been married once. We divorced last year."

"So you live alone in Wyoming?"

"I have family a few miles from my place. I'm getting married again this November. My new wife and her daughter will live with me then." He sat back in the chair and sighed. "Why don't you think about coming out for a visit? I'd fly you out and back. "

Brian grinned. "Would that be safe?"

Michael returned the smile. "I always have a co-pilot with lots of experience."

"I'd love to go to Wyoming." Brian hadn't planned to say those words. Only after they were out of his mouth did he realize their honesty.

"What were your plans after the audition?"

"I have to take Jo home on Tuesday. If I get the job with the band, I'll come back here. If not, I'm supposed to start a roofing job."

"My daughter, Katie, lives on Long Island with her mother. I'm picking her up Friday and we're flying back on Saturday morning. Why don't you think about coming with us? I'll bring you back Monday evening."

"I'll talk it over with Jo and let you know."

Brian turned off the bedroom light, slipped under the covers beside Jo, and sighed.

Jo nuzzled closer, rubbing his chest lightly with her fingertips. "I like Michael."

"I could tell — you flirted all day."

"I was nervous Brian. I wasn't flirting. He's your father, for heaven's sake."

"He's only thirty-six years old and he's great looking. You were flirting."

Jo ignored him. "He looks like you, or vice versa I guess. It was amazing to see you two together. The whole thing was so easy, wasn't it? I mean, like you've always known each other. I can't wait to go to Wyoming. I'm calling Mom in the morning."

Brian didn't hear everything she said. His thoughts drifted, rerunning the highlights of the day. Jo stopped talking when she realized he wasn't listening.

"Are you okay? "

"Yeah, sure, I'm just thinking."

"You like him, don't you?"

"I guess. It just feels so strange. I spent all those years alone. Suddenly I've got you, two stepfathers who actually like me, and a biological father that wants me in his life. I don't know what to do with all my resentment. It's sort of like losing a lot of weight overnight and I have all this excess skin just hanging there."

"You sound scared."

"It's so unreal to me, Jo. I'm afraid, if I reach out for it, the whole thing will evaporate and I'll be back where I started."

Jo took his hand, guiding it up the warm bare skin of her hip to a breast. "Not gone yet." she whispered.

Brian's breathing immediately quickened when she wrapped a cool hand around another, more intimate body part. "Max is in the next room," he whispered.

"Don't worry," she laughed. "I'll cover your mouth with kisses when you moan."

The audition was in a Manhattan nightclub at two in the afternoon. Max drove Brian and Jo to prevent them from getting lost again. Brian drummed his fingers on his thigh, staring out the window while Max and Jo chatted easily.

Max parked next to the curb and Brian jumped out. He opened Jo's door then looked down the street toward the club and took a deep breath.

"Are you nervous?" she asked.

Brian shook his head and walked away. Jo and Max exchanged glances and smiled. She called Brian's name several times then let loose an earsplitting whistle.

Finally he turned, frowning at her. "What Jo? You're going to make me late."

"Don't you need your guitar and amp?"

A young woman showed them into the dark interior of the club then pointed to tables near the stage. Once Brian's eyes adjusted to the dimness, he saw the stage, Todd Cahill and two unfamiliar men sitting at a table near it. Todd Cahill, Amanda's boyfriend, rose as they approached.

Brian accepted Todd's outstretched hand then shook the hands of the other two men. The first was a man named John Argent. John was a sweaty, overweight, tacky dresser and the owner of the club. The second man, a nervous, wiry looking fellow, was Stan Young, the manager for the band. Brian wondered if any members of the band were going to be there.

"Sit down, Brian," Stan said. "We'd like to talk a bit before we hear you play."

"Are you a member of the musician's union?" John asked abruptly.

"No, before today, there was no reason for me to be."

"If we decide to let you play here you'll have to join immediately. Understand?"

Brian met his watery brown eyes and nodded.

"I want to ask a few questions about your skill, Brian." Stan told him with a thin smile. "Do you read music?"

"Yes."

"Ah, then you don't play by ear."

"I have pretty good pitch Mr. Young, but I've been reading music for about six years."

"And where did you receive this training?"

"In school, private teaching, church."

"We were certainly impressed with the tape you sent us." Stan continued. "What instruments do you play?"

"Guitar and piano."

"All right, enough with the chit-chat. Let's go," John said, waving a beefy hand at the stage.

Brian hesitated uncomfortably. "Aren't any members of the band going to be here?"

"Certainly not yet," Stan laughed. "If we think you're good enough, you may have a second audition."

"You didn't tell me this would take all day," Brian began.

"Don't worry kid, it probably won't," John told him gruffly. "You could be out of here in a minute, if you don't shut-up and play,"

Brian bit back the angry words that sprang to mind. He looked to Stan. "Did you want me to play something specific?"

"Play one of your own compositions, like on the tape."

"Yeah," John sighed dramatically. He glanced at his watch before folding his hands over his fat stomach. "Dazzle us."

Brian smiled and his blue eyes sparkled. "I'd really like to dazzle you, Mr. Argent," he said.

John laughed and his great belly shook, "Just play, smart ass."

Brian climbed to the stage, plugged in Kenny's amplifier, warmed up a little, and played without hesitation. On the periphery of his vision he saw Jo twisting and fidgeting anxiously and forced his focus away from her. He finished and waited.

John turned to Stan. "If they don't want to hire him, you'd better convince them or you'll be a very foolish man."

"I don't know John. He's only eighteen. "

"He's a gold mine. Didn't you hear that voice?"

Todd Cahill held up a hand, stopping the bickering. "We have to see what Sammy thinks."

All three men turned and peered into the darkness.

"Well?" John asked.

"Have him use a different amp and see if he can play Betsy's Blues," a woman called from the shadows.

Stan jumped to his feet and handed Brian sheet music. "Plug your guitar into that amp back there. Run through this a few times then sing while you play it. "

Brian stared at the page in his hand for a few minutes. He placed it on top of a music stand and began to read and play, slowly with no mistakes. He played it in time, again without mistakes and murmured the words to himself.

"Turn on the mike," John yelled to the darkness.

Brian adjusted the height of the microphone and dared a glance at Jo before he began in earnest. The loving confidence in her gray eyes gave him the courage he needed. When he started the chorus, the woman from the back began singing harmony with him and he hesitated, losing his place.

The woman laughed. "Come on kid, keep up. "

A slender woman in a tight, black leather jumpsuit emerged from the shadows and took the stage next to him. "Start again," she said.

After they finished the song, she threw her arms around Brian. "You're wonderful!" She pulled back and poked him in the chest with a forefinger. "Was that full throttle or do you have more in there?"

He grinned uncomfortably and the woman stuck out her hand.

"My name's Sammy Cahill. Welcome to Sanguine Heart."

"Sammy," Stan interrupted. "We can't just hire him like that. We have to discuss a contract and…"

"Money," she finished the sentence for him with a sigh, turning to the manager. "You'd better get busy, Stan. I want him here with me when we open next Thursday night."

"We'll see, Sammy. He's got to join the union."

"I don't want to hear any bullshit, Stan. Do the job you're paid to do. The only thing I want to hear is Brian Burnette on this stage with me next Thursday. Make it happen."

Sammy turned back to Brian and smiled again

"Stan will take care of anything you need, including a better amp. Be here for rehearsal Tuesday afternoon."

"I have a better amp, but I won't be available until Thursday," Brian told her without hesitation.

She regarded him for a moment, her light green-brown eyes were slightly upturned at the outer edges and she reminded him of a cat scrutinizing its prey.

"Hell kid, I thought you wanted to be a musician."

"I am a musician."

"Then you better learn to put the music first. It's a tough lesson, but if you can't make yourself available then you shouldn't expect us to take you seriously."

"I was told I wouldn't be expected to play until the end of June if I got the job."

She tilted her head a little to the right and looked him in the eye. "You were told wrong."

Brian sensed she was testing him. He drew in a slow deep breath and decided to gamble. "Give me the music. I'll be back, ready to play on Wednesday. That's the best I can do."

Sammy smiled broadly and patted his cheek. "We're going to get along just fine, blue-eyes."

chapter 8

ON SATURDAY MORNING Max dropped Brian and Jo off at Michael's apartment in Manhattan and the doorman directed them to a private elevator with a courteous smile.

Once the doors of the elevator closed, Jo looked at Brian and giggled. "Do you think he's rich?"

Brian grinned at her, "The doorman?"

Jo rolled her eyes. "Michael."

"Well, Max said he was."

The doors opened quietly in a private hall. Directly in front of them was an open set of double doors. A little girl with dark hair and big blue eyes peeked around the corner. She giggled and ran inside.

"Daddy! Daddy! They're here."

Brian and Jo stood immobile in the foyer in awe at the grand hall before them. Michael came down the curved staircase to their left, buttoning the cuffs of a long sleeved shirt. The girl sat on the bottom step, watching Brian and Jo intently.

"Good morning," Michael said pausing at the bottom of the stairs. "Didn't Max come with you?"

"There was a problem with a tenant's plumbing. He had to get right back," Jo said, looking up at the domed ceiling.

"That's too bad." Michael held out a hand to his daughter. "Come meet Brian, Katie."

After he introduced them, Katie looked back to her father and cupped a hand in front of her mouth as if to whisper.

"He's just like you," she said loudly.

Michael laughed and scooped her up in his arms. "That whispering still needs some work."

Brian and Jo got a second hint of Michael's wealth when the limousine stopped near a Lear jet. The door was open and a crew waited with professional smiles. Katie squealed, climbed inside, chose a seat nearest the cockpit, stowed her small backpack, and buckled her seat belt. She waited patiently with Brian and Jo while Michael and the copilot prepared for takeoff.

After fifteen minutes, Katie looked over at Jo, sighing deeply. She cupped her hand in front of her mouth and rolled her eyes. "Daddy is so slow sometimes."

Michael laughed, glancing over his shoulder at them. "I heard that,"

Brian barely heard them. He concentrated on a piece of sheet music, his eyes scanning slowly. He should have cancelled this trip. He should be somewhere in a room practicing. This was no time for mistakes or he would be back in Pennsylvania putting on roofs in the summer heat.

They arrived in Jackson Hole as dusk settled over the landscape. They transferred their bags to a Jeep and drove southeast toward the Wind River Mountain Range. Katie and Jo fell asleep in the backseat, but Brian stared speechless at the brilliant colors of the sky.

"It's so beautiful," he said.

Michael smiled and turned to him, keeping his voice low. "I'd better explain a few things before we get to the ranch. Sam and Nellie Parker took me in when I was eighteen and became the parents I never had.

"You are an orphan?"

Michael shook his head, "My family was a mess."

Brian didn't know what to say, so he just nodded.

"You can consider Nellie and Sam your grandparents, if you'd like. I guarantee that's the way they'll treat you."

Michael turned off a straight, two-lane blacktop onto a private road and the sprawling property he called home. In the distance, soft yellow light glowed in the windows of a two-story log house. After the penthouse and Lear jet, the simple ranch house was a surprise.

"Is that your house?"

"No. We're having dinner with Nellie and Sam."

Katie immediately woke from her nap and squinted out the window, "Are we there?"

"Almost."

Katie giggled excitedly. "Nellie's on the porch. See her, Daddy?"

The moment they stopped, Katie unhooked her seat belt and clambered out of the vehicle. She squealed Nellie's name and ran for the woman's open arms.

Brian and Jo got out slowly, watched Katie hug a heavyset woman then turned their attention to the remote beauty around them.

"I've never seen anything like this." Jo yawned and rubbing the sleep from her eyes.

Brian kept his eyes on the fading ribbons of crimson over the mountain peaks. "I don't think we're in Kansas anymore."

Michael introduced Jo while Brian continued to soak in the beauty around him. Finally, Michael touched Brian's arm, drawing his attention.

"I'd like you to meet Nellie Parker."

Brian guessed Nellie to be in her middle fifties. Her plump figure and rosy cheeks reminded him of pictures of Mrs. Claus. Her auburn colored hair had been wound into a bun at the back of her head. Surprisingly, her clear blue eyes were teary.

"Looking at you takes me back to the first time I saw your Daddy standing in that very spot," she said in a choked voice.

Without any warning, Nellie bestowed the first motherly hug Brian had received since Mrs. Clifford all those years ago in Cleveland. The sensation was so extraordinarily comforting it shocked something to life, something old and distressing. Embarrassed, Brian took a tiny step back and caught the look in Michael's watchful eyes. Brian saw Michael understood the complete impact of Nellie's loving arms.

"You've made your Daddy such a happy man by giving him this chance," Nellie smiled, gracing his cheek with a gentle stroke. "God gave you a good heart."

An older man came around the side of the porch. Katie ran to him and hugged him with enthusiasm. He bent to hug Katie and spoke quietly with her for a minute, before letting her go.

As he drew closer, the man turned a set of warm brown eyes on Brian, he pushed his hat back a little and a small smile played on his lips. Soft, silver hair brushed the top of the collar on his blue jean coat. He stopped next to Nellie and offered his hand to Brian. "I'm Sam Parker. Welcome to Wyoming."

Brian immediately understood one thing about this silver-haired cowboy — Sam Parker meant what he said.

Nellie ushered everyone inside to a meal of roast beef, mashed potatoes, fresh vegetables, homemade bread and pies. While they ate dinner, someone entered through the back door, into the kitchen.

"Hello?" A man called.

Brian had just taken a bite of bread, but forgot to swallow when a big Native-American male filled the doorway between dining room and kitchen, ducked his head under the frame and approached the table.

"I brought the harness back. Mary says thank you."

His dark-eyed gaze fell on Brian and Jo, who stared openly. He grinned, flipping long, black hair over both shoulders and offered a hand to Brian. "You must be Mike's boy. I'm Red McDonough, Nellie's little brother."

Brian nodded and stood to accept the hand that dwarfed his.

"You'd best swallow whatever you got in your mouth son before you choke," Red said, then turned to Michael. "Didn't you warn them about me?"

Michael shrugged. "I forgot."

"That's real flattering nephew. Thanks a lot."

Nellie got to her feet and waved a hand at him. "Sit down and have a piece of pie, Red."

"I'd better not. Mary's got me on another diet. I'll take some coffee though." He sat across the table from Brian. "My wife thinks I'm too fat. How much do you think a six-feet-seven inch Indian ought to weigh?"

"Whatever he wants?" Jo said.

Red roared with laughter at the old joke. "What's your name Honey? Nobody bothered to introduce us, did they?"

"You never shut-up long enough for anybody else to say anything," Nellie said placing a cup of coffee in front of him. "This is Brian's girl, Jo Fields."

"I'm pleased to meet both of you kids." He winked at Brian. "Boy, you're the spitting image of this lonesome kid I dragged home years ago as a peace offering to my sister."

Nellie placed a hand on her brother's shoulder and smiled at Brian. "He is, isn't he?"

Red nodded and glanced at Michael. "He's even got the same look in those big blue eyes."

"What look would that be?" Jo asked, expecting another joke.

"As if life's been a little rough around the edges," Red said.

The room was suddenly quiet. Brian looked down the table to catch Michael's reaction. Michael simply stared into his coffee cup for a minute. Finally, he raised his eyes and met Red's dark gaze head on.

"He doesn't need a history lesson, Red. Leave him alone."

Red raised a big hand and waved it in Michael's direction. "Don't go getting all puffed up. I was just saying you and the boy seem to have a lot in common."

Michael got on his feet and patted Red's big shoulder. "It's been a long day for us. I'd better go on to the house and get Katie to bed."

Michael took them an additional five miles down the road. His home sat high on a plateau overlooking a long, deep valley and the mountains. The curved, rambling house had multiple levels with an abundance of windows each with breathtaking views.

Michael was not as casual about the sleeping arrangements as Max. He showed Jo and Brian their separate bedrooms on the third level of the house then helped Katie get ready for bed in her own room.

Jo and Brian were sitting on the bed in Brian's bedroom when Michael knocked softly on the open door. He wore loose fitting sweat pants, T-shirt, and tennis shoes and still looked like he belonged on the cover of GQ.

"Do you want the guided tour now, or would you prefer to call it a night?"

Brian grinned at him. "Don't you have maps?"

"Nope, all you get is this one brief tour. After that, you're on your own — I'm going to work out."

Jo stretched her back and yawned. "I think I'll just go to bed. I'm still on East Coast time."

Brian followed Michael down a spiral staircase to a lower level and down three corridors before they reached the gym. There was a small basketball court, nautilus room, sauna and hot tub in a separate room on the lower deck.

"You don't have a track for running," Brian joked.

"Sure I do." Michael waved a hand at the moonlit landscape. "Weather permitting, of course."

"I feel like Alice in Wonderland or something."

"Well, Alice, there are extra clothes in the dressing room if you want to work out."

Michael pulled his shirt over his head and tossed it on a weight bench. His strong, muscular torso reminded Brian how young this man was. After stretching for a while, Michael bent forward, placing his chest against his thighs, head on knees, hands on the backs of his ankles.

"You're in really good shape. Have you always worked out?"

Michael straightened up and contemplated the vast land for a minute, as if Brian's question required deep thought.

"Physical exertion used to be the only thing that gave me any relief from the things I found intolerable. I used to run till I dropped. Now, I just keep it steady." He gave Brian a sideways glance. "Know what I mean?"

For a minute, neither of them moved. Brian knew exactly what he meant and nodded slowly, holding on to the connection. Michael smiled then went back to stretching.

The two days in Wyoming went by quickly. Michael's house, lifestyle and most importantly, the people, made the stay comfortable. Having relatives that wanted him around seemed odd, but he couldn't help warming to their honest affection.

He was grateful Max made the call and gave him this opportunity. Still, part of him couldn't relinquish the old hurt so easily. Michael O'Mara had looks, brains, money, and love. A man this wealthy could have used his money and influence to find his long lost child if he really wanted to.

Saying goodbye at the airport in New York proved to be the most awkward part of the week. Michael gave them money for the cab ride to Brooklyn and Jo hugged him goodbye without hesitation. Michael stepped toward him and Brian offered his hand.

"Thanks for everything," he said.

Michael seemed surprised and it took him a minute to accept the handshake.

"If there's anything I can do to help you get started, let me know." He released Brian's hand and looked him in the eye. "Good luck with the band."

"Thanks."

Michael nodded and started away. Jo nudged Brian in the spine with a sharp poke.

"Is that all you have to say? Jesus, Brian, tell him you'll stay in touch or something."

Brian picked up their bags and shrugged. Jo slapped his shoulder and cupped her hands in front of her mouth.

"We'll call you!"

Michael turned and smiled. "I hope so."

He waved one last time and merged with the crowd. Jo turned on her heel and stalked away from Brian.

He hurried to catch up with her. "What's the matter with you?"

"You're mean."

"When was I mean?"

"Think about it."

They waited in line for a cab in silence and Brian grew more irritable.

"I don't know what you expected, Jo," he said.

"Forgiveness would be a good place to start."

"All right," he said then shrugged, "I forgive you."

Jo looked up at him slowly, narrowing her eyes. "Not funny."

"Oh, come on. What did you think I would do — throw my arms around him the way you did?"

"I expected you to display a little warmth toward your father."

"Max is my father."

She shook her head. "Wrong."

"Excuse me, but I think this is my decision."

"What makes Max more important?"

"He gave me his name."

Jo opened her mouth, snapped it shut then opened it again, without making a sound. Finally, she shrugged and looked away. "All right, maybe he did, but everything else came straight from Michael."

"Yeah, including the childhood from hell."

"Oh, grow up. He didn't have any control over that."

A cab pulled to the curb and they stepped forward, but a man jumped in front of them. Brian grabbed the man's coat and yanked him back. "Get in line jerk."

He climbed in behind Jo and gave the driver Max's address. Jo turned on the seat and faced him, but he looked away, out the window.

"Look, it's stupid to argue about this," she said. "Be reasonable."

"The hell with being reasonable. While I was going hungry, he was living a life of luxury. He has no idea what it's like to have to choose between stealing and starving."

He still wouldn't look her way and Jo touched his arm gently. He shook her hand off and she moved away.

"I don't understand, Brian. I thought things were going so well."

"Jo, please, this is hard, okay? I've got a lot of things to work out."

"I thought you liked him."

"I do, At least until I start remembering then I want some answers." He was quiet for a minute. "I want apologies."

"He's not your mother."

"No, he's worse."

"That's the most outrageous thing you've said so far."

"Why? He's got a decent personality, he's rich, he seems sane — none of these things can be said about my mother. Why shouldn't I blame him? Why shouldn't I expect him to apologize?"

"Because if you push this thing you'll be losing something much more important than an apology."

"What?"

Jo turned away, "My respect."

After spending the night with Max, it was time for Jo to go back to Pennsylvania. Max loaned Brian his truck so he could bring his clothes and amplifier back.

Brian had two days to learn the music before his meeting with Sammy and the rest of the band. It would take most of those two days to get Jo home and return with his things. He had no idea when he was going to find the time to do what he promised Sammy.

Back in Pennsylvania, his mother stood near the kitchen sink, eyeing him coolly as he carried the first box up from his basement room.

"Don't plan on calling here asking for any handouts when you fall on your face," she said.

Brian started out the door. "Don't worry, I won't."

"Don't go behind my back and ask Harlan either. I keep the check book."

Brian dropped the box on the table and eyed her angrily. "I know how to take care of myself."

"Oh, that's right," she smiled. "You're a good little thief when you need to be, aren't you?"

His face flushed crimson. "I won't need to be anymore, Mom. I'll be living with my father this time." He laughed at the shock on her face. "Guess what? He actually likes me."

"Who are you talking about?"

"Take your pick."

He wasn't proud of the statement. It left him feeling childish and mean. Jean said nothing as he and Harlan finished loading the truck.

"Well, that's everything," Brian sighed when he reached the top of the stairs with the last box.

Jean leaned against the counter top, smoking a cigarette and studying the pattern on the floor.

"We're sure going to miss you," Harlan said. "Promise to write and if you need anything don't hesitate to call, Brian."

He shook hands with the shorter man and the tears in Harlan's eyes were almost more than he could bear so he wrapped his arms around him. "Thanks for everything, Harlan."

Brian looked to his mother, unsure of what to do. Jean's hard stare told him all he needed to know. There would be no last minute apologies, professions of love, or tearful good-byes from her. The moment he dreamed of for all those years arrived, but there was more pain than pleasure in it. The fresh hurt angered him and he turned to the door.

"Jean, for God's sake," Harlan began.

Brian closed the door behind himself, shutting out the rest of Harlan's plea.

Their moment of separation loomed closer and Jo grew gloomy. Brian reminded her she could come see him over the summer, and, if he got a break, he'd come to her. He promised to call, write, and be faithful. Still Jo cried as if her heart was breaking.

They spent the last hours of the night in the tree house, at the back of her mother's property, sitting high above the world in the stately, ancient tree. Kenny built it with the help of their father the year he left his family for another life with another woman. Kenny lost interest in it long ago, but it was special to Brian and Jo.

This was the place they went to be alone. Many nights, they snuggled warmly in an old sleeping bag, talking the comfortable talk of young lovers. Tonight they didn't talk. Jo cuddled against him and wept quietly.

At four that morning, Brian forced himself to leave her. She stood on her mother's front porch under the ugly yellow bug light waving good-bye with tears rolling freely down her cheeks.

The last thing Brian wanted to do was leave Jo standing there. He would miss her more than anyone or anything in his life. He wanted to take her with him, but reminded himself they were doing the right thing. He would pursue his music and she would finish high school. Still, he couldn't imagine life without her to be anything but bleak.

Brian arrived at Max's flat early Tuesday afternoon. They unloaded the truck then talked for a while over a pizza. Finally, Brian went to the spare bedroom and practiced the songs on his electric guitar without the amplifier. When he finally put the guitar away hours later his hands ached and his fingers were sore. He lay down on the double bed, too exhausted to think about removing his clothes, and slept deeply until Max woke him.

Brian arrived at the club at noon and met the rest of Sanguine Heart. The bass player was a young woman named Mary. Mary's blond hair stuck out in wild disarray. She wore heavy mascara, eyeliner, and red lipstick, but nothing to hide the milky white of her skin. She sported short blue jean cutoffs, no bra, and a white T-shirt with holes in it. Brian counted seven earrings in her ear lobes. She switched a long-necked bottle of beer from her left to right hand and shook hands enthusiastically.

The keyboard player was a redhead named Tara. She was softer and more feminine than either Sammy or Mary, but she was all business. Tara explained that she and Sammy started the band in their college days. They co-wrote most of the music. Sanguine Heart was their band; everyone else was considered hired help. His percentage of the house would be fifteen percent to start.

Nick, the drummer, was the only other male. He sported short, neat, sandy-colored hair, tortoise-shell glasses, and looked like he belonged in an office trading stocks and bonds, not sitting behind a set of drums.

Sammy arrived with Stan the manager nipping at her heels. Sammy stopped at a table near the stage, threw a garment bag over a chair and wheeled on the small, nervous man.

"Shut-up, Stan!"

Stan stared blankly as Sammy turned to the stage. Seeing Brian, Sammy's mood shifted quickly. "Welcome back, Kid. Are you ready to be a musician now? May we begin?"

"He was here on time like the rest of us," Tara said mildly, her eyes scanning a page of music. "We're waiting for you, as usual,"

Undaunted by the soft reproach, Sammy hopped onto the stage. "Well, I suppose everybody's met everybody then. Let's start with Betsy's Soul."

Sammy picked up her guitar, adjusted her amp, and got ready to play rhythm. Brian began the lead. Tara, Mary, and Nick watched while Sammy joined in and Brian turned up the volume.

Betsy's Soul was about a young woman's death from a drug overdose — told from the viewpoint of her brokenhearted lover. Still reeling over his separation from Jo, Brian delivered the fury and heartache of the words with passion.

Finished, he stepped away from the mike and Sammy grinned at him. "To think there were some who doubted you'd get a feel for the music. You just played that song the way I heard it when I wrote it. Thank you."

He turned to the other three and waited for their comments. Mary chewed a wad of gum and studied him as if he were an alien. Nick nodded and gave him the thumbs-up signal.

Tara offered a tiny smile. "For the last week, Sammy has talked of nothing but the potential she saw for this band because of your talent. She swore you had lightning in your fingers, rhythm in every step, and a voice straight from the gods." She glanced at Sammy and the little smile widened. "It appears for once Sammy hasn't exaggerated."

While standing backstage Friday night, waiting for their introduction, Brian suffered his first serious case of stage jitters. He shoved his hands into the front pockets of his jeans to still the shaking and ward off the stiffness in his cold fingers. By show time, the club was almost full. Nick went on first, followed by Tara, Mary, Sammy, and finally Brian. The stage lights blinded him, but the hot glare blocked out the faces of the audience. He listened to Sammy greet the crowd then for Nick to kick off the first song. Once Brian started to play, the fear slipped away.

After their first set, they took a fifteen-minute break. Sammy grabbed him once they left the stage and hugged him with enthusiasm. She kissed his cheek with a loud smack. "You nailed it, you little son-of-a-bitch! I've been trying for three years to get that right. You just open your mouth and out comes that one sweet note that makes that song tick. Damn you're good!"

"Which song?" He sang lead on three and didn't know which one she meant.

"Sweet mercy, have you got range!" she continued, as if he hadn't spoken.

"Thank you."

"Let me buy you a beer."

"I'd rather have ice water."

Sammy kissed his cheek with another loud smack and turned happily. Tara was right behind her, blocking the way. "Tara! Isn't this a beautiful night? Man, I love this kid."

Tara watched Sammy dance away then wiped the lipstick from Brian's cheek with a tissue. "No one would know you were shaking like a leaf just before you walked out there." She gave him a serene smile. "You're going to work out fine, Brian."

Ice water in hand, Brian headed for the back door and some fresh air. Mary and her boyfriend were locked in a heated embrace near the door and didn't see him pass.

Sitting there on the steps, the first sudden longing for Jo blindsided him. Back home, in Pennsylvania, she was always right there beside him during the breaks. He decided calling her during the next break would ease the heartache.

The second set was rowdier. A capacity crowd now packed the club. Sammy had labeled this their power set. Brian and Tara sang back-up harmony, as Sammy belted out the first tune — a sexual, coming-at-you song. Tara took the lead on a humorous song about a bad day gone sour.

Brian was next. Sammy wrote the song and its title, "Sorry...Well, Maybe," was vintage Sammy, sarcastic and rocking. He sang the first two bars a cappella, slow and with feeling. His clear, low tenor drew the audience in and held them. They were quiet, and attentive, sensing this wasn't just one more bar band.

Nick slapped the snare drum and Brian brought a quick scream up from his gut and they shot into the fast paced song. Sammy joined him at the microphone and they belted out the quick lyrics together in a tight harmony. The crowd drew in around the stage as the band took them on a ride.

When they finished that set, Brian called Jo, but her mother said she was spending the night at her friend Amy's. Brian asked her to tell Jo he called. This time he accepted the beer Sammy pressed in his hand and stayed inside and mingled backstage with a few people from the audience, quietly pocketing the phone numbers from several young women who were no more than a brief image.

They finished at the club around two-thirty that morning. Tara had a date, Nick disappeared the moment the set concluded, and Mary slipped away with her boyfriend. Brian placed his guitar in its case and accepted Sammy's invitation to breakfast.

She studied him carefully while he looked over the menu.

Feeling her steady gaze, Brian looked up slowly. "Is there something you want to ask me?"

"There are a lot of things I want to ask you," she said, then laughed. "I just don't know where to begin."

Brian sipped a soda and waited patiently. He had been incredibly tense all evening. Now, as the adrenaline rush ebbed, exhaustion crept in and he yawned.

Finally, Sammy seemed to arrive at a decision. "How old are you again?"

"Eighteen."

"And how many phone numbers did you get tonight?"

Brian sat back, slipping a hand in a front pocket of his jeans and pulled out several crumpled pieces of paper. He tossed them on the table and thought of Jo.

"Four," he said.

"Has anyone warned you about adoration?"

This woman was way out there. He chuckled, "Adoration?"

"With your talent, that body and face, people are going to want to get close to you, touch you, sleep with you, and consume you. Just remember — you aren't some demi-God, no matter what anyone tells you. I want you to learn how to keep your feet on the ground before we start moving forward."

Brian focused on the last sentence. "Do you really think we have a shot?"

"I have a gut feeling you're our ticket. With you on board, we can elevate this band from bar status to something much finer." She reached across the table and gripped his hand. "Brian, when you touch the strings of that old guitar, you pick the world up and hold it in your hands like a gentle angel. That alone is truly a gift, but you take it one step further. You look your audience in the eye, open your soul, and free a voice that immerses us in perfection."

Brian lit a cigarette and sat away from her. A hot blush crept up his neck and he hoped she would stop soon, but Sammy was never short-winded or distracted. She certainly didn't miss his embarrassment.

"Look at that blush! The real beauty of you is that you are still so humble." She took a sip of coffee and shrugged. "With or without Sanguine Heart, you're going to skyrocket. All I want is my chance to jump on for the ride."

"You've written some great songs. My talent isn't any more special than yours."

Sammy laughed and took one of his cigarettes, "Right."

chapter 9

Sanguine Heart practiced Tuesday afternoons and all day Wednesday; they played Thursday, Friday, and Saturday nights. Brian's cut was sixty dollars a week. To survive, he worked part-time at a convenience store near Max's flat.

One Wednesday rehearsal ran long and Brian was late for work. He hurried into the store and behind the counter and listened to the manager's quick admonition with half-interest. Three people waited in line and he checked them out quickly. He didn't notice a fourth customer until the man spoke.

"Pack of Marlboro Lights, please."

Brian reached overhead and tossed the pack of cigarettes on the counter then looked up to accept the money. The guy stared hard for a minute then his gaze drifted to Brian's nametag.

"So, you're Brian."

"Yes sir."

"My name's Bob O'Mara." He smiled casually and picked up his pack of cigarettes. "Welcome to the neighborhood."

Brian arrived home after midnight and found Max in front of the television. Brian slumped onto the sofa and sighed wearily.

"Tough day?"

"Nothing went right at rehearsal and the store was crazy all night."

"It's the full moon," Max said, keeping his eyes on the television. "It makes everybody nuts."

"Max, this guy came in tonight and introduced himself as Bob O'Mara, is he Michael's brother?"

Max studied him for a minute then nodded.

"So, Michael has relatives living around here?"

"A whole slew of them. Are you ready to be part of an Irish clan?"

Brian shook his head. "I don't belong with them — my last name's Burnette. I was just curious."

Max sat forward quickly. "Listen to me — you belong anywhere you want. I don't expect you to choose between Mike and me. We both love you and I'd like to think we're mature enough to share."

"He doesn't even know me."

Max laughed softly. "He probably knows you better than you know yourself."

"What's that supposed to mean?"

"You know that old phrase, 'Walk a mile in my shoes?' "

"Sure."

"Well, Mike's been where you've been and then some. All you see is a man who has everything. I see someone who paid his dues."

"How? What are you talking about?"

"I'm not the one to tell you that. Ask Mike."

Bob O'Mara dropped by the convenience store frequently. If Brian wasn't busy, Bob bought a soda and struck up a conversation. He never mentioned their link. Brian got accustomed to the visits and learned to like the uncle he couldn't bring himself to acknowledge.

Bob was older and shorter than Michael, and carried a little extra weight around the middle. Beneath his careful gaze, his less dramatic blue eyes held just a hint of amusement. Bob was handsome, but his appearance would never startle the world — not the way his younger brother's did.

"I hear you play in a band over in Manhattan when you're not working here," Bob said.

They were outside the store watching storm clouds gather overhead. Brian looked up as thunder rumbled somewhere in the distance. The air was heavy with the threat of rain and he hoped it would arrive soon to break the heat.

Bob lit a cigarette and sat on the windowsill. "My younger brother, Michael, was quite a musician. He used to win awards playing the piano."

Brian gave him a sidelong glance and played along, "Classical music?"

Bob smiled broadly. "They said he was a genius with perfect pitch."

"Was?"

Bob pointed the cigarette at him. "I stand corrected."

"Sounds like you admire him."

"I do. Oh, he's not perfect or anything. He still gets on my nerves sometimes, but, overall, it's hard not to respect him."

A big, wet drop landed on the top of Brian's head. He grimaced and looked back to the sky. "I really hope that was rain."

Bob laughed and tossed his cigarette into the street. "I'll see you, kid. I'd better get home."

They were halfway through a song when Brian spotted Bob watching from the audience. He tripped over the words and closed his eyes to concentrate. The audience didn't catch the mistake, but Sammy walked over and tapped him with the toe of her boot. Brian finished the tune without additional errors and turned his back on the audience for a drink of water.

Sammy moved close. "What's up?"

"Somebody just surprised me."

"Friend or foe?"

"Mind your own business," he snapped.

"Lighten up, Junior."

Brian swung around quickly. "Don't call me that."

Sammy rolled her eyes and stepped away to begin the next tune.

On the break, Brian got a glass of ice water and asked Bob to join him outside for some fresh air. Staying inside the club meant enduring Sammy's curiosity and constant interruption from the audience.

Uncle Bob grinned at him, "I have to tell you how impressed I am. You're really good."

Brian studied him for a minute then looked away. "I heard your brother play — he's better."

"Different maybe, not better, I have no idea how he sings. Maybe that talent is yours exclusively."

Brian smiled a little and lit a cigarette. "You have your brother's knack for turning things around on me."

Bob nodded at the cigarette in Brian's hand. "You know those things are hazardous to your health, don't you?"

"I breathe in a hundred times this much up on the stage."

Bob lit a cigarette of his own and they sat side-by-side on the stairs, smoking in silence, until Brian glanced at his watch. Break time was nearly over. Sammy would be looking for him.

He got to his feet and looked down at Bob. "I'm sorry, I've got to go."

"Sure. I need to get going myself. I'll see you at the store."

Brian walked a few steps and turned. Bob's attention was on the keys in his hand. "Hey, Uncle Bob?"

When Bob raised his head, Brian caught the twinkle of satisfaction in the man's eyes and smiled.

"Thanks for coming."

Bob saluted him with a quick wave, "You bet."

Jo was needed to look after her younger brother and sister while her mother worked that summer and couldn't come to visit. Brian knew her mother, Amelia, was never fond of him and saw this separation as an excellent opportunity to put an end to their relationship. He didn't have the time to go to Jo, so he focused on music, worked, and did a lot of running.

He ran the streets in the early morning hours, before the sound of most alarm clocks began to pull others from their beds. The hypnotic pace of the workout always brought him peace. He composed music, dreamed of the future, and kept the situations he couldn't change at bay to the rhythm of his feet drumming on the concrete.

Michael called a few times over the summer, but the brief, uncomfortable conversations left a lot unsaid. In early September, Michael returned Katie to New York and invited him to dinner.

Brian wasn't sure he wanted to accept the invitation, but Max browbeat him into going. He put on his only dress shirt and tie, a sport coat he borrowed from Nick, the drummer, and drove to Manhattan. Michael was already waiting at a table when he arrived.

"I'm sorry, I'm late."

"You're not late," Michael said, eyeing his hair. "I was early."

Brian smiled, touching his longer hair absentmindedly. Sammy had encouraged him to let it grow.

"So, how long are you going to be in town?"

"About a week. I have some business to take care of and I want to see my brother while I'm here."

"Which one?"

His eyes narrowed a bit. "Bob."

"Did he tell you he's been down to the club to watch me play?"

"Does that bother you?"

"I thought you might be keeping an eye on me."

One of Michael's eyebrows lifted slightly. "Does someone need to keep an eye on you?"

"Hardly. I've managed just fine on my own for eighteen years."

Michael started to say something, but a waiter appeared and he let the moment pass. Their conversation was interrupted two additional times by people who recognized Michael and stopped by the table. He introduced Brian only by name and didn't tack on the word son. Oddly, the omission insulted Brian.

"Why didn't you explain our relationship to your friends?"

Michael's face remained impassive, but the blue darkened several shades. "I got the impression you wanted it that way."

"Well, I'm eighteen and I'm not sure of what I want right now. Excuse me."

Michael reached for his coffee and shrugged, "Deal."

Unnerved, Brian looked around the room, feeling the need to flee.

Michael nodded in the direction of the door. "The exit is on your left."

Sudden tears sprang to Brian's eyes. He pushed his chair back, but didn't rise. He looked back to his young father. "You obviously don't need me in your perfect life. What do you want from me?"

Michael eyed him for a minute and when he spoke, his gaze didn't waver. "Same thing I wanted all along. I want the opportunity to know and love my son."

Brian lowered his head and closed his eyes, willing the tears to dissipate. Not even his mother was capable of doing this to him. Michael's statement had reached inside and hit him where he was most vulnerable. Part of him needed this man after all, and, as usual, need intimidated him.

"I'm willing to do this on your terms," Michael said after a few minutes.

Brian sniffed and moved his chair close to the table again. "I don't have any terms."

"All right then. We can take it as slow as you want."

Brian laughed at that. "Any slower and we'll be at a complete standstill."

"No argument here."

Brian swallowed some ice water and cleared his throat then looked Michael in the eye. "Okay, how about this — you introduce me as your son, but I continue to call you Michael, at least for the time being. I'm not sure I'll ever be able to use the word Dad or father, I think I'm too old to try."

Michael nodded and looked away. His handsome face spread into a slow smile and his eyes sparkled with tears. That said more than any words could have and forced Brian to realize his own selfishness.

"I'd really like it if you'd come down to the club and listen to me play."

"Thanks for asking. I'd love to."

"Thursday is probably the best night. The crowd's not quite so rowdy."

"I'll be there."

On Thursday night, he scanned the audience, expecting to see Michael's face, but Michael didn't show. After the last set, he joined Sammy for breakfast and managed to keep the bitterness at bay. Still, on the drive home, disappointment got the best of him.

The television was on and Max was asleep in his chair when Brian opened the door. He woke with a start and sat up straight.

"Hey, you're later than usual."

"I went out to eat with Sammy after the show."

Max stood and stretched. "I'm too old to sleep in that chair, I guess."

"I don't know why you wait up."

"I like knowing your home before I go to bed. Oh, hey, I almost forgot. Mike called right after you left this afternoon. He said something came up and he couldn't make the show. He said to tell you how sorry he was and that he'll try again tomorrow."

"Sure he will. Goodnight Max."

Brian worked the next morning and Max was out when he got home. He showered and hurried out to meet Sammy before the evening show.

In the middle of the second set, Michael and Bob walked in the door. By then, Brian was too angry to care. He made sure not to look their way.

At break time, he headed for the back door and gulped ice water. The second set was hard on his vocal cords and the cold water numbed his throat. He heard voices and looked up as Bob and Michael turned the corner.

"I told you he'd be back here, sitting on the steps like an old farmer," Bob said good-naturedly.

"I sit here to cool off," Brian shot back, glancing at Michael. "I figured you went back to Wyoming."

"I told you I would come to hear you play."

"Hope it wasn't a disappointment after all your effort."

Bob frowned at him. "You mad about something, Brian?"

"Yeah," Michael said, his attention riveted on Brian. "Me."

Brian grunted and got to his feet. "Why would I be mad at you? I don't give a damn if you ever hear me play. I've always known where I fall on your list of priorities."

Michael turned and walked to the front of the building. Bob looked from father to son.

"Brian, our mother had a heart attack yesterday. They don't expect her to make it. We both tried getting hold of you, but you're a little hard to pin down."

Brian grimaced. "I'm sorry."

"Tell him. He's the one that needs to hear it."

Brian approached Michael and called his name.

Michael turned, revealing a raw frustration that set Brian back on his heels.

"I called Max," Michael said. "Didn't you get my message?"

"He said you couldn't come — that's all. Did you tell him more?"

"I didn't think you cared to know more."

"Shouldn't that be up to me after I have some of the facts?"

Michael's eyes narrowed a little. "Are you making these rules up as you go along?"

"Rules? I wasn't aware there were any rules for this sort of thing. I'm just doing the best I can."

"Well, it's frustrating as hell," Michael said loudly, then sighed. "Sometimes, I get the impression I should just stay away."

"That's not what I want."

"Then tell me what you want. I'm confused."

Brian threw up his hands. "I want you to be patient."

Michael laughed shortly. "You could benefit from a little patience yourself."

"I have a lot of patience. I spent most of my life waiting to get away from my mother."

"And you spent the rest of the time resenting me for not rescuing you."

"I didn't hate you until I realized how well you were living while I suffered."

Michael inhaled sharply, as if he had been sucker punched. Brian wanted to take those words back, but, of course, it was too late. Bob joined them now, watching Michael carefully.

"I didn't mean that the way it sounded," Brian offered. "I don't hate you."

"Shut-up, Brian," Bob said. "Enough is enough."

"Could you give us a minute, Bob?" Michael spoke softly, without looking at either of them.

Bob nodded and left them.

Michael looked to Brian. The pain etched on his face added years to the handsome features. "I'd change everything if I could, but I can't Brian. I'm sorry, but all we have is now."

"I didn't mean what I said. I'm so sorry."

Sammy came out the back door and called his name.

"I've got to go. Would you please apologize to Uncle Bob for me?"

Michael nodded and looked away again. Brian started toward the club, but paused halfway and looked back.

"Would it be okay if I called you?"

Michael met his gaze and nodded, "Anytime."

Brian was running the next morning when he encountered Bob, sitting on the porch of his home only a few blocks from Max's flat. Brian waved and intended to keep going, but Bob asked him to wait.

"I need a favor."

"Sure."

"After you finish your run, would you meet me at this address?" He held out a piece of paper.

Brian read the address and frowned. "Whose house is this?"

"My mother's. There won't be anyone else there but the two of us. I think this is something that would do you a lot of good."

"Maybe I should go now, before I get all sweaty."

Bob smiled at him. "How considerate. I knew there was something about you I liked."

They walked six blocks to a two-story brick home on one of the quieter streets and paused in front of the stairs.

"This is where we grew up."

"Nice house."

Bob looked up at the place and considered it for a minute. "I guess that depends on your perspective."

Brian stepped inside, eyed the clean home, the polished wood floor of a long hallway, and looked up the stairs toward the second level. Bob motioned for him to follow down the hall and opened a door. He flipped on a light and Brian followed him down the stairs to a small brick basement.

"This," Bob said, waving an arm around the dimly lit room, 'was my father's favorite place to beat the hell out of Mike. He usually started with his fists. Mike used to walk around with black eyes, split lips, and so many bruises he looked like a boxing veteran." He sighed. "Only Mike didn't get to fight back."

Bob pointed to a support post in the center.

"See that?"

Brian nodded, waiting.

"My father use to drag Mike down here — well, sometimes he saved time by throwing him down the stairs. He made Mike strip and grip that post then beat him with a leather shaving strap until he couldn't stand."

"Was he cruel like that to all of you?"

Bob looked him in the eye and shook his head.

"When Mike was four, my parents discovered he had a high IQ and turned him over to my father's youngest brother, a priest named Frank. Frank took charge of Mike's life and drove him hard, as if it were a personal challenge to see how much he could take."

Bob paused to light a cigarette and stared into a dark corner. "Frank was a twisted son-of-a-bitch who had no business being a priest, let alone in charge of a gentle kid like Mike. When Mike was twelve, he and Frank had a showdown, two days later Frank hung himself and Dad blamed Mike."

Brian's mouth dropped open slightly. He snapped it shut and shifted his weight. Bob took a deep drag on his cigarette and pointed at a corner.

"There used to be a wooden bin there. It was about three by four feet and was once used to store coal. After my father beat Mike, he would lock him in that bin. Sometimes, Mike was down here for days."

Brian swallowed hard, "Days?"

Bob nodded solemnly. "In the beginning, Dad had the only key to the padlock."

Brian's insides were churning. He wanted to run up the steps and out of this house. He held up his hands and took a deep breath.

"I don't want to hear anymore of this."

"No one wants to hear this. I remember sitting at the kitchen table with the rest of my sisters and brothers, listening to Dad scream, and punch, and kick, and beat him with the damned strap for what felt like an eternity." He paused and shook his head. "My mother actually expected us to eat."

Brian turned and headed for the stairs. Bob came right behind him.

"Are you going to be sick, nephew? You're looking a little pale."

"I've got to go."

"Let me show you one more thing."

Bob took him to the living room and showed him a mantle full of pictures.

"Most of these are of us when we were kids." Bob handed a photo to Brian. "That's him when he was twelve."

Michael was dressed in an altar boy's cassock and looked right at the camera. His wide eyes expressed a profound sadness Brian couldn't bear. He handed the picture back quickly, as if it were hot.

Bob replaced the photograph and stared at it for a minute. "I don't want to get into anymore of the details with you Brian, but I want you to understand — Mike wasn't living on easy street while you suffered. He carried a lot of scars away from this house and he's still trying to recover."

He looked Brian in the eye. "Next time you want to punish my brother, you just remember that picture. You weren't the only one who had it hard."

chapter 10

MICHAEL WAS MARRYING a woman named Beth Thomas on the day before Thanksgiving in a west Texas town called Silverpail. Brian received an invitation with a plane ticket enclosed. He flew to Amarillo with Bob and they picked up a rental car for the drive to Silverpail.

Bob unlocked the trunk and shivered in an icy wind. "I guess you're wondering why the wedding's in a little hole-in-the-wall place like Silverpail, Texas, aren't you?"

Brian tossed their bags inside and shrugged. "I assume that's where the bride's from."

They merged with traffic and headed northwest before Bob launched into the story of how Michael and his bride-to-be met.

"Back in 1967, Mike ran away from home and wound up in San Francisco. He spent about five months with all that other hippie nonsense then started hitching back to New York. A little west of Flagstaff, his ride pulled in at a rest stop and he hopped out, leaving everything he owned, including his coat, in the car while he went into the bathroom. When he came out there was a cop car in the parking lot and his ride was long gone because they were transporting about thirty kilos of grass to Chicago."

"Did he know about the grass?"

"Yeah, but he needed the ride. A few days later, Beth's brother, Kevin, happened to stop in the middle of a blizzard for a pee break and found Mike freezing to death under an overpass. Kevin took him home and probably saved his life because Mike had pneumonia. This was the day before Thanksgiving 1967.

"I was two weeks old," Brian said, thinking out loud. He didn't mean to interrupt. He wanted to link his history and Michael's together somehow. This seemed like a good place to begin.

"Well, hell, what day is your birthday?"

"November tenth."

"So you turned nineteen a few weeks ago and didn't say anything to anybody?"

Brian shifted in the seat and pulled at the safety belt to loosen it. "It doesn't mean anything to me. Why should I mention it?"

"You never know," Bob drawled, lighting a cigarette, "it just might mean something to somebody else."

Brian shook his head. "It hasn't up till now."

Bob glanced over at him in disbelief. "You mean exactly what you say don't you?"

"Most of the time."

"I mean now. You're not yanking my chain, looking for sympathy or anything. You really don't expect people to care about you."

"I've only met one person I could count on that way — she's in Pennsylvania."

"Oh yeah? What's her name?"

"Jo."

"When was the last time you saw her?"

Brian turned his head and looked out at the cold ground speeding by. "June."

They rode in silence for a few minutes, until Bob resumed the story of Michael and Beth. Brian was grateful for the diversion. Thinking about Jo made him restless.

"Beth's brother Kevin says that from the minute Beth looked into my brother's weird eyes she was in love, but it took Mike a whole minute longer to fall for Beth because he's a little on the slow side. Anyway, that's why they're getting married one day before Thanksgiving. It's sort of an anniversary."

"Why did they wait so long?"

"Back in sixty-eight Mike figured he had nothing to offer her but misery so he left Silverpail and it might have stayed that way if he hadn't taken a nose dive and fell apart a few years ago."

Bob took a deep breath and stared straight ahead, tapping the steering wheel. Brian waited impatiently for a few minutes then had to ask.

"What happened? Did he finally confront your father?"

Bob shook his head and poked the cigarette out the window. "After Mike ran away, he never spoke to Dad again."

"Then what made Michael fall apart after all that time?"

"Before committing suicide our Uncle Frank wrote a letter to Mike, but my father kept the letter a secret. When he was dying Dad's last request was that I make sure Michael finally received that letter, a request that I unfortunately honored. What I expected to be an apology from Uncle Frank turned into a final stroke of cruelty from both my father and Uncle Frank. That sadistic note and my father's vengeance brought all the rage and pain crashing down on Michael and he went on a binge that everyone was sure would end in suicide, but one day he smacked into the bottom and finally the truth got hold of him."

"He seems happy now."

"He's made some peace with that part of his life, but he has a long way to go. I think marrying Beth is the best thing that can happen to him."

Bob turned onto a two-lane blacktop. They drove for twenty minutes before swinging onto a private gravel road. Two houses, one small, one rambling, stood in the distance.

"This should be Beth's brother's place."

Though the temperature hovered around thirty degrees and a steady wind blew across the long, flat yard, Michael stood on the porch steps of the smaller house, talking with a bearded man that made Michael's six-foot-two-inch frame seem fragile.

Bob brought the rental car to a halt and a smile spread across Michael's face as he descended the stairs. This time he didn't offer Brian a handshake — he hugged him with enthusiasm.

"I'm so glad you could make it," Michael said. "I know how busy you are."

"Thanks for the airplane ticket."

Michael patted Brian's shoulder and looked at him squarely, "My pleasure."

Michael turned his attention to Bob and Brian dared a glance at the large, bearded man. The man considered him with black, penetrating eyes.

"Mike?" he called, in a deep voice. Michael and Bob stopped talking and looked to the giant on the porch.

"What?"

"You should've warned me about this."

Michael came closer. "What?"

The big man jerked a thumb in Brian's direction, "Him. It's like being yanked back about twenty years, well, except this kid's better looking."

Michael laughed and turned to Brian for introductions. "Brian, this is my friend, and soon to be brother-in-law, Kevin Thomas. Kevin, meet my son, Brian Burnette."

Kevin held out a hand and smiled. "Don't let him sell you that soon-to-be part. Ain't a damned thing soon about it, Brian."

Bob announced he was freezing and they moved the conversation inside. Kevin slapped Michael on the back. "Bethie ain't met your boy yet, has she?"

"No."

"I'm gonna go get her. I gotta see her face when she meets this spittin' image. Maybe I'll capture this Kodak moment on videotape."

"Kevin," Michael began.

"Shut-up, Mikey, you ain't in charge."

Michael closed the door behind Kevin and shook his head. "Brian, I'm sorry. He's really a nice man, just a little eccentric at times."

"I don't mind looking like you," Brian told him softly, meaning it. His mother might hate him for it, but if the resemblance hadn't been so obvious, he probably would have never known the truth.

"Hell, who would mind looking like you?" Bob shook an arm out of his coat. "I only wish I did."

Michael frowned. "What's wrong with how you look?"

Bob grinned, sitting down on the arm of an overstuffed living room chair. "You're kidding, right?"

Michael crossed his arms over his chest and fixed Bob with an irritated look.

"In case you haven't noticed," Bob said, "I'm older, shorter, and have ordinary O'Mara eyes. I've always had to work hard to have any kind of muscle. No female ever turned around to look at me and stare with lust in their hearts." He paused to grin at his brother. "I hate going anywhere with you, by the way."

Kevin burst through the door wielding the promised video camera. "Smile, Brian. Say hello to Texas.

Brian smiled self-consciously and waved at the camera. Michael asked Kevin to turn it off, just as someone else entered. Because Kevin's bulky body hid her from view, Brian heard Beth before he saw her and his first impression was that her sweet voice sounded like music.

"Kevin, for heaven's sake, what are you doing?"

Kevin swung around and backed up, aiming the camera at Beth's face.

Beth was tiny, maybe five-two at best. Her shiny black hair fell softly around her shoulders and oval face. Her big brown eyes found Brian and widened in surprise. The smile that lit her face was genuine and Brian immediately knew he would like his stepmother. This woman met the world with unswerving honesty and vigor. She switched her gaze to Michael and some private message passing between them brought him to her side in two steps. He wrapped an arm around her shoulders and gently introduced them.

"Beth, this is my son, Brian Burnette."

Beth stepped up without hesitation and embraced him. She pulled back, looked up at his face with an unreserved affection Brian knew he could trust.

"It is such a pleasure to meet you," she said.

A hot blush crept across his face and he smiled shyly. "The pleasure's all mine."

"So, what do you think Bethie? Ain't it creepy?" Kevin called from behind the video camera. "Doesn't this boy's face take you back a few years?"

Beth turned to her brother and put her hands on her hips. "Kevin, put that camera down. You're being rude."

Kevin lowered it immediately. He seemed confused and genuinely hurt, "How?"

While Brian listened to their friendly banter, loneliness dropped by for a visit. He didn't belong with these people. He was a stranger here. They were just being polite to some kid who pushed his way into their lives.

He didn't realize he was moving until he felt the wall against his back. After quietly excusing himself, he fought the assault with the only tool available. His legs moved him toward the door, away from Michael, past Bob, Beth, and Kevin.

He was almost outside when Michael's voice stopped him. "Want to take a walk out to the barn and see the horses?" The soft words didn't come from across the room, where Brian last saw him, but right behind him.

Brian nodded, too embarrassed to speak. Michael led the way through wind and snow to the barn. Brian welcomed the freezing wind in his face, willing it to drive away the old melancholy.

By the time they finished walking to the barn, he felt better, maybe even a little foolish. Knowing Michael recognized the all too transparent attack of discomfort was unsettling. The knowledge that someone, other than Jo, read him that easily made him question his ability to hide his feelings anymore. Maybe laying his soul bare through the music was doing something to his defenses.

Michael talked casually about the horses as they walked by the individual stalls. He asked if Brian ever rode a horse and made general, small talk. Brian sensed Michael was again saying one thing while his mind focused on something else. Finally, Michael leaned against a stall and looked him in the eye.

"I know meeting all these strangers must be difficult for you," he said quietly.

Brian shook his head quickly, "No, not at all."

Michael's left eyebrow lifted slightly and Brian knew his too perceptive father was about to nail him.

"That's odd," Michael began, "the look on your face back at the house seemed to say the situation rates right up there with a double root canal."

"I'm sorry."

"Don't apologize to me, Brian. That's not what this is about. All I'm asking you for is a little patience. We'll get beyond this, I promise."

"You've already gone out of your way," Brian said.

Michael shook his head. "Please, listen carefully. You're my son and this can be your family if you want it that way. You'll fit in, if you give it time." He shrugged his shoulders and sighed a little. "Who knows? You might even learn to like us."

Brian smiled back. "I already like Beth."

That left eyebrow came up again, but this time Michael's face relaxed into a smile. Suddenly, he glanced at his watch and grimaced. "I'm afraid it's time to meet the rest of the bunch over at Kevin's house."

Nellie and Sam arrived just before dinner. Brian was most comfortable with them. The softness of Nellie's hug and the straightforward acceptance in Sam's wise brown eyes were something he could count on if the panic came back.

The wedding ceremony was simple and elegant. A light, dry snow blew out of the north as the hushed crowd witnessed the marriage. When Beth and Michael gazed into each other's eyes and exchanged vows — something special and private passed between them. Brian understood the power of that kind of love. He felt it each time Jo's eyes saw him.

The sound of loud sniffling distracted him just as Michael slipped the ring on Beth's finger. Glancing around the crowd, he saw tears streaking Kevin's cheeks. Brian looked back to the ceremony just as the preacher pronounced them husband and wife. The crowd erupted into applause and Michael kissed his new wife.

After the honeymooners vanished down the blacktop, Brian asked Kevin's permission to use the phone and slipped away to the quiet of the kitchen. This day had turned up the volume of his need for Jo.

"She's not here," Kenny told him. "She went over to Aunt Mary's with Mom. How's the new band coming?"

Brian didn't want to talk about anything but Jo. "When will they be back?"

"Sunday. Are you making pretty good money with this new gig?"

"No, I'm still broke all the time. Do you think it would be okay for me to call your aunt's house and talk to Jo?"

"It's after ten. That's kind of late, don't you think?"

"I forgot the time difference," he mumbled, resting his forehead against the door of the refrigerator. "Would you please tell her I called when she gets back? Tell her I'll call Sunday at one."

"Sure. You okay?"

"Yeah," he sighed, "everything's fine."

He said a quick good-bye and replaced the receiver. Turning, he found Sam standing in the doorway, watching.

"I'm kind of restless," Sam drawled. "Do you play chess?"

"No sir. I'd like to learn though — if you don't mind a beginner."

Sam's face spread into a kind smile and his dark eyes wrinkled at the corners. "Don't mind at all."

It was still dark the next morning when Bob shook him awake. Brian rolled to the edge of the old sofa bed and sat up. Bob shoved a cup of coffee in his hand.

"Drink up, Nephew. We've got to get going. There's a blizzard outside and we got a long drive."

Fifteen minutes later, Brian was dressed, packed, and shrugging his shoulders into his old letterman's jacket. Still, Bob waited impatiently. They slipped away into the dark morning while everyone else slept in warm beds. Bob pulled a cassette from his pocket and tossed it in Brian's lap.

"Kevin told me to give you that."

"What is it?"

"Just put it in and listen."

Music floated over the speakers, piano then a young man's voice. Bob turned the volume up and gripped the steering wheel with both hands, staring straight ahead.

"I know this song," Brian said. He listened intently. "Angel's Blues. I heard it a lot when I was a kid, but that was a woman."

"Well, this is the original artist we're listening to."

Bob's bitter tone said a lot. Still, Brian had to ask.

"Who is it?"

"Your father."

Brian leaned forward and closed his eyes. This voice was young and passionate, full of raw hurt. The version he knew was sad and beautiful, well orchestrated, but this bare bones piece reached deep inside and squeezed, until his heart begged for mercy.

"When did he make this tape?"

"On his eighteenth birthday."

"But, that's before it was published."

Bob laughed softly. "Kid, you're as thick as a brick sometimes. Mike wrote that song. He doesn't like for people to know."

"Why not?"

"All I can give you is my opinion. I think it's a private goodbye to the childhood that never was. He's acknowledging the hell Uncle Frank and Dad put him through the only way he could back then."

Michael hit a long note and Brian's stomach tightened.

"Melissa Cole is probably the person you remember singing this song. Mike gave the song to her with the provision that she never connected him to it and she won a Grammy." He looked over at Brian and grinned. "When you win your first one, I want you to know you're taking more than your talent to the stage. For me, at least, you'll be giving my father and uncle the bird."

Brian grinned at him and rewound the tape. The sounds of Michael's young voice again filled the car and the fine hair on Brian's arms rose.

chapter 11

THE BAND'S FIRST tour began in January. They opened for a group who had just released their first album. Brian decided it was time to invest in a new guitar and amplifier.

Because of the limited budget and tight schedule, they did most of their sleeping on the tour bus roaring down the highway from one town to the other. They usually arrived just in time to clean up and make it to the stage for that night's performance.

When they did spend the night in a hotel, Sammy, Tara, and Mary shared a double room while Brian and Nick shared another. Their manager insisted on having a private room. Sharing a room with Nick proved to be another exercise in patience Brian could have lived without.

Nick always referred to him as "the teenager," and seldom spoke to him unless it was a necessity. Nick dominated the phone, talking for hours to his "people" back in New York. He thought nothing of throwing his personal belongings on Brian's bed. He used all the towels then tossed them in a wet heap near the base of the toilet. Brian either found the time to get more towels or did without.

Nick turned the television and lights on first thing upon entering the room and kept them on all night. If Brian turned a switch off, Nick immediately turned it back on. Nick usually ate his meals in the room and never cleaned up after himself.

Several times, Brian voiced his complaints to Nick. Nick listened, nodding as if he understood completely, but nothing changed. One bitterly cold night in Kansas City, Brian's tolerance disintegrated.

They did their stint on the stage and returned to the hotel at one. Typically, no one fell asleep until they descended from the adrenaline rush of performing. Nick, of course, hurried into the shower and Brian sat on the bed with his guitar. A new song hummed in his brain and he tried to concentrate, but the mess around him chipped away at his concentration.

Laying the guitar aside, he went downstairs and looked for a suitable box in the hotel dumpster. Back in their room, he threw in half-empty soda cans, candy bar wrappers, Styrofoam plates, a half-eaten cheeseburger, empty chip bags, newspapers, clothes, Nick's leather-bound daily planner, shoes, two address books — anything lying around went in, including the telephone. He printed Nick's name in bold letters on all four sides of the box, sat on his bed and picked up Michael's old twelve-string.

Nick emerged from the shower towel drying his hair with a second towel wrapped around his waist. He looked around the room in confusion, as if he stepped into the wrong room — until he spotted the box on his bed. He walked over and peered inside then swung around.

"Did you put all my stuff in this box?"

"I figure you can haul it around with you, Nick. All you have to do is root through it when you need something."

Nick lifted his leather organizer with two fingertips. A slice of tomato stuck to the cover dripped special sauce onto his foot. "Damn it, Brian."

"Wasn't that thoughtful of me? I thought you might appreciate a snack, while you're calling your 'people' in New York and keeping me up all night."

Nick shook with rage. After finding some clothes from the box, he dressed and marched directly to the manager's room to complain.

Sammy knocked on the half-open door and found Brian playing the guitar. She sat on Nick's bed, eyeing the box.

"Brian, we can't afford two rooms for you guys. I'd appreciate it if you'd try to get along with Nick."

Brian kept his eyes on the guitar and grunted. "I'm trying Mom, honest. I mean, gee whiz, I cleaned the room for him and everything."

Sammy laughed and lit a cigarette. "You're not one of those nit-picky people — are you, Junior?"

That single word brought his head up with a snap. "No, Sammy, it's sleeping with cockroaches, stepping over piles of his crap, never getting any sleep, and drying off after a shower with my own shirt that I find hard to live with. If you consider that picky that's too damn bad."

Sammy laughed shortly. "Whoa, where did that come from?"

"Don't talk down to me." He looked back to the strings of his guitar. "I'm not an idiot."

The song he played pricked her interest and Sammy temporarily forgot her mission.

"What are you playing?"

"I'm working on a new song," he responded flatly, wishing she would go back to her own room.

"No shit. Is it done? Do you have a title?"

"Fallen to Ashes."

"Oh, I think I like this. Got any lyrics?"

Brian sighed, summoning patience. "I wrote those first."

Sammy sat back on the bed, crossing her arms over her chest. "Okay kid, dazzle me."

Brian shook his head, and relaxing a little began to sing the ballad about losing the love of his life. Though starting out sarcastically, he shed the anger and performed the song with passion. He closed his eyes and allowed something deep within to fly to the wide-open freedom his spirit craved.

When he brought the song to a close, he opened his eyes and looked at Sammy, who seemed stunned.

"Damn," she whispered, blinking back tears. "You're unbelievable."

Brian got to his feet and laid the guitar in its case. The song was good — he didn't need Sammy to confirm that. In Fallen to Ashes, he allowed the world a glimpse of his most vulnerable place. Losing Jo would be the end of him. An inner voice insisted he tempted fate by opening this door. It took every ounce of courage he had to shut that voice away and move forward.

"Do you think it's too self-indulgent?" he asked casually, slipping on tennis shoes.

"I think it's one of the most beautiful songs I've ever heard. Where did this sorrow come from?"

"Jo," he answered softly, stretching, preparing to run.

Sammy frowned and came to him. "Did something happen?"

"Nothing exactly. There is just so much distance between us. I feel like I'm losing her."

Sammy tilted her head and narrowed her cat eyes, studying him for a minute.

"At the risk of being shredded by the sharp edge of your tongue again, I'd like to point something out to you. I think you are probably past your umm — limit. This song and the thing with Nick are just symptoms of a need. You know what I mean, don't you?"

Brian turned his back to look for a sweatshirt. "There's no connection between my being unable to tolerate Nick-the-pig and not seeing Jo. I'm in love with her Sammy. I miss her."

"You can deny the truth to me, but you can't deny nature. You need to be more in touch with your biorhythms." Sammy patted his chest and sighed. "You're in need of a good lay, my friend."

Sammy swept out the door and left him staring after her in disbelief. Brian pulled a sweatshirt over his head, tied his shoes and went out into the cold February morning to run.

An hour later he returned and found Mary asleep in Nick's bed. Nick and his box were safely tucked away in another room. There was a stack of clean, dry towels on his bed, courtesy of Sammy. Brian stripped in the bathroom, took a shower, and fell into bed.

At the end of April they played the University of Miami. This was a three-night stop and the idea of not getting right back on the bus sounded like heaven. They checked into the hotel at five in the morning.

At nine, the phone woke him. Brian reached for it automatically.

"Hi. Did I wake you?" Jo asked cheerfully.

"Jo," he murmured dreamily. Hearing the bathroom door open he looked up and saw Mary with a toothbrush in her mouth. He motioned for her to be quiet.

"I'm in the lobby," Jo said. "I wanted to give you a minute to wake up before I get there and jump your body. See you in a minute!" She laughed, and the line went dead.

"She's here! Jo's here. Mary! She's in the lobby." Brian threw back the covers and jumped out of bed, tripping over the sheet, and fell face down on the floor. After untangling his foot, he quickly slipped on a pair of jeans.

Brian looked at himself in the mirror and ran his fingers through his shoulder length hair. Mary emerged from the bathroom, picked up her bag and waved at him.

"I'll see you this evening. Enjoy yourself."

Brian rushed to the bathroom, brushed his teeth, and pulled a brush roughly through his thick hair, ignoring the pain. It wasn't until he stood in the hallway, waiting for Jo, that he realized Mary knew Jo was coming.

The elevator doors slid open and Jo ran out at top speed. She fell into his arms and he lifted her off her feet, kissing her mouth with hunger while he carried her into his room and closed the door with his foot.

After their initial embrace and kiss, Jo demanded he stand back for inspection. His wavy hair fell to his shoulders. He had also allowed Sammy to talk him into getting his left ear pierced — twice.

Jo smiled. "You seem to fill out those jeans better than I remember."

"I've put on about ten pounds."

She touched his earrings with a fingertip then tugged on a strand of hair. "You're certainly starting to look the part of a rock and roll singer."

"Do you hate it?"

Jo planted a long, warm kiss on his mouth. "You look good enough to eat."

Sammy was right. A weekend with Jo was just what he needed and gave him the boost to finish the tour with a lighter heart and more passion.

chapter 12

IN LATE MAY, Brian topped the final hill and pulled Max's truck to the side of the road. He slid out the door and leaned against the driver's side for a smoke while he surveyed the view of the town below. Both legs were stiff from driving all night and his tired eyes ached.

He thought back to the first morning he woke to this view, when his mother's slap blew the cobwebs from his sleepy mind. The town below hadn't changed much since then — not nearly as much as him. Dreams were coming true and his time to live was at hand.

Today, Jo was graduating high school. Tomorrow, she would kiss this place good-bye and they would be together forever. There would be no more bending to her mother's rules.

Before the brief interlude in Miami, he believed he knew exactly how much he needed Jo. That quick visit provided a deeper insight. Now, he understood — nothing was more important than Jo. He loved music and performing was now second nature, but if she were to ask him to give up the adventure, he would do so without hesitation. The band was going to the recording studio next week and the future looked bright, but he didn't need the predicted money or fame. While the money would be welcome and the recognition excited him, he could play music anywhere and be happy. His need for Jo was on a much higher plane.

Of all his requisites in life, need was the most simple to define. He needed Jo, music, food, water, rest and air.

He crushed the cigarette beneath the heel of his shoe and climbed behind the wheel. He shifted the truck into first and smiled. Only five miles stood between him and the girl he would spend the rest of his life with.

Jo's mother was on her knees in a flowerbed near the front door. Hearing the truck, she squinted into the sun and watched him approach.

"Afternoon, Mrs. Fields."

She stood, staring hard at his haggard appearance.

"Please, excuse the way I look. I worked last night and came straight here from the club."

"I hope you clean up before you attend the graduation."

Sighing, Brian turned his attention to the front door. "Is Jo home?"

"Where do you plan to stay? I ran into Harlan yesterday and he said you weren't expected there. You understand how inappropriate it would be for you to stay here don't you?"

Brian couldn't stop the anger from showing. "Mrs. Fields, I've been awake for twenty-four hours, and I'm really short on patience, so I'll make this real simple for both of us. If it weren't for Jo, I wouldn't spend one minute at your house. I have reservations at a hotel for the night."

Amelia Fields pointed her spade at him. "Don't even think about taking my daughter there."

Brian opened his mouth to respond just as Jo came up from behind, slipped a hand around his waist and hugged him tightly.

"Leave him alone, Mom."

Amelia's mouth curled into a tight knot and her eyes narrowed as she looked from Jo to Brian then back again. She pulled off her gloves, threw them on the ground, and stalked into the house.

Brian wrapped his arms around Jo and gave her a quick kiss on the lips. "I've missed you so much."

"Did you check into your room yet?"

He shook his head solemnly, "I came straight here."

"Let's go. I'll help you get settled and you can get some sleep before tonight."

"You'll give your mother a stroke if you come with me now."

Jo smiled and those light gray eyes caressed the starved places in him. "I can handle my mother."

He leaned against the fender of the truck and lit a cigarette while Jo went inside. All the windows in the house were open and their angry voices floated unimpeded through the screen and down to where he stood.

"You are not going, Jo. That's final."

"I'm going with him tomorrow anyway. What does it matter?"

"It matters to me! Maybe that son of a whore doesn't have any morals, but my children do."

Brian threw his cigarette into Amelia's tidy flowerbed and got into the truck, slamming the door. He backed down the driveway so fast the tires squealed. He didn't glance in the rearview window and didn't see Jo running across the lawn toward Amelia's old Buick.

She followed him to the motel parking lot and parked the Buick carelessly next to the truck. She was standing next to the truck before he got out.

"I'm sorry," she said. "Please don't be angry with me."

Brian frowned deeply and wrapped his arms around her. "I'm not angry with you, Jo."

"She didn't mean it, Brian. She's jealous."

He knew Amelia meant every word. He had heard it all before.

He stretched his back and surveyed his tired face in the mirror. After a quick shower, they had made love and sleep came over him without warning. He barely remembered Jo's soft good-bye kiss. Unfortunately, a few hours of sleep in thirty-six hours felt worse than none at all. He had exchanged one need for another and the price was written in dark circles under his eyes.

Exhaustion clouded his brain and he knew if he stopped moving he would crawl back into bed. Harlan was expecting him for breakfast at the cafe down the street the next morning, but the graduation wasn't due to start for two more hours so he drove by his mother and Harlan's home on impulse.

Harlan stood on the front lawn talking to a neighbor and grinned widely as Brian parked.

"Look at you, Boy. My goodness, you're really growing up."

Brian embraced him enthusiastically. "It's good to see you, Harlan."

"You too. Come on inside. Your mother's almost got supper ready."

Brian had no interest in seeing his mother. They hadn't spoken once in the last year. He called a few times and talked to Harlan, but Jean always seemed to be out or sleeping. Harlan promised she would call back, but she never did.

"I can't stay. I just had a few minutes on my hands."

"My God, look at that hair," his mother said.

Brian looked to the porch where she stood, hands on hips, the ghost look set on her face.

"You look like a mop, Brian."

"Gee, Mom, it's good to see you too."

"Well, since you're here, I guess you might as well come inside."

"Thanks for the gracious invitation, but I'll pass." Brian turned to Harlan. "I'll see you in the morning."

He had just opened the door when she spoke again.

"Arrogant little bastard."

He opened his mouth to respond, noticed Harlan's pained expression, and changed his mind. Jean went inside and slammed the front door.

"She's having one of her spells," Harlan said.

"Is she drinking again?"

"No, but sometimes she acts like she is."

"I don't know how you do it."

Harlan squinted up at him and that pained expression deepened. He shoved his hands in his pockets and glanced toward the porch. "She doesn't act like this all the time."

Harlan's unspoken explanation sunk in and Brian cursed himself for coming here. He smiled for Harlan's benefit and patted him on the shoulder.

"I'll see you tomorrow at seven."

At Jo's graduation party, he pretended to be interested in seeing old acquaintances for a while then drifted away to the tree house and fell asleep. Hours later, Jo's gentle kiss woke him.

"Time to move to Gotham," she said. "I'm all packed."

"You can't just run off without saying good-bye to your mother."

"We said our good-byes. She's up in her room crying herself to sleep." She kissed his mouth again and smiled. "Kenny helped me pack the truck."

Brian grinned widely, "Yeah?"

"All you have to do is drive. I'm all yours, Romeo."

"Jo, I promised Harlan we'd have breakfast."

"What time are you supposed to meet him?"

"Seven."

"Well, that's only about four more hours. Let's go to your hotel. I have an idea how we can fill up the time."

Max gave them a flat on the second floor and in many ways, became more of a companion to Jo than Brian who spent most of his time in a recording studio. If he wasn't recording, he practiced, performed at John's club, worked the part-time job, or slept. He knew this life in Brooklyn wasn't what Jo expected and promised her things would get better.

Jo frequently talked of marriage, but he wanted to wait until he had more time and money so they could take a long honeymoon. Despite his set ideas, Jo started planning a wedding with her mother for June of the next year.

Once the recording finished, Brian was free to pay more attention to his personal life. Unfortunately, this was too short-lived. Sanguine Heart was going back on the road to promote their first album on a whirlwind fifty-city tour. When he announced the news, Jo insisted she wanted to tag along which led to a marathon argument.

"Jo, we live, eat, and sleep on the run. When we're not on the bus, we're working. There won't be a lot of days off. You'd be bored out of your mind."

She was headed for the kitchen and swung around, glaring at him. "Yeah, well at least I'd know who you were sleeping with."

Brian stared hard at her. "I've never given you one reason to say that to me."

"Oh, come on. I've watched you perform, Brian. I've seen the way women look at you. Do you think I was born yesterday?"

"You don't know what you're talking about." He dropped to the used couch and sighed loudly. They had been arguing for over an hour. He hated to spend what little time they had this way. He decided to try again.

"Look, Jo, what I do on stage is a show. After we finish, I get on the bus with everybody else and go on to the next town."

Jo smiled slightly and sat on his lap. "Let's make up."

"No. We should talk about this. I want you to trust me. You have to trust me."

"I do trust you. It's just that I get afraid."

"Afraid of what?"

"I thought we'd be married by now."

He frowned at her. "How's that going to change anything?"

"I want to be your wife. Make a commitment to me."

"I have Jo. I've been committed to you since the first day you looked at me with your pretty eyes."

"You've made promises and half a commitment. I want your name."

"Fine. If you want to forget the big wedding you and your mother have planned, that's okay with me. I never wanted a big show anyway. We'll get married before I go on the road and fit the honeymoon in at the end of the tour."

Three days later, with Max and Sammy looking on, Jo and Brian got married in front of a judge.

Jo's choice to rush into marriage right out of high school was no surprise to her mother. Amelia told Brian she expected him to be a man now and put the needs of their marriage before his desire for fame. She then wished her daughter luck with a wild boy who was raised by a mother possessing fewer moral values than a whore.

Brian called Harlan to give him the news and didn't ask to speak to his mother. The call to Michael and Beth was the last on the list of parents.

"I thought you two were going to have a big wedding next year," Michael said.

"That was her mother's idea. Jo didn't want to wait anymore."

"Her mother must be exceptionally pleased with this decision."

"She blames me, as usual."

"Did you invite her, Brian?"

There was an odd edge to Michael's voice and Brian wondered if he had crossed the line again. "Are you mad at me?"

"No," Michael said, without conviction. "Will you at least accept a wedding gift from us?"

"I'm sorry we didn't let you know. It happened pretty fast."

Michael cut in quickly. "I understand."

"No, I don't think you do. We didn't plan this. We just went down and got married."

Silence was all Brian heard.

"Damn it," he muttered, rubbing his forehead.

"Look," Michael began, but paused for a deep sigh. "You just took me by surprise that's all. I'm happy for you. Jo is a wonderful girl."

Brian decided Michael covered his feelings the same way that he did. "You know what I'd like for a wedding present?"

"What?"

"I'd like for Jo to meet Beth. I'm going on tour at the end of the week, but I'll have some time off in November. Could I bring Jo out there for a visit?"

Again, silence from the other end.

"You still there?"

Michael laughed softly. "I'm in shock."

"You want to talk to Beth and get back to me?"

"I don't have to talk to Beth about this — I know what she'll say. You're welcome here any time. All you have to do is let us know it's what you want."

Brian stepped into the street and put one foot in front of the other until he fell into a natural pace. The pavement shined from a fine layer of fog and his voice didn't travel far as he worked out a new tune.

By now the route was so familiar he could run it blind. He passed Michael's boyhood home and a soft light coming from an upstairs room caught his eye, but he kept going. That single visit with Uncle Bob had left an odd sadness — like walking through another person's bad dream.

Uncle Bob had switched shifts at the cab company and they hadn't seen much of each other lately. Brian missed the gentle sparring. Bob's comments taught him a lot about Michael.

He crossed the street and ran six blocks out of his way, hoping to find Bob sitting on his stoop with the usual cup of morning coffee, but the house was dark and the cab wasn't there.

Brian ended his run at the convenience store just down the block from Max's. After catching his breath, he entered for a bottle of water and talked with the night clerk.

Back in front of the store, as he sipped water and cooled off, Uncle Bob eased the cab down the street and parked.

Bob smiled broadly and slapped him on the back. "Hey nephew, long time-no see. How you been?"

"I've been great. I'm getting ready to go back on the road next week."

"Come on, Kid, my brother tells me you got bigger news than that to share with me."

"Oh, yeah, Jo and I got married last week."

Bob studied him for a minute, then shook his head and lit a cigarette. "I hope she's more important to you than that sounded."

Brian smiled at him. "We've been joined at the hip from the minute we met. Getting married was just a legal formality."

"Where is she living while you're on the road?"

"With Max."

"Mind if I drop by and introduce myself?"

"No, go ahead. She knows all about you."

Bob grinned. "Bullshit."

"Truth, Uncle Bob."

"So, how come I'm important enough to talk about with your new wife, but you forgot to invite my brother to the wedding?"

So, Michael was hurt, a year ago knowing that might have brought Brian pleasure.

"It happened quickly," he said to Bobby. "We didn't plan anything."

"You know, my little brother just seems to be the kind of man who can handle anything you throw at him. Trust me, he's not. I wish you would be a little kinder."

Brian tossed his empty water bottle into a trash bin nearby. "It's good to see you again, Uncle Bob."

"Don't turn on me, you little shit."

"I'm not turning on you. Nobody seems to remember the fact that I'm not used to having parents."

"Hell, you don't have to think of him as a parent. Think of him as a human being."

"I do."

"Good, nephew, if ever there were two people who should understand each other it's you and him."

Brian patted him on the shoulder. "Thanks for the pep talk. Now, if you'll excuse me, I have to get home."

He was half way down the block when Bob's words caught up with him.

"We love you, Kid. Good luck on the tour."

chapter 13

THE FIRST NIGHT of this tour began in Memphis where another group opened for Sanguine Heart. Waiting in the dressing room drove everyone a little crazy. Sammy always got hyperactive before a show, but tonight she paced and talked so fast she was hard to understand.

Nick sat in a corner talking on the phone. Tara pretended to read, but her eyes weren't moving and she wasn't turning pages. Mary played solitaire, hummed, and chain smoked.

Brian warmed up by playing an acoustic guitar and exercising his voice. The roar of the crowd overhead made him edgier by the minute. Sammy's behavior didn't help. He put the guitar aside and got to his feet, drawing Tara's immediate attention.

"Don't go anywhere. We go on in five minutes," she said.

"I know that," he snapped. "I'm restless."

Mary flipped over a card and stubbed out a cigarette. "Who wouldn't be? Sammy's like a wild cat."

Sammy stopped suddenly. "Was I pacing again?"

"Yes!" They answered in unison, even Nick. Everyone laughed, except Sammy, who threw up her hands.

"Hey, excuse me if I get a little nervous before we go on."

"You look a lot nervous," Mary said. "I need to relax, but you keep reminding me we're about to walk on stage in front of ten thousand people."

"It's five thousand and we're all quite aware of what we're about to do," Tara said, putting her book aside and adopting the persona Sammy referred to as "the Holy Mother."

"I understand your nervousness, Sammy," Tara said. "You and Brian are the two every one of those five thousand will be staring at most of the time."

Brian laughed at the reminder. "Oh, thanks a lot, Tara."

She smiled and got on her feet. "How about a group hug?"

Sammy backed away from her and groaned. "What have you been reading this time, more of that psychobabble junk?"

Tara glided to the door and blew Sammy a kiss. Mary shrugged and followed, stretching her back as she walked. Nick glanced at his watch, but stayed on the phone.

Sammy glanced at Brian, "Ready to feed the lions?"

"Well sure, since you put it like that," he said with a grin.

"Wait." She turned suddenly and walked around him, looking him over head to foot.

Brian's smile slipped away. "What?"

"I was just thinking, you're filling out in all the right places. You really don't look like a boy anymore." She shook her head. "It's such a shame you're married. You might have had a lot of fun with such a magnificent body."

"Who says I'm not having fun?"

"Oh yeah, sure you are. Moving down the road at seventy miles an hour with a psychobabbelist, a part-time lesbian, a half-human, and Mary — well, I can't quite find the appropriate label for her yet — this is every hot-blooded male's dream."

"What part-time lesbian? Who?"

Sammy frowned at him. "Me. Didn't you know?"

"How would I know a thing like that?"

She shrugged and patted his chest. "You've never really tasted life, Brian. You're just a baby. Someone should have given you better advice than to marry so young."

Brian shook his head. "Jo is all I ever wanted."

Sammy studied him for a moment then turned for the door. "Come on, before Tara grounds us. Nick get your ass off the phone. It's show time!"

The band completed the road trip and had a three-week break before they were to return to the studio. Brian flew to the Bahamas to meet Jo for their delayed honeymoon. He arrived first and checked into a hotel. He ordered a room full of flowers and made arrangements for a candlelight dinner on the terrace of their suite. Jo's plane arrived a little after six that evening and he waited impatiently at the gate.

Jo pushed her way through the crowd to his open arms. The minute her body touched his, he pulled back and looked down at her pregnant abdomen. Slowly, he looked back to her face.

"Why didn't you tell me, Jo?"

"Please don't get upset. I thought I could convince you to take me on the road trip. I knew if I told you I was pregnant you'd definitely say no."

"How far along are you?" he asked loudly.

"Five months." She stopped smiling and cocked her head to one side. "What's wrong? I thought you'd be happy. "

Brian stepped back. "Is this why you wanted to get married at city hall and skip the big wedding?"

"Well, yeah, but…"

"I had a right to know."

He looked away in frustration and she burst into tears.

"I'm sorry. I didn't know how to tell you, after I made such a big deal about going with you and everything."

Five days later they flew to Wyoming. Michael met them at the airport in Jackson. As usual, Jo greeted him with a warm embrace and Brian ignored her curiosity when he too hugged Michael. Brian was still reeling over the news of her pregnancy and not her biggest fan at the moment. He had tried to engage in their honeymoon and be happy, but the sense of being manipulated and lied to struck old wounds hard. A bulky coat hid the changes in Jo's body and he didn't believe Michael had noticed. Brian wasn't sure when the best time would be to tell him he was going to be a grandfather.

"Beth sends her apologies for not meeting you with me," Michael said. "She's got a cold and has been running a fever. We'd better hustle, there's a strong storm brewing and I'd like to get home before it hits."

The contrast from tropics to snow storm thrilled Jo. Brian's attitude was less than enthusiastic. At this moment, he didn't want to pretend to be happy or excited about anything. He needed some distance to think.

They found Beth building a snowman with her daughter, Emily, in front of the house. She smiled and pulled off her gloves as she approached the Jeep.

"You're supposed to be in bed," Michael said.

"Oh, stop fussing, Michael. I'm fine." Beth kissed his cheek, softening her admonishment and turned to Brian with open arms. "Hey you, congratulations on your marriage."

Brian accepted her embrace and introduced her to Jo. The two women hugged and Beth jumped back, looking from Jo to Brian, then back again.

"Are you two going to have a baby?"

Jo smiled widely and Brian looked away just in time to catch the wounded expression on Michael's face. Michael turned his back and walked toward Beth's daughter.

"We haven't told anyone yet," Brian said, more to Michael than anyone.

Beth threw her arms around Jo and then Brian, "How wonderful. Michael? Isn't this wonderful? You're going to be a grandpa."

Michael wrapped an arm around Emily's slender shoulders. His blue eyes flicked over Brian once then moved on to Jo and he forced a smile.

"Absolutely."

Beth led Jo and Emily inside while Michael and Brian unloaded their bags. Michael drove the Jeep down the driveway and parked it inside the garage. Brian looked up at the dark sky and the storm clouds moving in over the mountains. The cold wind seeped through his coat and chilled him, but he didn't want to go inside. Emily's snowman drew him like a magnet. He ran a hand over the icy surface of the head and old memories of Stacy and her snowman stirred.

Michael joined him and watched in silence as Brian scooped up a handful of wet snow and sculpted ears onto Emily's snowman.

When the job was complete, Michael smiled, "Great idea."

Brian ran a fingertip over the top of the smooth ice and without warning, tears stung his eyes. He hadn't thought of Stacy in such a long time. The residual weariness from the road trip and wrestling with the disappointment of Jo's secret had weakened his defenses.

"I'm sorry I didn't tell you about the baby sooner," he said, then turned, looking at Michael. "I don't mean to hurt you."

Michael drew in and released a long breath. "If that's what you believe is wrong, you're missing the point."

"No, right now, I think you're the one who's missing the point. I'm still in shock. I didn't know we were having this baby until four days ago. Jo didn't bother to tell me. I don't know if I'm ready to be a father." He stopped abruptly, embarrassed by his sudden outburst. He shoved his hands into his pockets and shivered. "I'm not sure what I think right now."

Michael studied him for a minute, then looked at the snowman, and finally back to Brian. "Being a grown-up can be tough."

He grunted. "I've been a grown-up all my life."

Michael shook his head. "You were a survivor, Brian. Being a grown-up's a whole lot different, trust me."

Michael bent and picked up a handful of snow, shifting it right, then left, forming a ball and there was a hint of mischief in his eyes.

"The biggest tragedy is you never got to be a kid," Michael said.

Brian realized what was about to happen and ducked a little too late. The snowball got him in the shoulder. Quickly, he scooped up a handful of snow and the fight was on.

Later that night, while Jo slept peacefully beside him, Brian thought about that moment of fun in the snow. Michael was right — childhood had passed him by. The picture of twelve-year-old Michael sitting on his parents' mantel came to mind and Brian knew Michael understood that loss intimately. Somewhere, inside both of them, was a little kid who still needed to laugh and play.

chapter 14

Sanguine Heart was back in the recording studio for their second album. On the second day, Sammy walked in waving a magazine in the air. "Has anyone read this bit of fluff?"

"What's that?" Tara said.

"It seems Sanguine Heart has one of the best front men in the business." Sammy announced, looking directly at Brian. She walked toward him slowly, quoting from the piece, her voice heavy with sarcasm.

"He stood up there looking like Adonis come to life and I wanted to hate him. I found it hard to believe that anyone with his face and body could have talent for anything other than attracting lust. I was wrong. This front man has the energy and immeasurable talent that raises Sanguine Heart above the rattle and hum. The audience can't get enough of Brian Burnette and neither can I. Blah, blah, blah."

Brian's guitar rested on his lap. Outwardly, he appeared completely re-laxed and unaffected by Sammy's attitude — inside he was churning. When she finished, he held out a hand.

"Can I see that?"

"Hell no, Mr. Front-man, buy your own copy."

"You can't blame Brian for what someone else said," Nick said.

"I don't blame him for anything other than being another crowned prince of the boy's club. I wish I'd been born with balls. Maybe they'd see me as more than a set of thirty-eight's." Sammy threw the magazine on the floor at Brian's feet. "Go on, read."

Brian put the guitar aside, stepped over the magazine and into the hall for a smoke. Behind him, Sammy began a familiar tirade about the music business, its prejudices against women, and how hard it was to break the code.

After a few minutes, Tara jumped up from the piano bench. "Oh, Sammy, shut up. If someone praises the way he plays, it's because Brian has extraordinary talent. If they say he has a powerful and exciting voice, it's the truth. I still get goose bumps when he punches that high E in Betsy's Soul. We all have talent, but Brian's better than that. He's what puts us over the top and you know it. Stop punishing him."

"I'm not mad at Brian."

"No, you're jealous. Now, go find him and apologize, so we can get on with this. I don't want to be here all night again."

The first Sanguine Heart album was a great success. Betsy's Soul was the first single released and the song rose to the top ten while they were on the last tour. One of Brian's compositions currently held the number one spot and Betsy's Soul went platinum. The swift pace of events thrilled and terrified him in equal proportions.

Nothing, except Jo, came close to the pleasure he found in playing, writing, and entertaining an audience. He never gave a lot of thought to fame, but found himself confronted with the issues accompanying success in the entertainment business. The worst part was how intrusive the attention became. Sammy loved the recognition. For Brian, the demands were too sudden and unwelcome.

He spent most of his twentieth birthday in the studio recording Fallen to Ashes. Today the words had new meaning. Life moved with a will of its own now. Jo's pregnancy was only the beginning. Alone in front of the mike, he allowed the fear inside to surface, giving the song even more emotional punch. Sammy watched through the control room window and when they had the final cut, she joined him as he took a long swallow of water. She didn't say a word, just stood there and stared.

"What?" he asked finally.

"There is so much depth to you it frightens me."

He rolled his eyes and reached for his coat. "I'm exhausted."

"Did you know Jo was pregnant before we got back from tour?"

Startled by her question, he shook his head. "I found out in the Bahamas."

"Is being a father something you wanted right now?"

He sighed wearily. "No, not yet, but it is what it is, you know?"

She patted his back and smiled a little, "How about some dinner before you go home?"

On the last day of November, the phone woke Brian at three in the morning. Jo nudged him and he stumbled to the living room to answer it.

"I need help," Max said.

"What's wrong?"

"I got up to get some aspirin and this pain shot through my back. I lost my balance and fell. I think I might have broken my leg."

"I'll be right down."

Max had a fractured hip. The emergency room doctor wanted to do more tests and admitted Max to the hospital. After a few days of testing, Max was diagnosed with advanced bone cancer and the doctors gave him six months, at best.

Two days later, Brian accompanied Jo to the obstetrician on a routine visit and listened in shock when the doctor said he heard two heartbeats then a technician confirmed twins with ultrasound.

The final load on his shoulders came one rainy afternoon as the band rehearsed for a New Year's Eve date and Stan informed them they were leaving for a three-week European tour at the end of January. Brian put down his guitar and walked outside. Sammy followed close behind.

"I've got a special bottle of Cognac my Dad sent as a Christmas gift. Want to come over and try a glass?"

Brian stopped abruptly and started to tell her to leave him alone, but Sammy poked him in the side. "Come on, howl at the moon. It will do you good."

Sammy opened the bottle of cognac and went to the cabinet for two glasses. "Would you light the fireplace, Brian? I need to shake this cold from my skinny bones."

He got the fire going and sipped the Cognac while he rifled through her collection of old records. He hadn't eaten all day and the alcohol got to his brain quickly.

"Come on, pick something," Sammy said. "We need some background noise while you tell me what's bothering you."

Brian slipped a record over the post and adjusted the volume. The cognac was his first drink ever and offered a comfort he never knew existed. Right now, everything seemed barely tolerable. He closed his eyes and listened to B.B. King play Lucille.

"I love his style," he said, hovering in front of the speakers.

"Quit stalling, Brian. Tell me what is bothering you."

"Hush Sammy, the man is talking."

"People are starting to say that about you."

Brian waved her off and turned his back. He wanted to listen to one thing right then. The sweet music would drift over him like a net of freedom and carry him away.

After the last note of the first song faded, he joined her on the leather sofa and took another sip of cognac. Sammy pushed at an errant lock of hair on his forehead and, as usual, Brian flinched.

"Is it just me, or do you always respond that way when people touch you?"

"Everyone except Jo."

"Hey, you're something special Brian, but sex with you would feel like incest."

"I know you're not interested in me. I didn't mean it that way."

Sammy studied him for a minute. "Want to get something to eat?"

"No. I like the way I feel. If I eat, this feeling will stop."

"It's not going to last anyway. You should eat something or you'll get sick."

He groaned and put his head back on the sofa. "Sammy, pretty please with sugar on top, stop mothering me."

"Okay. You want to get stupid, go right ahead. Just make sure you tell Jo I tried to stop you."

"I should call her."

"Yep."

Brian balanced the glass on his thigh with one finger and stared into the swirling amber liquid. The truth was he didn't want to call Jo because that would only lead to an argument. She would never understand why he was here instead of at home.

He shifted his weight and pushed aside calling Jo for now. "How hard would it be to postpone the tour?"

"You worried about your stepfather?"

"He's so sick. I don't want to dump this on Jo, especially now."

"I wish I could help you, but we're committed Brian. It's only a few weeks." She patted his thigh. "Come on blues man, let's get out of here. I'll take you to a few of my favorite clubs. We'll have a night on the town."

Around midnight he went back to Sammy's and while she prepared a late dinner, he decided he should call Jo and explain. "Where are you?" Jo shouted.

"I went to a couple of clubs with Sammy. I'll be late."

"For crying out loud, it is already midnight. You'd better get home right now."

"Jo, please. I need a little time off. I'm getting crazy."

"You start this kind of stuff and you'll be alone and crazy."

"Just a few more hours, I promise."

"You're asking for my blessing to run around drinking all night with another woman — isn't this special?"

"Never mind," he said, sighing heavily. "I'll leave now."

"Hey, don't bother. Sleep any place you want."

The line went dead in his hand. Brian replaced the receiver and swallowed the rest of the cognac.

Sammy had reheated some Chinese takeout and placed a plate for each of them on the coffee table in front of the sofa. "Are you in trouble?"

He shrugged and felt a wave of disorientation rush through him. He swayed on his feet, drunk for the first time in his life.

Sammy squinted at him. "I am going to be honest with you. I know it is none of my business, but sometimes I just don't get your relationship with Jo." She stepped closer, her tone subdued and attitude sober. "I know she was your high school sweetheart and all, but why do you put up with her trying to control you all the time?"

"She doesn't try to control me."

Sammy's eyebrows shot up in disbelief, "Oh, really? What about keeping you in the dark about being pregnant?"

"Mind your own business," he said hotly.

"Most of us marry what we are familiar with you know."

The alcohol was taking control now and the room moved before his eyes. A rush of heat swept through his body and he closed his eyes, taking a deep breath. "What?"

"I get the impression your mother was a devilish piece of work."

He reached for the back of the couch, but fell forward instead landing with a solid thud. Sammy knelt next to him.

"Are you okay?"

He stared up at her, knowing down deep there was truth in her words, but not ready to admit any of it. "I love her, Sammy."

"I know." She smiled sweetly, as only Sammy could do. He understood her intention was to look out for him.

She put her hands under his shoulders and lifted with a little groan. "Come on, let's get you on the couch."

"I need to go home."

"You can go home in the morning."

The first stop on the European tour was Paris. The French loved Sanguine Heart and their enthusiasm buoyed his spirits. Though he performed that evening with vigor and didn't disappointment his audience, he remained quiet and withdrawn offstage. The obligations to Jo, Max, and the band weighed heavily on his shoulders. For the first time, music felt like a job. Michael's statement about being a grown-up haunted him like a constant headache.

At the post-concert party, Sammy pushed through the crowd, glass of champagne in hand. "Hey, did you see who's here? "

"Who?"

"My brother and Amanda, they're vacationing in Europe. Come over and say hello."

Amanda smiled slyly as he approached. She dropped her gaze to his feet and deliberately panned his body. Meeting his eyes, her lips curled into a slow, wicked smile that sent the fine hair on Brian's arms into static shock.

Amanda hugged him with over familiarity and kissed his mouth, leaving a smear of red lipstick.

"It's so good to see you again," she purred

"Thank you," he managed, shaking off his surprise and wiping his mouth.

"I guess marriage agrees with you, Brian. You're looking quite fine. How is dear Jane? I hear she's pregnant."

Brian ignored the stupid question. Amanda knew Jo's name well. He turned his attention to Todd, until Sammy announced they had to mingle and gently pulled on the back of his shirt.

Once they were away from Amanda and Todd, Sammy slipped her arm through his and led him outside to the balcony. "So, tell me about you and Amanda."

"There's nothing to tell, Sammy. What you saw tonight is usually the extent of every conversation we've had, minus the kiss, of course."

"I find that hard to believe Brian. After all, she got you the audition, didn't she?"

"She told Todd about me."

Sammy studied him for a moment. Brian let his attention wander to the magnificent view of Paris and wished Jo was standing next to him so he could appreciate the splendor instead of feeling lonely and selfish.

Sammy sighed and followed his gaze. "I don't think I'd let Amanda anywhere near my body if I were you. Jo wouldn't like it when she saw the bite marks where that bitch tried to eat you alive."

"I can see you like your sister-in-law," he said.

"She's breaking Todd's heart. So far, she's cheated on him three times."

He looked at her over his shoulder and grinned. "What's this Sammy, an attack of convention?"

She flipped up the middle finger of her right hand. "Let's get a real drink. I hate champagne."

When the phone woke him in London two days later, Brian picked it up with a great sense of dread.

"Hi," Jo said.

"What's wrong? Is it Max?"

"Relax, nothing's wrong. I called to tell you they did another ultrasound today. One of the babies is definitely a boy. Isn't that great?"

"Yeah, it sure is." He sat up in the bed, trying to shake the sleep from his brain.

"Why does it sound like you don't care?"

Every time they talked, they quarreled. Nothing he said pleased her. The last thing he wanted was to get into another heated argument.

"Jo, it's early in the morning here. I was asleep."

"You're a liar. You don't want these babies."

"No, it's not that."

Jo cut in loudly. "You're going to be a father in two months! I'd say it's time you got used to the idea, Mr. I'm-so-wonderful rock star."

"That's not fair. I wanted to wait a while. I thought we'd stick to the plan."

"Too bad your plan didn't allow for the curves of real life."

"I'm talking about the plans you and I made together. Remember?"

"Well, things change. You've got a dying stepfather and a pregnant wife. Grow up and deal with it."

She slammed the receiver down and the line went dead in his hand.

Brian was too frustrated to sleep, so he dressed and ran the foggy streets of London. After a shower, he decided to call Jo, but there was no answer. Six months ago he would have been concerned that she didn't answer. Now he knew she simply wasn't answering to punish him. On impulse, he called Michael.

"It's good to hear from you, Brian. How's the tour going?"

The question stunned Brian. They hadn't spoken since he and Jo visited Wyoming yet Michael knew what he was doing.

He took a stab at a reply. "The tour is great."

"I'm surprised you'd be up this early. Isn't it only six in London?"

Michael not only knew he was on tour, but exactly where he was — a detail Brian wasn't always sure of himself.

"How do you know where I am? Did you talk to Max or Jo?"

"No. I have some contacts in the music business."

"You're keeping tabs on me?"

Michael laughed softly. "Yeah, just in case you need me."

Brian heard the sarcasm, but stepped around it. "Do you know about Max?"

"Bobby told me."

"And about Jo having twins?"

A long, dreadful silence ruled until Michael finally responded.

"No."

"We saw them on the ultrasound. There are definitely two and one is definitely a boy. I guess it really does skip a generation, like they say. Of course you had a sister…"

"What's wrong, Brian?" Michael said. "You didn't call me at the crack of dawn to discuss this, did you?"

Michael's ability to read between the lines struck a deep chord in Brian and something cracked. He couldn't stop the flow of words. "I feel like I'm heading straight for a brick wall at ninety miles an hour and picking up speed."

Afterwards, Brian realized he had talked for nearly an hour. Michael had listened, but didn't offer any advice — probably because he didn't ask for any. Still, the man managed to diffuse the panic and the pressure found a release. Brian told himself he should call Michael more often, when things weren't so negative.

He returned from Europe in late February. This was the beginning of the ninth month, but Jo looked more than ready. Max was in a period of remission the doctors didn't expect to last and Brian spent every available moment looking after the two of them.

Some evenings, he joined Tara at Sammy's apartment to work on the songs for their third album. The trio was finally a perfect mesh and the project came together easier than the other two. Four of ten songs were those he wrote alone. He collaborated with Sammy or Tara on most of the others.

By this time, everyone in the band respected his opinions and permitted him a generous amount of latitude in deciding which direction the band should take. Sammy swore he could listen to a piece of music then tighten all the loose ends until the result was art.

Sammy wrote a rhythm and blues number entitled "Blind Burden" for him. She envisioned a little bass, Tara on piano, a soft drum, and her on acoustic guitar. Brian need only step up and sing. Sammy said this slimmed down, acoustic piece had one purpose — it was time the world heard him wail.

The first time he saw the song was late at night in Sammy's Soho loft. Tara had left for the day and Jo slept on the couch. Sammy handed him the sheet music and asked him to run through it then disappeared to the kitchen while he sat at the piano. He ran through slowly then began again, shifting the key and singing the lyrics.

The music flowed from him, carrying him away to a familiar plane. He didn't need to think in this place. Didn't need to work or reason, plan or execute anything for anybody. This was as simple as his life got — rhythm, rhyme, and fingertips on cool keys. His right foot rose on the pedal and vibration bubbled up his spine.

Sometimes, music was on the same level as making love to Jo. Their love-making lifted him just like this — to a place beyond limitations. He didn't need to see her eyes then — he could feel her love caressing his soul. That blessed feeling suspended him in a timeless place where their spirits blended into one.

As the last notes slipped from his fingers, he nodded. He turned and found Sammy and Jo nearby. Jo had tears on her face and he jumped to his feet, hurrying to her side.

"What's wrong?"

Jo smiled at him and wiped at her face. "That song's way over the top."

Brian hugged her and stroked her soft hair while he smiled at Sammy.

"Looks like you did it again," he said.

"Oh, yeah, me. As usual, you're incredibly blind, but thanks anyway."

chapter 15

ON MARCH 31, after twelve hours of labor, Jo gave birth to twin boys. Brian stood next to her, soothing and coaching her, grateful he was around to witness his sons come into the world. One was quiet and one complained from the first breath. A nurse handed Jo the quiet one and presented Brian the cranky, tiny bundle. The baby quieted the moment Brian held him close.

Jo smiled wearily. "He likes you already."

The baby opened his eyes and seemed to focus on Brian's face.

"I think he's staring at me, Jo. Isn't he too young to do that?"

Jo's giggle drew Brian's attention away from the baby.

"What?"

"You think I'm an expert just because I'm the mom."

Brian shrugged and looked back to the baby. "I've never been around little babies — you have."

"You're going to be a very interesting father."

Brian brushed the baby's cheek with his fingertip and swallowed the sudden lump in his throat. "I've been thinking, maybe I should quit the band. You know — find something else to do for a living, so I can be around more."

"I can't believe you said that, especially now."

"This is the perfect time."

"Brian — look at me."

He raised his head and groaned when he saw tears rolling down her face. "What did I do now, Jo?"

"Promise me you won't quit. You're just hitting your stride, Brian."

"You and these boys are more important."

"No," she said firmly. "We're a family, with equal rights. If you were a failure at what you do, I'd go along with this idea of quitting. There is no reason for you to stop. We can work this out. You can have it all."

Jo insisted on naming the first born Michael Brian and the second Maximillian Joseph. Brian strongly opposed the name Maximillian, but she put the name on the birth certificate anyway. She insisted they would never call the boys by their whole names anyway. Everyone would call them Mike and Max.

Brian returned from the hospital and found Max senior asleep in a wheelchair near the front door. He had dressed himself and his coat lay across his lap. Brian touched his shoulder gently to wake him. Max opened sleepy eyes and peered into Brian's weary face.

"I want to go to see the babies," Max said.

"We're bringing them home day after tomorrow. Don't you think it would be better to wait?"

"Brian, I know you've been up all night, but I can't wait. Will you please take me?"

Brian didn't argue. Some time, some year, there would be time for sleep. He took a quick shower, put on fresh clothes, and drove Max to the hospital.

Max was weak and enduring incredible pain, but held his namesake and kissed the newborns tiny cheek, putting on a good show for Jo. As Max thanked them for their gift of love, Brian saw a shift in his dark eyes and knew Max wouldn't live to see the babies come home.

Brian took Max home, helped him into bed, and stayed beside him through the night. Eventually, exhaustion took over and he fell into a deep sleep in a chair next to the bed. Near dawn, a car alarm on the street below sprang to life and he woke with a start, looking to Max immediately.

Max's face seemed peaceful in the early morning light and Brian knew he was gone. He reached out and checked for a pulse, then covered his face with the sheet, and went outside to the fire escape.

The sun rose behind gray clouds and the cold wind blowing down the alley chilled him. He smoked a cigarette and gripped the metal rail so tightly his hand ached. He didn't know being twenty wasn't supposed to feel this old.

Brian walked in Jo's hospital room late that morning and took her hand. "I've got bad news."

"Is it Max?"

"He's gone, Jo."

Her soft-gray eyes filled with tears. "Are you okay?"

"I'm glad he's out of pain," he said, turning his attention to the hallway. "When do they bring the babies around?"

"In fifteen minutes or so." She squeezed his hand gently. "Brian?"

He shifted his eyes to her face and Jo opened her arms. "Hold me."

Later, as Brian held baby Max and talked on the phone to a funeral director, Jo held out a bottle of formula. He pressed the receiver between his ear and shoulder, and accepted the bottle with a shaky hand. The small glass bottle slipped from his fingers and shattered on the floor at his feet. He lowered his head and tapped both feet in frustration. The receiver slipped from his ear to the chair and bounced off the floor.

Jo pushed the call button as Brian backed his chair away from the mess, stood, and turned his back, holding Max to his chest. He took deep breaths and closed his eyes, fighting for control.

Brian was sleeping for the first time in two days when the sound of knocking invaded this peace. A glance at the clock told him it was eight in the morning.

He pulled on a pair of jeans and T-shirt then stumbled to the door, expecting one of the tenants. Michael and Beth stood side-by-side waiting expectantly.

Beth smiled a little. "Surprise."

"Please, ugh…come in."

"I tried to let you know we were coming last night," Michael said, following Beth inside. "I didn't get any answer."

"It was kind of a rough day. I stayed with Jo until they kicked me out."

Beth patted his arm gently. "You look tired."

Brian shrugged. "There's a lot going on."

"That's why we're here," Michael said.

Brian met his eyes. "You know about Max?"

"Bob called."

Beth slipped off her coat and looked around. "Where's the kitchen? I'll make a pot of coffee."

He directed Beth to the kitchen and looked back to find Michael watching him. He ran a hand through his tangled hair and waved a hand at a chair.

"Please, have a seat. I need to clean up. I'll be right back."

After washing his face and brushing his teeth, he changed clothes. He needed to shave, but put that off until later. He found Michael in the babies' nursery. There was only one crib and he didn't want Michael to think they didn't have the money to provide for their children.

"It's kind of cramped," Brian said. "We plan on moving to a bigger place soon. We'll set up the other crib then."

Michael turned, examining him as he spoke. "You don't need much space with newborns."

"Do you want to see them while you're here?"

Michael's blue eyes flickered and Brian knew his careless words had inflicted a new wound.

"I mean this morning…today," he stammered.

"Well, they are my grandsons." Michael picked up a tiny pair of baby shoes and smiled.

Oddly, something gave way inside Brian and he found he could breathe a little easier.

Michael put the shoes down and eyed the single crib. "I was surprised you chose to name one of them Michael."

"We're going to call him Mike. Wait until you see him — he's feisty."

Michael looked back at him and grinned. "Maybe you should have named him Brian."

Michael took charge of Max's funeral and helped Brian settle Max's estate. Max left everything he owned to Brian and Jo. Sorting through the personal belongings was the most difficult part. Looking back, Brian wasn't certain he could have handled everything without Michael's help.

Beth hovered over Brian, Jo, and babies like a mother. Her joy and gentleness eased the weight on Brian's shoulders.

After they left, Jo confessed she was now completely in love with his soft spoken father, especially when she saw Michael's tenderness for his grandchildren. She didn't understand why Brian couldn't accept his father's love and affection with open arms.

"He just feels guilty, Jo," Brian said, hoping this wouldn't be a long discussion.

"So? Are you going to let that go on forever? You can't make him pay for everything that happened to you."

Brian sighed loudly, keeping his eyes on the television screen. "I'm not trying to make him pay for anything."

"Yes, you are. You reject him to get even for what your mother put you through."

He grunted and rolled his eyes. "Gee, thanks for explaining."

"Forgive him, Brian. He deserves it and so do you."

Three months after Max's death, Jo decided it was time to move into a home with more room and fewer reminders of Max. She chose to tell him on a day when Brian spent fourteen hours working on a video and came home in a foul mood. He sat at the kitchen table and she placed a plate of spaghetti in front of him, then launched into the plan she had worked on all day.

"I want to sell this brownstone and move back to Pennsylvania."

Brian stopped chewing and looked at her in disbelief.

Jo hurried in before he got angry. "I want to be near my mother and friends when you're on the road. With Max gone, I have no reason to stay."

"I'm not reason enough?"

"Don't be ridiculous. You'd come to Pennsylvania when you're not on tour."

"And when I'm recording?"

"Well, you'll just have to come back here for that. Brian, it will be hard for me to take care of two babies alone. I need to be where I know people will help me when you're gone."

He sighed and pushed the plate away. "It's just that I never wanted to move back there. I hate it."

"You hate it that our mothers are there."

"Good point."

"Just remember we're adults now and I don't have to take my mother's advice. As for your mother, well, I don't see that she'll be a problem unless you go over to her house."

In the end, Brian didn't put up much of a fight. She had a right to some help. In six weeks, he would start his longest tour. The only people they knew in Brooklyn were the O'Mara's and he wouldn't contact them for help. He sensed that Michael would see it as a betrayal if he were to reach out in that direction. Jo would be better off in Pennsylvania.

Out of a growing need for privacy, he wanted to have a home built outside the town where they would have plenty of space. Jo wanted to live in one of the older, elegant homes, on Snob Hill. Brian found it amusing when she chose a house around the block from Amanda Cutler's parents, but kept the irony to himself. After Jo's brother Kenny pointed out the obvious to her, Jo decided to have a home built after all.

He was two months into the tour when she changed her mind and hired a contractor. Her plan was that she and the boys would stay with her mother until the house was finished some time the next year.

"Find a house to rent. I'm not about to stay with your mother when I get time off."

"When you come to town, we'll get a hotel room. By the time you join us for any extended length of time, the house will be ready."

In the middle of the tour, Sanguine Heart received two Grammy nominations for their first album. Simultaneously, the second album went gold. The pace of life kicked into a new kind of overdrive. In addition to touring, they were popular guests on talk shows and music news. On Saturday night, they played New Orleans. On Sunday morning, Brian joined Sammy and Tara for an interview with a popular entertainment magazine reporter. At the conclusion of the interview, the reporter mentioned they were sending a photographer to Pennsylvania for pictures of Jo and the twins.

"My family is off limits," Brian said.

The reporter gave him a small, thin smile. "Mrs. Burnette has already consented."

Brian returned that smile with one that had nothing to do with humor or good will. He didn't raise his voice. He leveled his gaze on the reporter and hammered him softly.

"My family isn't part of this deal. If you go anywhere near them, I'll personally hunt you down and break the hand that knocks on my door."

"Are you threatening me?"

Brian's steady gaze didn't waver.

The reporter glanced at Tara and Sammy for support and finding none, shifted his weight and cleared his throat. "There's no need to be hostile."

Jo joined him in New York for the Grammy ceremony. The band won two — best album and best single in the pop/rock category. Sammy and Tara made long-winded thank you speeches and Brian had little time. He quickly rattled off a list of people he wanted to thank, the first being Mrs. Clifford and the congregation of the First Baptist Church of Cleveland.

Jo hated the parties that followed and Brian kept his promise not to stay all night. They caught a ten o'clock flight to Pennsylvania the next morning and went directly to their unfinished home.

Brian visited the construction site only one time before and hadn't seen their home yet. He turned the car into the sloping half-moon drive and parked in the front. He got out of the car and stared, speechless.

Jo nudged him after a minute. "Well?"

"It's going to be beautiful."

She held out her hand and led him to the wooded property behind the house. Jo had insisted the construction company leave as many trees around the house as possible. She stopped, smiled broadly, and pointed to the treetops. Brian looked up and saw a tree house.

She wrapped her arms around him and Brian reveled in the familiar comfort of her body.

She pulled back a little to look up at his face. "Know what it's for?"

His smile widened. "I love it."

"Beat you to the top."

She ran laughing to the spiraling staircase that wound to the first floor. Her laughter reminded him of the girl he fell in love with over six years ago.

The tree house was much more elaborate than the old one at her mothers. This one had two levels. The bottom was wide and the top level provided a roof. There were benches around three sides and a few tables. The second level was open to the sky and a magnificent view. The rolling mountains formed a large inverted-V in the lush, green valley.

Jo turned from admiring the view and expressed her love with those wide, exquisite eyes. Brian put his arms around her and kissed her mouth hungrily. Jo pulled away from him and giggled.

"There's a sleeping bag and a bottle of wine in the trunk of the car. Would you go get them?"

Brian kissed her again then reluctantly backed off. "I'll be right back."

They made love, drank all the wine, and made love again. Later, lying together contentedly, staring up at the clear sky, Brian wrapped her in his arms.

"This has been one of the most perfect days of my life, Jo." He turned and pressed his lips against her temple. "Thanks for having the tree house built."

"No need to thank me. I did it as much for myself as for you. When we're apart, I'll come up here, watch the sun rise and feel more connected to you. This is the place where I will talk to you spirit to spirit."

The identical Burnette twins had dark hair and their eyes were a blend of Jo's gentle gray and Brian's deep blue. At first glance, it was difficult to tell them apart, but for anyone who spent time with the boys, it was completely clear which twin was Mike and which was Max. Mike was the more assertive of the two, the most mischievous, cried the loudest, and was the first to laugh. Max was cuddly, slept more, and had an even, happy temperament.

The twins were eighteen months old the first time Brian spent any extended time with them. They quickly learned he was not as tolerant as their mother was. When it was naptime, they stayed in their beds. When it was time to eat they didn't play, they ate or they left the table. Most importantly, when Dad said no, he wouldn't take it back.

They also learned that sitting in the big rocking chair with their father meant he would read or sing to them and that he was strong. He could toss them high in the air, and carry or swing them both at the same time. He always let them play in the tub until their skin wrinkled. He enjoyed wrestling on the floor, slurping spaghetti into his mouth, taking them down the slide, and long rides in a convertible, which always ended with the treat of ice cream. Best of all, the house filled with music and laughter when he was home.

Returning to Pennsylvania had drawbacks Brian found nearly intolerable. The first and most significant disadvantage was contending with Jo's mother.

Amelia readily shared her thoughts and beliefs on any subject that she considered significant. Her favorite topics regarded their extravagance and not-so-subtle reminders that Jo should maintain a higher profile in his life. Amelia was full of opinions from raising the twins, how they spent their money, Brian's occupation, even their sex life. Jo was skilled at ignoring her mother. Brian usually walked away rather than argue. Amelia seemed to gain a sense of power from his silence and pushed harder and harder. The inevitable confrontation was something Brian didn't look forward to.

One morning, he returned from a long run to find Amelia sitting at the kitchen table with a fresh cup of coffee in her hand, ready for battle. The boys had just finished their breakfast when he entered. Jo was busy wiping Max's face and Mike squealed, holding out his arms.

Brian picked him up then kissed Max's cheek and poured a glass of orange juice before sitting at the table. Amelia looked him over, head-to-foot in a slow pan of disapproval.

"Don't you think you should shower before you hold the babies so close?"

"Mom, don't start," Jo said.

Brian ignored Amelia and lifted Mike into the air, making him giggle.

"He's sweating, Jo. It's very crude."

Brian kissed Mike and put him back in the high chair, then picked up his orange juice and drank it all before facing his mother-in-law.

"Amelia, this is our house. If you can't show me a little respect, take your opinions home and stay there."

He pushed the swinging door to the kitchen open and disappeared. Amelia's face puckered and she started to cry, but she received no sympathy from her daughter. Jo walked her to the front door and promised to call.

Late that year, near Christmas, Brian had a break in the current tour and met Harlan for their ritual breakfast. Harlan had already ordered coffee for both of them before Brian arrived and slid into the booth.

"You look tired. Living on the road must be rough."

"Not as tough as staying up with Mike all night."

"What's wrong with him?"

"He got into the Flintstone vitamins with iron and ate all the Barney's. The doctor said not to worry as long as he continued to throw up."

Harlan smiled. "How's Max?"

"He didn't indulge. Are you coming by for Christmas?"

"Well," Harlan said, shifting his weight uncomfortably, "we need to talk."

"What about?"

"Your mother wants to see the boys. She asked me to talk it over with you."

Brian was speechless. Since their birth nearly two years ago, Jean hadn't acknowledged her grandsons.

"What does she want — a private audience, without me around?"

The bitterness of the question startled Harlan. He shook his head quickly. "No, nothing like that. We'll come over to your place, if that's okay."

Brian sat back in the booth and looked around at the crowded cafe. "Why?"

"What do you mean?"

"Nothing's changed, Harlan."

"She has, Brian. She's trying anyway. The episodes have stopped, for the most part. She needs this. She has no one except you and me."

Nothing would have pleased him more than to never see his mother again. She could rot for all he cared. Saying no to her would have been easy, but saying no to Harlan was impossible.

Jo bathed and dressed the twins and brought them to the music room where he sat at the piano.

"I'm going to take a shower. Keep an eye on the boys, all right?"

Brian kept his head down, concentrating and Jo shook his shoulder.

"Did you hear me?"

He lifted his fingers from the keys and looked at her blankly. "What?"

Jo sighed loudly. "I have to take a shower. Watch the boys."

He nodded and went back to the keyboard. "Close the hall door so they can't escape."

The boys played quietly with a pile of Legos, lulling him into a false sense of security. His attention drifted until he paused to scribble a few notes and the silence in the room alarmed him. He looked to the spot he last saw them and saw nothing.

Standing, he looked frantically around the room. "Mike? Max?"

"Daddy," Max said.

He found them under the piano. They smiled in harmony and Brian groaned. Their hair, faces, arms, hands, legs, shoes, clothes, and the hardwood floor around them were covered in chocolate. Mike held out a mushy remnant from what must have been the largest Hershey bar in the world.

"Good," Mike said. Max nodded in agreement.

Brian had to smile. "Looks like it."

"Oh, no!" Jo stood in the doorway, wrapped in an old terrycloth robe and her hair in a towel. "You were supposed to watch them."

"They're fast, Jo."

"Well, you'd better hope they're a chip off the old block. You're mother and Harlan will be here in half an hour." She turned and started toward the stairs. "Good luck cleaning them up."

Brian was upstairs when Harlan and Jean arrived. He slipped a shirt over Max's head and Mike took the opportunity to jump on the bed.

Brian snapped his fingers and pointed at the bed, "Down."

Mike dropped to the bed with the skill of gymnast and turned his attention to the appliqué on the front of his denim overalls. He frowned, trying to pluck it away.

"Leave that alone," Brian said.

"Off, Daddy."

"No."

That single word brought tears to Mike's eyes and his lower lip quivered. Brian finished dressing Max and picked Mike up for a hug.

He set the boys down at the foot of the stairs and let them run ahead to the kitchen where he heard Jo talking with Harlan. Brian couldn't hear his mother and hoped she had decided not to come.

Unfortunately, Jean sat at the end of the oblong kitchen table watching Harlan make a fuss over her grandsons with a real smile on her face. She switched her eyes to the door when Brian entered and her smile faded.

"Good afternoon," she said coolly.

Mike tapped Brian's leg. "Look."

Brian looked down and saw the gift Harlan and Jean gave each boy—red wagons filled with stuffed animals and small toys. Max pulled his wagon over the top of Brian's foot, but Brian didn't notice.

Never, in all his years at home, had his mother bought one gift for him for any occasion, including Christmas. He always spent most of the joyous season wondering why no one loved him.

One particular night was burned into his memory. He spent Christmas Eve in the backseat of a car while his mother and current lover drank inside a rundown tavern on the outskirts of Buffalo, New York. He buried his body under a mountain of clothes and eventually fell into a light sleep. Somewhere near midnight, he heard his mother laugh and wiped off part of the window to see. Jean and her current lover walked past the car and down the street to a hotel.

He threw off the heavy pile of clothes and ran after them. By the time he reached the hotel, his mother had disappeared inside. He took a tentative step toward the lobby just as the night clerk rousted a bum that had wandered inside. The clerk pushed the bum toward the door and spotted him standing there.

"Get out of here, kid. Am I going to have to call the cops on all you good-for-nothing scum tonight?"

Brian turned quickly and ran back down the steps to the sidewalk and slipped on a patch of ice. His feet flew out from under him and he struck the back of his head on the sidewalk. He woke sometime later to the sound of church bells announcing the arrival of Christmas. His body was covered with a fine layer of snow and stiff from the cold. There was a knot the size of a baby's fist on the back of his skull and his head felt like it might explode. He hadn't eaten or slept in a bed for almost two days, but the lonely sound of those bells was the last straw. He lay there on the sidewalk and cried so hard that he couldn't breathe.

That night wasn't the worst or loneliest, but it was his breaking point. Only forty-five days past his ninth birthday and he understood his place in the universe. He dusted the snow off, wiped the tears from his face, and moved on.

Some of the holidays were worse, but none were better until he met Harlan. He looked back at his mother and the anger rose freely. She had no right to come here bearing gifts and a benevolent smile for his children.

She looked his way and immediately sat straighter in the chair. Brian felt like throwing her out the door.

Harlan smiled at him. "You're mother picked these toys out all by herself," he said.

Jean rose slowly. "Let's go, Harlan. This was a mistake."

Brian leaned against a counter and crossed his arms over his chest, ignoring Jo's curious look. He refused to take his eyes off his mother. Harlan helped her into her coat and they started for the front door.

"Harlan, you're welcome to come back any time," Brian called.

He didn't move from his post until he heard the car pull away then dropped into a chair at the table and watched the boys play with their new toys. Jo returned from the front door and watched him.

"Want to talk about it?"

"No."

Jo stepped over the toys to rub his shoulders then kissed his cheek.

Michael and Beth visited frequently. The boys adored this set of grandparents and Jo taught them to call them Grandpa and Grandma. She also informed

Brian that even if he never brought himself to say the words father or dad, their children would extend the respect and love Michael deserved.

"Are you saying I don't treat him with respect?"

She laughed outright. "Try indifference. You want to prove you don't need him. Everything he does tells you he's more than willing to be a bigger part of your life if you'd let him."

"I let him," he said sourly.

Jo usually knew when to back off. Sometimes she heeded the warning. When it came to Michael, she pursued the subject with zeal.

"You should be ashamed. You make him stand out on the porch like some beggar and allow him to peek in through a crack of the door when you're feeling generous."

Brian was wrestling with a new string in the old twelve-string guitar, but the wire slipped and whipped away. He put the guitar aside and got on his feet as Jo continued.

"You don't treat him much better than you did your mother."

"Stay out of this, Jo. I'll work it out."

"Brian, honey, love of my life, being an asshole is not working it out. He was just sixteen when he had sex with your mother. If society punished women for this kind of thing, the way they punish men, she would have gone to jail."

Brian threw up his hands. "All right, I promise to be nicer."

chapter 16

Sanguine Heart received their third Grammy nomination for Fallen to Ashes while they were on tour. They were in Houston at the time, but flew in to perform one number from their current album and to accept the award if they won.

This time Brian attended the ceremony without Jo. She hadn't been feeling too well and he insisted she stay home. They did their song and he was still backstage with Sammy when it was announced that they won.

Since Fallen to Ashes was his song, the rest of the band let Brian go first. He quickly rattled off a list of people he wanted to thank, including producers, their record label, and of course the fans. He paused for a breath and smiled broadly at the audience.

"Fallen to Ashes is about the gift of a woman's love." Looking straight into the camera, ending his brief speech by speaking to a certain set of loving gray eyes. "Thank you Jo, I love you with all my heart."

After celebrating at a party that night, Brian squeezed in a few hours of sleep and took an early bird flight to Philadelphia the next morning. To his surprise, Jo's brother, Kenny, met him at the airport, instead of Jo.

"Wow, you look tired," Kenny said.

"Where's Jo?"

"She's at Mom's cooking up a special celebration dinner."

Amelia's home was the last place Brian wanted to be after two months on the road, but he didn't say so to his brother-in-law. He tossed his carry-on bag over his shoulder and followed Kenny to the car.

Brian lay back in the seat and tried to relax. A nap sounded like good news. He closed his eyes as Kenny merged with traffic on the interstate.

Kenny nudged him gently. "Hey, I'm playing music again. Did Jo tell you?"

"No."

"We're playing down at the Tap Room. Why don't you get Jo to ask Mom to watch the kids tonight and come hear us?"

"I don't know Kenny, I'm really beat."

"Well, we've got a three-hour drive. Take a nap."

Brian nodded and actually slipped into the edge of sleep before Kenny spoke again.

"I know this band can go places if we can just catch a break, Brian."

Kenny was hinting for direct assistance. Brian didn't have the heart to speak the truth. Kenny's talent at best was mediocre. He told Kenny to work on a demo and that he would see what he could do. After that, Kenny let him sleep.

The minute he walked into Amelia's house, the boys ran to him. He scooped them up and hugged them tightly, giving each son a kiss on the cheek. Jo entered from the kitchen and it felt like the floor dropped out beneath him. She was pregnant again.

She hugged him quickly and led him away to the kitchen, telling her family they needed a few minutes of privacy.

Brian sat at the table and stared at her in disbelief.

"I know it's a shock," she began gently.

"Shock? Jo, I thought we agreed there wouldn't be any more kids right now."

"I know, but..."

"When did you stop taking the pill?"

Jo studied her hands. Brian sensed he wasn't going to like this answer.

"Last year when we moved here," she said.

"Damn it!" He jumped to his feet and walked away a few steps.

"Shh! Everyone will hear you."

Being quiet wasn't a request he could accommodate right then. He felt like stomping, screaming, and breaking things.

"Tell me why? Why did you do this, Jo?"

"I want more children!" She got to her feet as well. "I don't know what you're worried about. We can certainly afford it."

"It's not the money and you know it." He shut his eyes and inhaled slowly, hoping to tap into some patience. "Jo," he began again, softly. "I want to be a real father — not the kind who visits a few times each year. I just can't be that right now. Don't you understand?"

"I understand you're selfish. I sit here waiting while you're out there partying and becoming a living legend. Can't you let me have this?"

Brian chose to ignore the sarcastic assessment of his work. "How far along are you?"

"Five months."

This truth infuriated him. "Then what's the point about asking me if I'll let you have this? It's pretty clear you made the decision for both of us."

Jo's expression switched changed from hurt to anger, "Were you thinking of an abortion?"

"No, I'm thinking I need a vasectomy."

"I can't believe how selfish you are! Don't bother considering a vasectomy, Brian. You won't be sleeping with me for a long, long time."

She turned and stalked into the living room. Brian wasn't about to follow. He walked out the back door.

Half an hour later, Jo found him sitting in the old tree house, smoking a cigarette. She looked up and pulled her coat tightly about her.

"You know you're not supposed to smoke," she said.

After a bout with bronchitis, he signed a contract with the recording company promising to refrain. This was the wrong time for her to remind him of that agreement.

"Too bad," he said.

"Can we talk about this rationally?"

"Just because I disagree with you doesn't mean I'm irrational."

"I meant your reference to a vasectomy and my brilliant exit line about not sleeping with you."

His expression softened a little as he flipped the ashes from the cigarette into the cold wind.

"Explain it all to me again. Why do you hate to see me pregnant?"

He glanced at her, then away quickly — thinking, searching for patience. "I'm not doing my job as a husband and father. This isn't the way I wanted it to be."

"Brian, sweetheart, look at our twins. Look at me." She smiled and waved a hand at her swollen abdomen. "You definitely find time to do your job."

He met her eyes with a steady, hard gaze. "I wasn't talking about getting you pregnant and you know it."

She threw up her hands, "This conversation again? Why do we have to go over and over this?"

"Because I'm pretty sure you never hear what I say."

"Which is?"

"I want to be an active part in the lives of my children."

"Then stop being a musician who tours three-quarters of the year."

"It's going to slow down, if you'll just be patient."

"No, I won't. Sorry, you can't have it all Brian. I get to make some of the choices."

He couldn't keep his anger at bay and glared at her.

Jo glared right back. "I hate it when you look at me like that."

She turned and walked away from him a second time.

Brian watched her walk back to Amelia's house, but couldn't make himself follow. He was afraid he would have another screaming fit so he walked toward town, where he called his old friend, Mark, from a payphone at 7-Eleven.

He envied the simplicity of Mark's life. Mark worked Monday through Friday for a delivery company and shared a modest home with his most recent girlfriend. He took a two-week vacation every year and life was running steady without the highs and lows that ruled Brian's life. Over a bottle of tequila, he told Mark that Kenny's band was playing at an old haunt and allowed Mark to talk him into going.

Brian seldom got out in the real world anymore and didn't know what to expect of people. They ordered drinks at the bar and after the third round he believed it possible for him to blend in with the crowd.

Unfortunately, Kenny spotted him through the dense haze of cigarette smoke. Brian hoped Kenny would come over, talk discretely between sets, and not announce his presence. When they finished the song, Kenny talked to the other band members for a minute then went back to the microphone.

"We'd like to try something a little different tonight. We don't normally do this song because there's really only one person who can sing the damn thing right. Tonight we thought we'd take a stab at it anyway. This is a little tune a friend of mine won a Grammy for last night. It's called Fallen to Ashes."

The audience applauded and Kenny began to pick out the lead on the guitar. He stepped up to the microphone, looked at the audience, opened his mouth, but snapped it shut again. He shook his head, smiling. "I can't."

The crowd clapped and whistled encouragement. Kenny glanced at Brian and shrugged, trapping him.

Kenny grinned. "You know, there's an old buddy of mine in the audience who could help me out, if he would be so kind."

"Damn it," Brian mumbled as a spotlight swung onto his face, blinding him.

"Ladies and gentleman, our own claim to fame — Brian Burnette!"

The crowd stepped back forming a path to the stage. They shouted, clapped, and whistled until Brian moved toward the band. Kenny offered him a hand and smiled widely. "Thanks brother-in-law."

Brian put his back to the audience. "How mad is Jo?"

"Well, during the blessing, she mumbled something to God about castration. This might be your last performance as a whole man." Kenny slapped him on the back. "Guess you'd better take it to the limit."

Brian turned around and raised the microphone to accommodate his height.

He offered the audience a slight smile. "I hope you'll bear with me. I don't usually sing this after consuming a fifth of tequila."

The audience erupted with rowdy enthusiasm.

Kenny played the introduction and as the house lights dimmed, Brian thought of Jo, sitting at home angry, disappointed and, God bless her, waiting for him to come home one more time. A wave of regret roared through his brain, rocking him body and soul. He put his head down and listened to Kenny begin the lead-in, let him pass the opening once and on the second round started to sing from this place of pain.

The band stuck with him as he stretched the four-minute song to seven and brought the audience to their feet. He climbed off the stage, refusing to do any more, and asked Mark for a ride home.

Jo was in the family room and didn't look up from her knitting when he entered.

"You smell like a bar," she said.

"Mark and I went to see Kenny play."

"Did you let Kenny talk you into playing?"

"Nope."

"I'm proud of you."

Brian slipped off his coat and tossed it on a chair. "Don't be. I let him talk me into singing."

Jo grinned girlishly, "Seems like you can be talked into anything, sometimes."

Brian didn't know what she meant and didn't care right then. He didn't want to talk about Kenny or music. He wanted to straighten things out between them. He opened his mouth to apologize, but Jo fixed him with a soft look and the words froze in his throat.

"I'm sorry you're so upset about this baby. It's just that I want a house full of children and I don't want to wait." She smiled sweetly. "Believe me our babies will know who you are and how much you love them. Just look at Max and Mike, they adore you."

"But to tell me this way, Jo, to just spring it on me not once but twice, I feel like I'm not really part of things." He sat on the couch and released a deep sigh. "I've always been estranged from everyone — there's always this distance between me and the world. The only time I feel connected is when I'm with you or lost in the music. Music allows me the freedom to bridge that gap and communicate without interruption. When I play or sing no one argues or corrects me. They can't make alterations or take off in another direction, because it's mine and I own it. It used to be that when I walked off the stage, nobody listened to me, but you. Now you're not listening either."

Jo considered the long statement for a moment, digesting his odd candor. Finally, she sighed and put her knitting aside. "Can we talk about your past without you getting weird?"

He shook his head. "That doesn't have anything to do with this."

"Oh, I think it does. I think you've always used music as an escape."

Brian stiffened, hating her analysis. "Escape from what?" he snapped.

Jo came to him and caressed his face tenderly. "The abuse your mother put you through."

Tears filled his eyes and she wrapped her arms around him and pulled him close to her. He held on, languishing in the comfort of her arms, too weary to argue.

An hour later, just as he was falling into a deep sleep, Jo rolled over and snuggled close to him. "By the way, did I tell you how proud I am that you won that Grammy?"

"No. We've been too busy arguing all day."

"I should have been there with you."

He pulled her closer. "You were right beside me, every step of the way."

"What are you going to do if something happens and I'm not around anymore?"

He flinched uncomfortably. Pursuing her "what ifs" always drove him crazy.

Jo kept pushing, "Well, what if you have to go on without me?"

He shifted his weight. "Quit."

"I mean with your issues about abandonment, wouldn't that be like the ultimate blow?"

"My issues of what?"

"Your parents, Brian. You still carry around a lot of anger and fear. It's plain as day, especially when you blame Michael."

"For the thousandth time — I don't blame him."

"Yes, you do, even more than you blame your mother."

Brian groaned. "Where do you get these theories?"

"I watch you. I listen. I know how you think. Give me a little credit, would you?"

"So, what am I thinking right this minute?"

"You're thinking maybe you could shut me up if we had sex one more time."

"Wrong," he laughed. "I don't have any energy left. I'm exhausted."

"I've heard that before," she said, reaching down to touch him.

"I mean it Jo!"

"All right, let's finish our discussion."

"No. Let's go to sleep. Please?"

"Your mother's a totally undeveloped person. She's stymied at about fifteen or sixteen years old. You know she's incapable, so you let her off the hook. Michael, well now, that's a different story. He's sane, sober, and mature. Still, he wasn't there for you."

Brian turned his back to her. "Please go to sleep."

"You think you're just like your parents. Every time you walk out that door for the job you love, you're torn in two. You think you abandon your children when you tour."

"No."

"Yes," she said firmly. She cuddled up to his back and slid her hand around him again. "You think that if you can abandon your babies then you have no right to point the finger at Michael and you're not through punishing him."

"Jo!" he yelled into his pillow, frustrated because she was slowly arousing him.

"Come on, Brian," she coaxed. "You know how I am when I'm pregnant."

Three hours of sleep took him a long way that day. The fighting, drinking, and making up had taken their toll. Brian was certain he had no energy left. Still, like always, she got to him. Finally, she let him go and he slept twelve hours straight.

Before leaving to finish the tour, he suggested it was time to hire a live-in nanny. Jo argued she didn't need help to raise her children, but he was adamant and for once she gave in.

chapter 17

TWO HOURS EAST of Denver the bus came to a halt, rousing Brian from a restless sleep. A glance at his watch informed him it was three in the morning. Across the aisle, Tara sat up and peered out the tinted window. Nick was talking to the driver up front.

"What the hell's going on?" Sammy asked from the depth of her bunk.

"I'll go check." Brian moved up the aisle, past Mary, who slept soundly through any chaos.

The bus driver and Nick watched the bus directly in front of them expectantly. That bus carried the Scott Engels' group, the other band on this tour.

Brian joined Nick and their bus driver. "What's going on?"

"I don't know," the driver said with a shrug. "They radioed back and said they needed to stop. So, I stopped."

Brian turned to the stairs. "Open the door, Lloyd."

The night air chilled Brian as he stepped off the bus. They were parked in an empty lot next to a baseball diamond. Just as he raised his fist to knock on the door, Scott stepped down and handed him a softball glove.

He grinned. "Get your group together, Burnette. Let's play a game."

"It's three in the morning."

"Pussy," Scott said with a grin.

Usually, Brian returned Scott's jabs, but he was short on sleep and patience. He started to hand the ball glove back when Sammy pushed her away in front of him.

"Who's a pussy?"

"Your front-man here," Scott said.

Brian knew Scott used the inflammatory phrase to provoke Sammy and threw up his hands as Scott drove the deal home.

Scott zeroed in on Sammy, "I made arrangements for us to have a private little ball game, but Mr. Front-man, Mr. Million-dollar-voice, thinks he needs his beauty sleep."

"We'll play," Sammy said.

Disregarding the look Brian gave her, she turned on her heel, heading back to their bus.

Brian followed close. "Will you be reasonable? We can't play against those guys."

"Quit whining, Front-Man. Go get the crew. We're going to kick that chauvinist in his itty-bitty balls." She bounced up the stairs to wake the others.

The road crew had been too busy playing poker and drinking to investigate the delay. They listened as Brian explained Scott's proposal and rose to the challenge. Scott's road crew beat every group they suckered into a game.

The crew chief slapped Brian on the back. "We would consider it a privilege."

Scott provided equipment for the game, several kegs of cold beer, and everything required for a barbecue. Sammy insisted on being catcher, Tara wanted second, Mary went to center, and Nick to left field. Brian pitched baseball in high school so he was elected to pitch. The road crew took the remaining positions.

Scott's team won first at bat. The first batter struck out with Brian throwing only one ball worthy to be called a strike. Scott was next at bat.

He pointed a finger at Brian. "This one's coming at your pretty face, Mr. Frontman."

Brian motioned him to bring it on. Scott promptly swung and missed three consecutive pitches. "Well, la-de-dah. You're pretty good Burnette."

"That's for waking me up." Brian grinned.

Sammy batted first for Sanguine Heart. She struck at the first ball and missed, drawing a loud chuckle from Scott. She swung wildly at the next ball yet managed to tap it with the very tip of the bat. It should have been an easy out, but the shortstop dropped the ball, and Sammy made it to first.

Brian stepped up and Scott instructed the backfield to move in, "Nothing to worry about guys. He'll wimp out."

Back in high school, Brian could hit a baseball out of the park and was fairly confident he could get a piece of the softball. He lifted the bat, anticipating the first pitch and kept his eyes on the ball.

Scott lofted one at him and it fell like a twenty-pound weight into the loose dirt at Brian's feet. Both the catcher and Brian looked down at the thing in disbelief. The catcher threw the ball back to Scott and asked what his problem was.

Scott jerked a thumb at Sammy. "I can't pitch with her showing off like that."

Brian looked down to first base. Sammy laughed and flung her shirt open. She believed she had great breasts and wasn't bashful about flashing them, especially when indulging in a little tequila, which she had been doing for the last half-hour.

"Knock it off," Scott grumbled.

"Go on and pitch, Scott" Brian said dryly.

Scott threw him a smooth, sliding fast ball. Brian knocked it over right field and out of sight. He dropped the bat and followed Sammy's flapping shirt-tail around to home plate.

Four innings and half a keg later, the game was fifteen-thirteen in favor of Sanguine Heart. Nearly everyone was getting loaded, including Brian. He stopped hitting the ball so hard in order to pause for a little flirting at third base with one of Scott's backup singers, a shapely girl named Cherie.

Lately, the enormous pressure of success and family had confined him to a very narrow space. Tonight, for just a few minutes, he was just a young man having fun. His alcohol-laced brain insisted he deserved one night off. He wouldn't do anything serious, just some joking around, laughing a little, flirting with Cherie, and playing ball like a kid again.

During the seventh inning stretch, he ignored the barbecue and opted to share a joint and several shots of Tequila with a few of the roadies and Cherie. Sammy watched every move he made, but he ignored her as well as his conscience.

Sanguine Heart won the game around five-thirty that morning. Nearly everyone was drunk by that time — except Sammy, who had stopped drinking back in the third inning.

Brian walked Cherie toward the road crew bus, intending to spend the remainder of the trip away from the scrutiny of his self-appointed mother.

Sammy tried coaxing him away from Cherie gently then resorted to pulling on his arm. Pulling nearly one hundred and eighty pounds of reluctant, drunken man was quite a job even for Sammy. He dragged his feet halfway to the bus then dug in his heels and refused to go further.

"What do you want Sammy?"

"I want you to pay attention. I know you're drunk, but you better focus — now."

He leaned down, smiling lazily, and crossed his eyes.

Sammy pushed him toward their bus. "Get in the bus and go to sleep."

Brian stepped away. "I'm not ready yet."

"Get on the bus, Brian."

"Hey, you know what? I'm a grown up. I go where I want."

She just shoved him harder. "Get on the bus!"

"Push me again and I swear I'll knock you out!"

"You hit me and I'll have your ass thrown in jail, Junior."

Brian's eyes narrowed to slits. "Why do you have to be such a bitch?"

Sammy stepped closer. "Will you please think with your brain?"

"Mind your own business," he said, turning away again.

"This is my business. What do you think you're doing out here, living in a bubble? You sleep with her, we all get screwed."

"What the hell are you talking about? I'm not sleeping with anybody."

"I'd say you're about seven inches from it."

His face spread into a white, angry grin. "So, now you know what I'm going to do."

"Yeah, sport, I do. Your hard-on at third base gave you away. Give it up. You have a wife and kids…"

"I know that," he snapped.

"Whom you love dearly, far too much to lose," Sammy finished then sighed tiredly. "Look, I know Cherie's pretty. She's got an incredible body and she's very willing. I also know we've been on the road far too long. You're over-tired, over-stressed, and looking for a little release from giving one-hundred percent to everybody except yourself, but you must step away. The only choices for a man like you are straight-and-narrow or cataclysmic heartache, there is no in between and you know it."

He looked over at Scott's bus and waved to Cherie then got on his own bus grumbling to himself. The next day he shamefacedly thanked Sammy for interceding.

One week later, Brian got his wake up call from the front desk at six-thirty in the morning. He rolled out of the bed and stumbled to the shower. At seven-thirty, he climbed aboard the bus with a splitting headache, a testament to an all night party in Scott's suite.

His thighs and back were very tender and felt strained. He couldn't imagine what he'd done to deserve it. He stuck a baseball cap on his head to hide his unruly hair because combing it only made his head pound harder.

After throwing his carry-on into a bin overhead, he lay down on his bunk and pulled the hat over his eyes. The headache throbbed in relentless, angry waves from forehead to crown, slicing like a razor through brain tissue. He didn't have any idea how much he had consumed the night before, but knew it was much more than he should have.

Sammy was next on the bus. She walked over and looked down at him for a minute, then swung a full, two-liter bottle of water at his crotch. Brian gasped and sat forward with a snap, putting both hands between his legs.

"I hope they swell to the size of softballs," she said.

"Jesus, Sammy, we don't need another soprano," Nick muttered. Pushing past her, he headed toward Brian who was now in the fetal position.

"Brian? Hey, you okay?"

Mary joined them, followed by Lloyd, the bus driver.

"Should I get some ice?" Lloyd asked.

Tara tried peeking around the group. "What happened?"

"Sammy hit him in the balls," Nick said.

Brian inhaled slowly and sat up. Instantly, bile rose in his throat and he lurched toward the bathroom, where he sank to his knees in front of the toilet.

Long after the bus started down the highway, he made his way across the rocking floor of the bus toward a bench seat.

"Feeling better?" Nick called.

He waved weakly in response and Sammy hissed loudly as he passed.

Brian carefully eased his body onto the bench. After placing a pillow against the window, he leaned into the softness. He had just closed his eyes when Sammy dropped onto the seat near him.

She leaned over, placing her lips close to his ear, "Still on top of the world, Stud?"

He squinted at her. "Why are you torturing me?"

"I know what you did last night," she poked him with her forefinger, "everyone knows."

Brian hoped she meant the drunkenness. He remembered little about Scott's party. Still, an inner voice kept reminding him doom was at hand.

Sammy folded her arms over her chest and studied him for a moment before speaking again, "Call Jo when we get to Seattle and tell her before she hears it on the wire."

"Hears what?" Brian hedged, holding on to a slippery fragment of hope.

"Stop it. I saw Cherie coming out of your room this morning."

He groaned and the pain in his head deepened another notch. "Please, tell me you're making this up."

"I never lie to you Brian."

"Damn it," he muttered.

"Yeah, damn it. You knew enough to stay away from Scott's parties. I can't believe you were determined to be that stupid."

"Jo will kill me Sammy. I can't tell her."

"You don't have a choice. Once she sees the photographs you're going to fry anyway."

"Photographs? What did I do, have sex in public?"

"That's pretty much the way I hear it. I'll spare you the details about the countertop in Scott's bathroom. Let's just say you performed with your usual flare and dazzled them."

They rode in silence for a few minutes. Brian slipped on a pair of sunglasses and stared at the landscape slipping by, ill from head to foot. He vaguely remembered meeting a reporter who was doing a story on Scott. Someone took his picture while he and Scott performed a raunchy version of the song Runaround Sue. Suddenly, he remembered Cherie sitting on his lap and giving him a French kiss and that was the beginning of his insanity.

Sammy's voice broke into his nightmare like fingernails on a chalkboard. "So, how are those testicles?"

"I'll get you back for that."

"Promise you'll call Jo and beg her forgiveness."

"I can't do something like that over the phone; she's almost seven months pregnant now."

"You slimy low life." She said this loud enough to draw the attention of the others. She popped him on the head with her palm and stomped her feet in frustration. "I'm so disappointed in you."

"Me too," he said.

Sammy jumped up and left him to his misery. The fangs of reality bit deep into his flesh, releasing an acidic truth that ate through every layer of tissue and made Swiss cheese of his bones which leaked marrow until he was a hollow shell of regret and self-loathing.

chapter 18

JO HIRED AN old acquaintance of her mother's to help with the children then had two rooms added to their home for the woman's private quarters and, while Brian finished his tour, the new nanny settled into their lives.

Brian walked into the house on a weekday afternoon, one day earlier than expected. He didn't see or hear Jo and the boys and entered the kitchen, surprising the nanny who was at the sink filling a teakettle. She jumped back and dropped the teakettle.

Brian smiled sheepishly. "Please, forgive me. I didn't mean to startle you. I'm Jo's husband, Brian."

The woman managed to smile and held out her hand. "I'm Theresa. It's a pleasure to finally meet you, Brian."

Brian grabbed a dishtowel and started to mop up the spilled water. "Is Jo out with the boys?"

"She's in back, watching them swim. You go on and say hello to your family. I'll take care of this."

Mike saw him first and Brian motioned him to keep quiet as he sneaked behind Jo, who was reading in the shade. Brian gently slipped his fingers over her eyes.

"Brian," she sighed happily. He knelt next to her and they embraced as the twins jumped on his back.

Late that night, after everyone else was asleep, Jo and Brian lay in bed catching up on what he missed while he was away. Jo traced the outline of his face with a fingertip and told him the doctor thought the baby might be taken cesarean.

"When will he know for sure?"

"Well, it depends on the next couple of weeks and how fast he grows."

"He?"

"Yeah, we're having another son. I guess you know that means we can't stop the way we wanted. I want a daughter."

He grunted and rubbed her back absentmindedly. She hadn't bothered to tell him the sex of the baby until just now. He knew she didn't exclude him purposefully, yet the omission drove him up the wall.

"Brian, there were a lot of nasty rumors about you and a back-up singer with the Scott Engles' band. I know I'm just being silly, but some of the pictures were pretty convincing."

Brian's heart pounded so loudly he figured she could hear it. He never lied to Jo, but telling her this truth scared him to death. When he didn't respond, she drew back and turned on the lamp on her nightstand, eyeing him in suspicion, then horror.

"My God, did you do this?"

He dropped his eyes and sat up to explain, but she threw off the covers and jumped out of bed.

She held up her hands and shook her head. "Never mind, don't tell me. I don't want to know."

Brian watched her move around the foot of the bed, coming toward him. He waited for her reaction with deepening dread. Suddenly, she grabbed a bottle of perfume from the dresser and hurled it at him. It exploded against the wall behind the headboard. Glass and perfume rained down on Brian and the bed.

"I want you out of my bed right now!" she screamed. She jerked back the blanket covering him and hit him with her fists. Brian grabbed her wrists and got to his feet.

"Let go of me!" she hollered. Wrenching a hand free, she slapped his face with blow that made him see stars. He released her and she backed away.

"How could you do this to me...to us?" Tears clouded her eyes and her voice cracked. "Damn it, Brian!" Then softer, "Damn it."

He shook his head to clear the ringing in his ears and Jo threw a pair of sweatpants at him. "Get out."

Brian pulled the pants on and walked out of the room without a word. He went to the stairs and made it to the bottom three where he sat. His legs were too weak to carry him further. Overhead, Jo slammed the bedroom door. He closed his eyes and leaned against the wall, overcome by the sorrow that a fool's fate demanded.

The grandfather clock struck two. Brian got to his feet and opened the front door to a blast of cold rain. Without hesitation, he walked out into the storm.

Jo came downstairs and stood on the porch, sheltered from the storm. She peered through the pouring rain at him.

"Have you completely lost your mind?"

He glanced back at her and held up his hands, shrugging.

"Get inside!" She came after him and grabbed his arm, but he shook her hand away.

"Go back inside. Leave me alone."

"Fine, maybe you'll get pneumonia. You can call the bitch you slept with to come nurse you back to health."

She went inside and slammed the front door so loud it shook the hinges.

Brian eventually came inside and fell asleep in Jo's rocking chair in the family room. He didn't sleep long. His wet clothes chilled him and he stripped them off and wrapped a scratchy afghan around his body. Apparently, Jo couldn't sleep either. He could see her sitting at the kitchen table with her daily journal. Jo had no idea he knew she kept the journals. Usually, he had no idea what she wrote. Tonight he was certain.

He went upstairs and dressed then peeked in on the boys. They had separate beds, but always slept together. Mike still clutched the fire engine Brian gave him that afternoon. He slipped the toy from Mike's grip and covered the boys and the pain of what he had done washed over him again.

He slipped downstairs to the family room and turned on the television, staring at an old movie with eyes that filled with tears. All that he loved was slipping away and he couldn't stop it. He covered his face with his hands and remorse took over.

He hadn't cried since he was nine years old. He even swore to Jo that he spent so many years shutting off emotion that he was now unable to shed even a single tear. Not even the birth of his sons, or Max's death, had disproved this theory. Losing Jo was more than he could bear.

Jo came in and sat on the coffee table and touched his shoulder gently. Startled, Brian sat back gasping for air, wiping at the tears on his face.

"I can't stand anymore of this," she said. "We'd better see if we can't work this thing out somehow."

"I'm sorry, Jo." He sniffed and cleared his throat. "I'm so sorry."

"I think that's obvious."

"It didn't mean anything. I mean she was..." He looked around the room and tried to catch his breath. "There wasn't anything between us."

"Stop it!" she commanded. "I told you I don't want to hear about it. Just knowing you did it is more than enough."

"Right," he nodded and pulled a few Kleenex from a box.

"Brian, I want to go on loving you, but if you ever do anything remotely close to this again I'll divorce you without hesitation."

He shook his head. "It won't happen again."

"I'm going to bed. You can sleep in the guest room."

She got to her feet and went upstairs without him. Brian desperately wanted to follow and crawl in bed beside her. Most of all, he wanted to forget the truth, return to the security of yesterday. Still, old hurts from her parent's marriage and divorce were in control. She probably thought Amelia's contention that men simply couldn't be faithful was true. It was going to take time for her to deal with the betrayal and learn to trust him again.

Brian stayed on the couch, staring blankly at the TV. Near dawn, Jo turned the television off and joined him on the couch.

"I have some questions," she said.

"Okay."

"Was this the first time you cheated on me?"

He took in a quick breath and nodded.

"What was her name?"

Brian eyed her curiously. "Cherie."

"Was it a one night thing or did you have a full-blown affair?"

Confused by this new tact, he didn't answer immediately.

Jo glared at him. "What are you doing, debating on a lie?"

"No, I'm just a little confused."

"Well, I feel like slapping you again for hiding things from me."

"Jo, we toured together all summer. We were constantly thrown together."

"Don't even think about giving me a list of excuses, Brian. Just answer me straight up, all right?"

"Sure," he snapped. "What was the question again?"

"Did you sleep with her all summer or was it just one quick blow job in the back of the tour bus?"

The crude question stunned him. "It was one night in my hotel room," he said slowly.

"One night, as in all night?"

"I don't remember."

"Bastard." She punched the couch with her fist. "What the hell were you thinking?"

"I'd say it's pretty obvious I wasn't thinking."

"I'll go along with that. Tell me why did you let this one get to you? I've seen beautiful women practically lay at your feet Brian. What made this particular woman so special?"

"She wasn't special. I got completely wasted at one of Scott's parties and let the stupid in me come out."

"The only time you drink on tour is when the stress gets to you. I wish you'd learn to call and talk to me when the pressure gets too great. I would have come to you Brian. I'm your partner, remember?"

His eyes filled with tears, but he smiled at her. "I love you, Jo."

Jo started crying and he pulled her into his arms. "I'm so sorry."

"It's going to take time for me to forgive you."

"I know."

"I can't stand the thought of another woman touching you. You let some stranger touch what was mine."

"Do you want me to move out?"

She pulled back and looked at him in horror. "Move out? My God, we're going to have another baby in three weeks."

"I thought it might be easier for you without me here."

She smiled, "Easier for you maybe."

They named their third son, Jesse. The baby was an immediate star with his older brothers. To Brian's chagrin, Jesse was blonde like his mother.

The next year Sanguine Heart finally had a lighter schedule. Brian spent nearly half the year with his family. In February, the band won a Grammy for their third album. Most of the songs were Brian's and Sammy grumbled that his talent was leaving the rest of them in the dust.

In March, Jo told him she might be pregnant again. This time he was with her the moment the doctor confirmed her suspicions. In the fourth month, the doctor told them they were having a girl and Jo promised that this baby would be their last.

chapter 19

ON LABOR DAY, Sanguine Heart joined a host of other entertainers in Washington, DC, for a concert to benefit the homeless. Brian did his stint and when he walked off the stage found Michael waiting in the wings.

"What a pleasant surprise!" Brian shouted above the extended applause. "I can't believe you're here!"

Michael stepped back to allow the others to pass and didn't return his smile. Brian scrutinized his sober expression and realized something was wrong just as the crowd roared for an encore.

Sammy pulled on his arm. "Come on, Brian! Let's go!"

"What's wrong?" he shouted, stepping closer to Michael, but Sammy pulled him back on stage.

He slipped the guitar strap over his shoulder, glancing to the wings and saw Michael speaking into their manager's ear. Stan stepped away, looked up at Michael open mouthed and shot a quick glance at Brian. Stan then took Michael by the elbow and guided him away. Brian forced himself to perform although instinct screamed something was terribly wrong.

The moment he exited the stage Stan grasped his arm firmly and guided Brian through the backstage crowd.

"Where did my father go?"

Stan looked directly at him more serious than Brian had ever seen him. "He's waiting in the dressing room."

Michael stood in the middle of the dressing room, head down, and hands in his pockets. Stan closed the door, leaving them alone. Slowly, Michael raised his head and the strain on his face was clear.

Brian's heart pounded, "My God, Michael, what's wrong?"

"About two this afternoon your house caught fire," he took a deep breath and his eyes watered. "They found Jo in the bedroom. Apparently, she was taking a nap..."

"Oh, no," Brian said. He backed away, shaking his head, as Michael continued.

"They took the baby, but it was too late." He stepped closer, placing one hand on Brian's arm. "They're both gone."

Brian moaned. "Oh, no..."

His legs were suddenly too weak to support his weight and without Michael's strong arms around him, he would have fallen. Michael eased him to the floor and held tight as he cried.

"I'm sorry," Michael said gently.

Brian pulled back suddenly. "What about the boys?"

"They were out with Theresa."

"She can't be gone," he whispered, pleading. After taking a deep breath, a new thought occurred to him and he smiled at Michael. "There's probably been a mistake."

Michael studied him for a moment then he shook his head.

Brian blinked and looked around the room in shock. The band on stage brought their first song to a close and applause roared.

"I need to get out of here."

"Stan arranged for a car to take us to the airport. It's waiting just outside for you. Do you think you can walk?"

"I'll make myself."

By dawn Brian was temporarily calm. His eyes were bloodshot and burning. He seemed to be out of tears. During the night he had spoken with Jo's mother and her brother Kenny. Beth had taken the boys to Wyoming for him to leave them in Nellie and Sam's capable hands before returning. He wanted the boys away from the circus that lay ahead.

Michael walked with him every step of the way, his strength buoying Brian, keeping all the fragile pieces together. Jean, of course, offered no form of compassion. While Michael went to the airport to pick up Beth, Harlan stayed with Brian at the hotel.

Brian couldn't sleep. The moment he closed his eyes he saw Jo waving goodbye at the front door of their home yesterday morning and the image sliced through his heart. He wanted to die along with her.

The funeral was torture. The diligence of the press made it even more of a nightmare. Brian asked that Jo and their unborn daughter be buried in the same casket.

At the funeral service, Beth stood on one side of him and Michael stood on the other. Sammy put on a conservative black dress and sang Amazing Grace in a clear, sweet voice, bringing any dry eye in the chapel to tears and her best friend to his knees.

There were so many people crowded into the small church some had to stand at the back and around the sides of the pews. Brian didn't register the presence of most that spoke to him, including Amanda Cutler-Cahill, who gave him such a long, overly-affectionate embrace Sammy intervened.

Immediately after the services, Michael took him back to Wyoming where the boys rushed to him with open arms. Brian knelt on the floor and hugged them tightly as tears came one more time. Max patted him on the back and Mike cried. Jesse watched the scene with big, sad eyes, and cuddled close to his chest.

Brian moved through every day in an unshakable stupor. He had to force himself to get out of bed every morning and perform even the simplest routines of life. He had no appetite and lost weight. He didn't want to wallow in this grief, but it consumed him, and his sanity seemed to be slipping through his fingers.

He was careful to be attentive to the boys and allowed them to sleep with him for the first time. He kept his sorrow to himself as much as possible. He knew his grieving was hard on those around him. No measure of comforting would help anyway. He needed Jo.

Sanguine Heart had a concert scheduled in LA that January. When they spoke on the phone, Brian told Sammy he wasn't sure he could manage to perform and she promptly flew to Wyoming to talk to him.

After observing the social amenities with Michael and Beth over dinner, Brian took Sammy to the enclosed deck, just off the living room where they could talk privately. Sammy stood at the window looking out at the breathtaking view and Brian moved to a chair, sipping a cup of coffee.

Sammy slid a look at him and tears filled her eyes. He caught her staring and frowned.

"Stop looking at me that way."

Sammy turned away and drew in a deep breath. "I talked to everyone else and we've decided to cancel the concert in LA."

The underlying message stirred something old in him. The expression in her eyes reminded him of the worst days of his childhood, back when he learned to set his feelings aside and made hard choices in order to survive. He had seen that look plenty of times in Mrs. Clifford's eyes and in the eyes of people who knew of his struggle with his drunken, vicious mother. The expression was pity and he couldn't endure that.

"No," he said, looking to the mountains. "I'll be there."

Brian left the boys at Michael and Beth's and flew to New York to start rehearsals. His voice was weak at first, but after a few days, he forced away the melancholy, and retrieved some of his verve.

Four months after Jo's death, he went on stage for the first time and faced a sold-out crowd of thousands. Waiting in the wings, his hands were so cold they turned stiff. He seriously considered backing out. Sammy saw the panic coming over him and pulled him into her arms. She gave him the warmth of her body and, for a moment, he stopped shaking.

Nick went on stage first, then Tara, and Mary. Sammy grabbed Brian's hand and didn't let go until they were center stage before a roaring crowd that was on their feet. Brian drew in a deep breath as Tara began the introduction to their first song and Sammy greeted LA. His heart was pounding so hard against his ribs it was difficult to breathe. Sammy sang lead on this song and he could play until he joined her on the chorus.

They did two of their standards then it was Brian's turn to do a song from their new album. Tara and Sammy wrote the song specifically for his vocal talents and it took a lot of control. To Brian's surprise, he carried it off without faltering.

Tara played the introduction of Betsy's Soul and the house lights dimmed. Brian stepped up to the microphone, sang the first two lines and tears sprung to his eyes. Closing them, he forced himself to concentrate on the song. At the end of the soft refrain, Nick began the shuffling cue on the top hat. Choking, Brian turned around and faced Nick. He put his head down, taking a deep breath fighting the surge of grief.

Without missing a beat, Sammy walked to Brian, as Tara and Mary began to play along with Nick.

Tears rolled down Brian's face. Sammy wrapped an arm around his waist.

"Hey kid," she said, leaning in close. "I thought you wanted to be a musician."

Brian straightened a little and looked directly at her. Sammy flinched and her face puckered in pain. She kissed his cheek quickly.

"I love you so," she said. "Now, turn around, tears and all, and sing for these people."

"I can't," he said desperately.

"Yes, you can."

"My throat is too tight Sammy. I can't."

"Your voice will work once you get started." She nudged him with her hip. "Let's go, Junior."

She turned around and began the song, slowing the pace to a ballad. She walked to her microphone and addressed the audience quietly, "Ladies and Gentleman...Brian Burnette."

Slowly, Brian turned, as the crowd applauded softly. He walked back to his microphone and a white spotlight found him. He began to play again, cleared his throat, and raised his head. With tears still falling, he began to sing.

The audience listened intently without a sound. He finished the last haunting note and stepped away from the microphone without ceremony. The crowd was still quiet as Sammy walked over to him and kissed his cheek. The applause began slowly then rippled in waves toward them until it became thunderous.

In the fall, just after the first anniversary of Jo's death, Brian purchased a beach house in Malibu and Theresa the nanny joined him and the boys. California seemed the perfect place to start again. Here, there were no memories to jump out of the shadows and hammer him back to his knees.

The boys loved the beach. In addition to Theresa, Brian now employed a full-time housekeeper and a part-time sitter for Theresa's much deserved time away.

Many nights, after the boys were tucked in, he sat on the deck of the beach house and listened to the rhythm of the surf. This jagged pain seemed to have no end and he begged God to give him strength to carry on.

chapter 20

IN THE SPRING, Tara married her long-term fiancé in New York City. Brian, the boys, and the nanny arrived in New York three nights before the wedding. The next morning Brian took the twins to a fitting for the tuxedos they would wear as ring-bearers. Tara wanted to include Jesse, but Brian refused. His youngest son was now two and a wild man. Tara pleaded with Brian to include Jesse as a guest. The nanny opted to come along and assured Brian she could handle Jesse, still he knew who would end up with the job.

Brian watched Mike and Max coming up the aisle and heard whispers about the adorable twins in their little tuxedos. The boys seemed to be rising to the task and he breathed a sigh of relief. Mike smiled broadly at everyone like the little ham he was. Max offered a shyer grin and looked to his father for reassurance.

As they approached Brian and Jesse, Mike opened his mouth, revealing a red Lifesaver balanced on the tip of his tongue. Jesse immediately began to wail and Brian placed him on his lap and talked softly in his ear until he quieted. Jesse rested his curly blond head against Brian's chest and slept contentedly through the rest of the ceremony.

Though Brian insisted he was doing better, Sammy stuck by his side the entire day. At the reception, when the music began, Mike ran to the dance floor. Mike loved music and didn't dance because he wanted to show off, he danced because he had move.

Max stood close to Brian, watching, tapping his foot shyly. At Sammy's suggestion, Mary took Max's hand and led him to the dance floor. Max looked over his shoulder and smiled at Brian. The look slammed Brian hard. He dropped his eyes and his leg began to bounce as he tried to breathe.

Sammy touched his hand. "Let's go outside and get some fresh air."

Brian shook his head and tapped his feet. "I'll be okay. Give me a minute."

"What happened?"

Brian looked at his sons then over at Sammy with wet eyes. "Sometimes, they look just like her."

After the wedding he took the boys to see Jo's mother. She had made him feel guilty about never allowing her to see her grandsons. He didn't want to go, but he had to face this someday. He rented a car at the airport in Philadelphia and drove straight to Amelia's house. He tried to ignore the constriction in his chest and pounding headache, but the condition worsened with every mile.

The day was nothing short of torture and he grew more and more tense as it ground slowly by. Finally, at seven, he took the nanny and the boys to their hotel. Once the children were asleep, he left them in the care of the nanny.

At nine-thirty, he was on the seedier side of town in a rundown bar. He had tequila in one hand, a cigarette in the other and had just realized he was in this bar once before, a long time ago, looking for his mother.

That had been one of the few times he ever looked for her when she was on a binge and on this occasion had the misfortune to find her. She had been sitting in a booth along the wall. She was intoxicated and letting some stranger put a dirty hand up her skirt.

Brian stood nearby, unable to turn away or go forward.

"Hey Kid! What are you doing in here?" The bartender called.

Brian glanced at the man, but didn't respond. Turning back, he faced Jean's anger.

"Yes, what the hell are you doing here?" she asked.

Her companion squinted through the smoky haze at Brian. "Who's this?"

The guy still had his hand up Jean's skirt and Brian wanted to punch him.

"My kid," Jean told the jerk flatly, removing his hand with a toss.

She grabbed Brian's coat sleeve and pulled him to the door. Brian shook off her hand and followed on his own terms.

Once they were outside, she wheeled on him and slapped the side of his head. "What the hell are you doing following me?"

Brian drew in a sharp breath and stepped away, mostly to keep himself from striking back.

"Harlan's looking for you," he said tightly.

"That's funny, you don't look like Harlan."

A woman approaching the bar paused near them and grinned stupidly, "He's kind of young for you, ain't he?"

"Shut-up, Karla. This is my kid."

"You don't have a kid." Karla challenged. She stepped closer, looking up at Brian, and licked her cracked lips with a pointy little tongue.

Jean's next words stung him harder than the slap to his head.

"Trust me, whether I like it or not, this is my kid."

Brian turned quickly and walked toward his car.

"Why is Harlan looking for me?" Jean called.

"Your father died," Brian tossed back, hoping the news hurt her.

"What? When?"

Brian kept walking to his car and she started running.

"Wait a minute!"

"No."

He jerked open the door of his car and she threw a shoe at him, just missing the back of his head. He wheeled around and faced her. "If you want to know anything, call Harlan. I don't give a damn anymore."

"Of course not, why should you? We're only talking about my father. I wouldn't expect his death to have any impact on you, you cold-hearted bastard."

"If I'm cold, it's because I have you for a mother."

Jean looked like she wanted to slap him and even took a step forward. She looked at him carefully and lowered her hand, settling instead for another twist of the knife.

"Well, boo-hoo, life's just a bitch. Mommy isn't perfect. Why don't you grow up, Junior?"

"Why don't you kiss my ass," he hissed, opening the car door.

"I did the best job I could!" she shouted at him.

"Yeah, well, your best was pathetic, Mom." He fired up the engine of his old VW and left her standing there feeling sorry for herself.

That was one of the longest dialogues he ever had with his mother and it summed up their whole relationship. Now, he was sitting in the same damned bar, nursing a drink and just about as lost as his mother.

There was a hockey game on the television over the bar, but he paid no attention. His brain was overloaded and there seemed to be a low humming in his ears, creating a pressure he couldn't escape. He needed relief, at least until the morning and then he was getting the hell out of this town.

Though the bar was almost empty, someone with heavy perfume sat next to him. Brian didn't turn to look. He didn't feel like company.

"Buy an old friend a drink?" a woman asked.

Reluctantly, Brian turned and recognized Amanda Cutler-Cahill. She had changed dramatically. In that other life, before Jo's death, Sammy had told him that Amanda's marriage to Todd was over and that Amanda had turned to booze and drugs for solace. The change was not so much on the outside, though there was plenty of that. The fundamental change was a hard, vacant look in her eyes.

"You look awful," she said.

"Thanks."

She took a cigarette from the pack on the bar. "Got a light?"

Brian lit her cigarette and motioned for the bartender. "What are you drinking?"

"Gin and Tonic." She puffed on her cigarette and glanced up at the television. "So what brings you to town? Did you just have to come back and reminisce?"

"Jo's mom wanted to see the kids." Brian sighed, crushing out his cigarette.

"So what are you doing in here?"

"Getting drunk."

"Now, you're talking about my forte. Just ask anybody."

"I've heard." He picked up his glass and finished it before the bartender got back with the next one.

"Courtesy of the lesbian no doubt."

"She's not really a lesbian." It was the truth. Sammy said so herself. It was a phase in college. These days Sammy was into men.

"Right and Donald's really not a duck," Amanda snorted.

The bartender placed their drinks before them and Amanda held hers up in a toast. "To the boy voted best body 1986."

He frowned at her. "What?"

"All the senior girls voted you as our unanimous choice." She leaned closer, touching his arm. "You could have been laid twenty-four hours a day and they'd still be waiting in line, but you never looked left or right," she pursed her lips and pointed with her finger at him. "No, you just looked straight ahead, giving it all to her."

Brian lit another cigarette and wished she would shut-up. He deliberately looked up at the hockey game, ignoring her.

"I always envied her, you know," she continued. "I wanted someone to love me the way you loved her."

"I'd appreciate it if you'd stop talking about, Jo," he said.

"Want me to move on?"

"No." He picked up his glass and shot back all of the tequila in one swift gulp. He wiped his mouth and motioned for another. "Change the subject."

Two hours later they stumbled from the bar into the pouring rain and Amanda drove them to her parents' home. Her mother and father were away for a few weeks and she had the mansion to herself. Brian followed her up the winding staircase, ignoring all the warning bells in his head.

Sex with Amanda was not gentle or kind. They plummeted into the act in a hungered frenzy without preamble. Brian lost himself completely, neither thinking nor caring. Desperate for a release from the torment, he swan dived into the fire.

He backed her into a wall, shoving his hands under her blouse, finding her soft breasts. Amanda cried his name and pulled at his clothes. Brian lifted her off her feet and opened her long legs. He buried himself in her so deep he met resistance. Amanda moaned in his mouth, welcoming the pain.

He rocked her against the wall until his body peaked. His mind went completely numb during what felt like an interminable explosion. Amanda dug her nails into his back and repeated his name as if in a trance.

A clap of thunder woke Brian one hour after passing out next to Amanda. Though he had consumed enough alcohol to knock him out under normal circumstances, he was far from that pleasure tonight. He dressed and stumbled out into the stormy night.

The cold rain sobered him a little and he came to a decision on his walk back to the bar. Storm or no storm, he knew what he had to do.

He walked back to the bar and purchased a fifth of tequila for his quest. The bartender told him a pretty woman with eyes like a cat had come in looking for him. Cursing Sammy under his breath, he climbed into his rental car and drove to the ruins of his life.

It was after five when Sammy climbed the stairs to the tree house and found him on the rain-soaked wooden floor of the upper level. He was sitting against a wall and gripping the neck of a half-empty bottle of tequila. He was soaked, muddy, and very much awake.

"So," he said quietly, "you find me at last."

"Not an easy task."

He held out his bottle, "Tequila?"

"Get up and come back to the hotel with me."

"Can't, I'm here on official business."

"You're just torturing yourself."

He shook his head. "Sammy, go on. I'll be where I'm supposed to be when I'm needed and I'll do what I'm supposed to do when it's time, I promise."

"Is that why you think I'm here? To make sure you come back to work? If it is, you can kiss my ass, Brian Burnette." She snatched the bottle from him and took a long pull. "It's cold out here. Stop being so stupid and get up. I'm out of patience."

He shook his head. "I can't go yet. There's something I have to do."

Sammy frowned. "What?"

Brian got to his feet and looped a cold, wet arm around her shoulder, leaning down to whisper in her ear. "I have to say good-bye to Jo."

"Jo's not here. She's not in this place," she said gently.

"No, she's there." He nodded toward the rolling valley below them. The sun peeked over the mountains filling the world with light.

Brian's bloodshot eyes filled with tears, but he smiled. "See her smile?"

"Sweet Jesus," Sammy whispered.

Brian laughed softly, "Him too."

Brian arranged to have the house bulldozed and the land put up for sale. He told Jo's mother if she wanted to see her grandchildren in the near future, he would pay the airfare for her to come and visit them. He did not intend to come back for a long time.

chapter 21

SANGUINE HEART FINALLY had a long hiatus. Nick and Sammy followed Brian's lead and moved to LA. Sammy started work on a solo album and Nick landed a part in a movie.

Brian accepted the invitation of a group of veteran musicians to join them for a concert tour and album. He considered being asked by them to lend his talent to the notable project the highest compliment he had received to date.

After he accepted the project, Sammy dropped by to spend the evening and chided him about jumping ship for the "Boys Club."

"I'm not jumping anywhere, Sammy. This is a one-time deal."

"You start going out on your own like this and people will think you're tired of Sanguine Heart."

Brian grunted and propped his feet on the lower railing of the deck. The kids were asleep and the rest of the night was his. The pleasant breeze and the soft sounds of the surf relaxed him too much to argue.

Sammy on the other hand seemed to have an agenda. "You know you scare the rest of us, don't you?"

"Can't we just sit here and be quiet?"

"No, you have to listen. Don't bail on us, Brian, not yet."

He sighed and turned his attention to the ocean view as she continued.

"This new adventure of yours is going to make everybody stand up and take notice of how deep your talent goes." She kicked the leg of his chair. "People will try to convince you to leave us."

He sighed loudly. "You know I'm happy with Sanguine Heart."

"Yeah, but when you go out on tour with these guys and all that adulation comes pouring in you'll get a big head."

He grinned at her. "What's the matter with you?"

"I've been putting off this conversation for a long time. This is very hard for me to tell you. My ego keeps getting in the way."

He groaned loudly. "What?"

"Working with you is a privilege I don't want to lose. Please don't leave me. I'm not ready."

"You're the one making the solo album."

"My talent is not in the same class as yours! When will you get a grip?"

He had heard all of this before. Sammy's compliments always came back to bite him. He didn't feel like playing this game right now and allowed his attention to drift. He closed his eyes and let the soft breeze wash over him. Finally, life offered a measure of peace for the ripped and torn places.

"Brian?"

"Hmm?"

"I never knew I could love a man the way I love you and not want more than this."

"You do want more. You want me to promise I'll stay in Sanguine Heart until we've got one foot in the grave and we're doing those sad tours that make people say 'I thought they were all dead.' "

"I want you to stay until the rest of us get some of what we want. Money's not everything, you know."

"I could've told you that when I was six."

"What does a six-year-old know about money?"

"You'd be surprised."

"Hey, Brian, I've met your father, remember? When did you ever have to worry about money?"

"He wasn't around when I was a kid. All I had was my mother."

"Double yuck."

Brian laughed. "A bachelor's in the arts and that's the best you can do?"

"How about bitch?"

"Now you're talkin'."

Sammy reached over and took his right hand, rubbing the fingertips lightly. "Are you going to try and fall in love again?"

"I'm right where I need to be anything else hurts too much."

"You're too young to live like this."

"Please, don't."

"You're a beautiful man, Brian. Please, consider living again."

"I don't have time."

"Remember our little talk about biological needs? There's no way you're getting those met when your only sleeping companions are your sons."

Brian jerked his hand from hers and kicked at the rail with his heel. "Damn it, Sammy, I'm trying to relax."

Sammy allowed a moment of silence before continuing. "I nag because I love you."

"You've got to let me do this my way."

"Your way is too slow. You're going to get so lonely some woman will come along and you'll mistake a great orgasm for true love."

He chuckled at that notion. "You know me so well."

"I never want to see you hurt again, that's all. It almost killed me the last time."

"Daddy?"

Brian looked over his shoulder to the little shadow in the doorway. "What's up, Buddy?"

"I had a bad dream."

Brian waved him out the door and Mike crawled onto his lap, snuggling against his chest. Brian wrapped an arm around him and gently wiped the tears away. He kissed the top of Mike's head and looked back to Sammy.

"Like I said, I'm right where I need to be."

Brian spent most of the winter working with the collective band putting together a package of new and old songs by each artist. Brian exercised his versatility by playing piano on some of the songs and took turns with lead and back-up vocals. His favorite was the closing tune. All five members put down their instruments and sang a cappella. The harmony of their voices glided deep inside, all the way to his bones, rejuvenating his creativity and finally he felt alive again.

Two weeks before the beginning of the tour, the phone woke Brian before dawn. He reached over Max who had crawled into bed with him sometime during the night and grabbed the receiver.

"Hi, it's Amanda. Did I wake you?"

"Amanda?"

"Yeah, you remember me, don't you? I'm the quickie you had in Pennsylvania about a year ago."

"Are you drunk?"

"Of course I'm drunk. It's what I do best," she paused for a false giggle. "Well, there is that other thing I did with my tongue, you seemed to think that was special."

Max stirred restlessly and Brian interrupted Amanda's walk down memory lane. "What do you want?"

"I wanted to see if you'd make time for an old friend. See I have this need and it just won't go away. You know what I mean, don't you?"

"Amanda, I don't have time…"

"Don't start that with me!" she hollered, then laughed, and returned to her normal tone. "You're free to do a lot of things to me, just don't lie to me, Brian."

"Okay, I have no intention of dropping by ever again, how's that?"

"Go to hell!"

She slammed the receiver down and just as Brian lay back, the phone rang again.

"It's me," Amanda told him. "I forgot to tell you something."

"How did you get this number?"

Amanda's laugh raked over raw nerves and Brian sat up in the bed.

"Come on," she cooed. "Come, come, come to me. I need you so bad, music man."

Brian dropped the receiver into its cradle and swung his legs over the side of the bed. He slipped on a pair of sweat pants and took Max to his own bedroom. He had just returned to his room when the phone rang again.

"Damn it, Amanda, stop calling my house!"

"Ooh, bring that anger to me. Come on, Baby, bury it all the way to the bone and punish me all over again."

Brian dropped the receiver on the bed and put his face in his hands.

"Who's that?" Theresa asked.

The nanny's voice startled him and he jumped three feet off the bed. He went to the dresser for a T-shirt. "Please, don't answer the phone, Theresa. I'll take care of it."

Theresa didn't move. "I thought I heard you say Amanda."

"I did."

"Amanda Cutler?"

Brian frowned, "Yeah why?"

"She used to call Jo sometimes."

"Why would she call Jo? What did she want?"

"All I know is the calls upset her."

Brian picked up the receiver and the line was dead. He put it back on the cradle expecting it to ring immediately. He and Theresa stared at the phone for a few minutes, but it remained silent. Theresa told Brian she was going to make a pot of coffee.

Brian was following her down the stairs when the phone rang and he ran for it. He was breathing hard when he answered.

"Yee-haw, gotcha running now, don't I?" Amanda laughed.

He peered out the bank of windows facing the beach expecting to see her.

"Tell me, do you give the old wham-bam to Theresa too?"

"Go to bed, Amanda. Sleep it off."

"Now that Jo's jealous ass is out of the way you can go on and do them all, Brian. Just make sure you come by and see me. I'd hate to get nasty."

She hung up again and Brian wanted to scream. He called information and tried to get Amanda's parent's phone number, but it was unlisted. It was now six on the East Coast so he called Jo's mother, Amelia, and after explaining about the phone calls asked her to see what she could find out about Amanda and call him back.

Half an hour later, the phone rang again. Brian was out on the deck pacing. For once, it was a relief to hear Amelia's voice on the other end.

"She moved out to the West Coast a few months ago. Her parents don't have a number for her and don't want one. She stole some of her mother's jewelry and quite a bit of money from them. Apparently she's abusing cocaine now."

"Thanks Amelia."

Brian called his attorney that morning and the attorney hired a private detective to find Amanda. Brian increased the security at the beach house immediately. He also changed his phone number.

Before leaving on tour, he took the boys to Wyoming for a long visit. He let Beth talk him into taking a horseback ride while the boys attended church with Nellie and Michael finished some work in his study.

With Beth leading the way, they chose the path behind the stable where the land sloped into a long meadow then to their right where the land rose again. They paused on the edge of a plateau. Miles and miles of land stretched before them — all of it Sam, Red, or Michael's property.

Red's two-story home rested in the valley just below the plateau. A lazy plume of smoke rose from the chimney and drifted toward the deep blue sky. Beth raised a hand to shield the sun from her eyes and spotted Red going to his old truck. She put two fingers to her lips and whistled loudly, drawing his attention. The big man spotted them and waved.

"He's huge even at this distance," Brian said.

Beth laughed. "Sort of like Paul Bunyan meets Geronimo."

Brian sighed and tilted his face up, bathing in the warm sun. "I love it here."

"Right here, this spot, or Wyoming?"

"This whole place. I hope he never sells this piece of heaven. Coming here is the closest thing to peace I know."

"Brian, Michael will gladly give you a portion, if you want it."

Brian smiled brightly. "I'd love that. I want this place, right here." He waved a hand at the landscape. "I want to look out my window and see all of this."

"Are you sure? It's only a mile from us, you know, and Red's just down there."

Brian watched Red's truck weave and bounce down the gravel road that led away from his home. "The thought of having you guys as neighbors and Geronimo Bunyan in my backyard makes me feel safe."

"This will mean a lot to your father."

In the past, whenever Beth referred to Michael as his father, she always called him by name. On this visit the rule was altered to include frequent references to Michael's status as a parent.

Brian didn't need the hint. Since Jo's death, Michael had forever altered their relationship with his gentle, if reticent, support. Only one problem remained. Though Brian now thought of Michael as his father his tongue simply wouldn't let loose of the word.

He and Beth rode further and Brian considered Michael's lean brand of communication.

"I wish he'd talk to me," he said, thinking aloud.

"Try not to take it personally. He's never been long on words. He's improved a great many of his bad habits since we first met, but this habit of silence seems to be the one thing he can't change."

"Do you think it comes from what happened when he was a kid?"

Beth reined in her feisty horse and turned toward him, patting the mare's neck. "How much do you know?"

"Uncle Bob gave me a thumb-nail sketch."

Beth nodded and looked back into the wind, toward her home and heart. "I know most of the facts and still can't comprehend what he went through, Brian. I think the only one who ever will is Michael."

She sighed and switched her warm gaze back to him. "I'll give you a suggestion for some common ground. Hand him the guitar I gave him for his last birthday then pick up that old twelve-string you love so much and start a tune. Don't worry about him not knowing the song, he'll keep up." She smiled sweetly. "Listen closely because when the music takes over, Michael talks your ears off."

Brian tried Beth's advice after dinner. At first, Michael seemed unsure of what to do. He watched Brian begin Sammy's blues song, following his fingers on the strings. After a few bars, Michael joined in and what he added to Sammy's rhythm and blues piece gave Brian goose bumps.

The stimulating session lasted nearly an hour and he smiled broadly when Michael put his guitar aside. Finally, Brian felt closer to him.

"You're incredible. Would you consider playing on stage with me sometime?"

Michael shook his head, "That's not for me."

Brian didn't press the issue. Having private, musical conversations with his father would give new depth to his visits to Wyoming.

The collective band opened in Denver, to a sold-out house of 30,000 and the tour began with glowing reviews. A few weeks into the tour, he called Sammy from New Orleans.

"Hey, it's about time," she said. "Congratulations on that gig. You guys are making big waves."

"It's going pretty well. How's the work on your album coming?"

"It's kind of scary not having you around to smooth out the rough spots, but we're making progress. Hey, I ran into Nick the other day. His part in that movie turned out to be a walk-on. He's really disappointed."

"Not me, I don't want a new drummer."

"How selfish of you, people do need to move on with their lives you know."

Brian laughed. "Can I quote you?"

"Nick's recovering nicely though. He got himself a new sugar and seems to have lost his mind over this one. Maybe a good affair will keep him satisfied until we're back on the road."

"So what have you been up to?"

"Well, I saved the best news for last. I met the most incredible guy. His name is Jason. He's the reigning hunky doctor on that nighttime soap opera Mercy Lake."

"This is the name of a show?"

"Well, it's something like that. Anyway, this beautiful guy is just about the most perfect thing I've ever met on two legs. He's got an incredible tongue."

Brian laughed. "Sammy, I'm certain I don't want to hear about his tongue."

In Baltimore, Brian glanced up from the keyboard to the crowd and saw a snowman floating above everyone's head in the first few rows. At first, he thought it was an optical illusion. He stared into the darkness, beyond the glaring lights, but couldn't find it again.

At the post-performance party, a waiter handed Brian a note. He said the note was from the young woman in the blue dress, waiting at the bar. Brian looked to the bar, but could see no woman in a blue dress. He unfolded the paper and found a hand-drawn snowman with ears. His heart started pounding double-time as he surveyed the room looking for Stacy.

Through the milling crowd he caught a glimpse of blue dress and pushed his way through until he encountered her big brown eyes and a smile that still warmed him. Without thinking first, he wrapped his arms around her, lifting her off her feet.

"Stacy, I can't believe your here." Brian put her down and smiled. "I never thought I'd get to see you again."

"You should try walking in my shoes. I've been looking at you in magazines and those music videos. I hear you on the radio and know that every time I try to see you somebody will stop me. I've been trying since I first saw you play in Miami back in eighty-seven."

"You were in Miami?"

"Right up front. I called your name until I lost my voice then cried my heart out for weeks because you didn't hear me." She leaned closer and grinned. "I lied like a rug to get in here tonight."

Brian wanted to touch her again, but fought the urge. This was no little girl standing in front of him.

"Thank you," he paused, making himself take a deep breath. "Listen, I have to talk to a couple of people then we'll get out of here and go somewhere private to catch up. Can you wait a few minutes?"

Stacy laughed and her brown eyes twinkled. "Are you kidding?"

He took Stacy to his suite at the hotel and ordered dinner for them, tacking on a pot of coffee as an afterthought. He was tired and wanted to spend as much time with her as possible. Coffee would keep him awake.

"Would you like a drink?"

"Just a glass of wine. I need something to calm my nerves. I've been dreaming of this day for so long, now it feels strange, kind of embarrassing. You're not like I imagined you'd be."

Brian frowned a little. "What did you expect?"

"Wilder and arrogant I guess." She dropped her eyes and lowered her voice. "I didn't think you'd want to see me again."

Brian set her glass on the table and lifted her chin with a forefinger. Her big brown eyes still contained incredible vulnerability. Two tears spilled down her cheek and she closed her eyes. Brian wiped the tears away then kissed her cheek.

"I'm so happy you found me," he said.

Stacy smiled a little and he wrapped his arms around her again.

"I'm usually more in control than this," she said.

Brian released her and laughed. "Sometimes, being in control has to give in to bigger issues. Trust me I learned the hard way."

Stacy studied him for a minute. "I'm sorry about your wife. That must have been very hard."

Brian nodded. "Why don't we sit down?"

Stacy picked up her drink and sat on the couch.

Brian sat a cushion away. "Tell me what happened when they took you away."

"I went to a foster home, then another, and another. I ran away from the last one when I was seventeen with a boy I thought I'd live the rest of my life with. That didn't last long though. I was soon on my own again." She took a sip of her wine and smoothed her dress. "I met this older man, his nick name is 'Tap' because he used to be a boxer and liked to aggravate his opponent by tapping around a while before he clobbered their face."

Brian grinned. "Sounds like a nice guy."

Stacy grimaced. "We got married a few years ago."

"Sorry." He took a few swallows of water. "So, where's Tap this evening?"

"Either drinking or hunting for me — his two favorite past-times."

Brian figured she was getting to something here. "Does he get violent with you?"

"He can," she said softly, then squared her shoulders and looked him in the eye. "I left him five months ago. He thinks I'm his personal property and he can beat me into coming back."

"Did you notify the police?"

"I've got a restraining order, but they're not worth the paper they're printed on. He does whatever he wants and all the police do when I call is ask him to leave. He leaves until they disappear then comes right back."

"Why don't you move?"

"I moved from Boston to Baltimore and three times since I've been here. He still finds me, but I'm determined to see this thing through. I'm in nursing school and I want to finish."

"How much time do you have left?"

"Eighteen months."

"Would you let me help?"

She bristled immediately. "I didn't come here for help."

"Why don't you come with me to California? I have a big house with lots of room. You could finish out there."

"Brian, I needed to see you again because you're the closest person to a relative I have. Please, stop."

"I didn't mean to offend you."

She smiled a little and her eyes misted, reminding him of a little girl calling his name from the back of a government car.

"You didn't offend me," she told him gently. "It's just that I want to do this on my own. It's important that I take care of me for a change. Once I'm finished with school, I'll come for a visit. Okay?"

Brian shrugged his shoulders. "Okay, but if you ever need me I want you to call."

Stacy was twenty-two now, but she still seemed incredibly young and vulnerable. Brian wanted to hold her next to him and shield her all over again. They talked until the sun came up and when it was time to go the only thing she would accept was his phone number.

She drove him to the airport in an old car that didn't have much life left. Brian was the last passenger to board the private jet and had to bite his tongue to keep from begging her to come with him.

He closed his eyes as the plane lifted off the ground. He could still see her face — so sweet and vulnerable. The night they took her away in the backseat of that police car still haunted him. He had to find a way to help her.

At the end of the tour, Brian took the boys back to Wyoming where Michael surprised each grandson with the gift of a small horse. Max immediately fell in love and tried to talk Brian into allowing him to take the horse back to Malibu. Jesse held onto the reins and laughed happily while being led around the corral. Mike rode, fed and groomed his horse occasionally, but preferred to stay inside and play Grandpa's piano.

Brian met with Michael's architect about the type of house he wanted to build and finally, it was time to get back to California for the business of Sanguine Heart.

Back in Malibu Theresa took charge of the boys and the housekeeper handed him a stack of messages. He leafed through the stack until he came to one from Mrs. Clifford's son, John Clifford. There was no message, just a phone number in Ohio. He glanced at his watch and saw it was still early enough to call. The man on the other end had a smooth, quiet baritone.

"Mr. Burnette, I'm Louise Clifford's son. Mother wanted me to contact you when she passed."

"I'm sorry."

"Thank you. I know how close you two were back when you were a boy. She told me you thanked her personally when you got one of those Grammys."

"I owe her a lot. When are the services?"

"Tomorrow afternoon." He sighed deeply. "I know this is short notice, but it took us a while to get your number. She wanted you to sing at the service, Mr. Burnette."

"Please call me Brian. What time do I need to be there?"

He concluded the call with Mrs. Clifford's son and called Stacy's number, but her roommate in the dorm said she was out. He left a message about Mrs. Clifford and that a ticket would be waiting in Stacy's name at the airport.

He walked to the podium of the old Baptist church and faced some of those he had known as a child. The pianist began the opening for Mrs. Clifford's favorite hymn, In the Sweet, By and By, and just as he began to sing a woman walked in the back of the church. He didn't recognize the face behind dark sunglasses but the corn silk hair was familiar. He took a deep breath and looked away from Stacy.

After the graveside ceremony, he talked with Mrs. Clifford's son a little and some of the other members of the congregation before he got away to talk to Stacy. She stood on the edge of the group, wearing dark sunglasses and a black hat, twisting a handkerchief in her left hand, the right arm was immobilized by a cast. Up close the bruises on her face were evident.

Brian didn't speak. He wrapped her in his arms and held tight.

"He found me." Stacy sounded like she had a mouth full of rocks.

He pulled back and fought the anger welling in his chest. "Is he in jail?"

She shook her head and Brian looked away in anger.

"He's dead," she said. "He ran right in front of a car when the police showed up."

"I want you to come live with me, Stacy. Let me make it easier."

She looked up at him and tears fell. "I'm not your responsibility."

He kissed her tear-stained cheek. "Come home with me."

The red-eye flight to LA lifted off the runway and Stacy looked out the window. The left side of her face was swollen and nearly unrecognizable. Her wrist was broken, so were two ribs. She lifted her hand and brushed away a strand of hair.

Once they were airborne, Brian pushed his seat back and closed his tired eyes. "I need a nap."

Stacy slipped earphones on and took the newspaper Brian had been reading. A few minutes later, she laughed.

Brian stirred and squinted at her. "What?"

She slipped the headset over his ears. He listened for a second then groaned and pushed the headset away.

"It's so ironic to hear you singing and see you sitting there beside me. It's like some dream. I love your voice, Brian. I could listen to you sing twenty-four hours a day."

He grinned at her. "We're going to have to get you a good therapist."

By the time they arrived at his home in Malibu it was after two in the morning. Brian led Stacy upstairs to the boy's rooms. Jesse was sleeping peacefully in his own bed. His tiny face was so sweet and angelic it brought a smile to Stacy's battered face. Brian opened the door to the twin's bedroom and saw only one boy.

He motioned her to follow, leading the way down the hall to his own room. Stacy peered around him and saw Max sprawled in the middle of Brian's bed wearing only a cowboy hat, boots, and superhero underwear.

She leaned close to him, whispering softly. "How do you tell the twins apart?"

He grinned. "We make Max wear the cowboy hat."

He took her back downstairs and showed her his studio. The oblong room had thick, insulated walls. Seventeen guitars rested against the wall and a studio grand stood in the middle of the floor. There were amplifiers, keyboards, reel-to-reel recorder, microphones and miles of black electrical cords.

One end had a large desk surrounded by shelves of sheet music, a fax machine, copier, and computer. Three Grammy's rested on a bookcase behind the desk. A cardboard box near the side of the desk contained other awards he hadn't gotten around to displaying.

Stacy ran her hand over the smooth, lacquered surface of the piano. "Would you sing 'My Girl' for me sometime?"

Brian's face relaxed into a slow smile, "Of course."

chapter 22

BRIAN SENSED HIS life was much more domestic than Stacy expected. Every morning he ate breakfast with his kids, drove the twins to school, then ran on the beach for at least an hour or worked out at a nearby gym. After a shower, he locked himself in the studio until lunch. For a few hours every afternoon, he attended to the business side of his career. For the rest of the day he worked in the studio or played with his sons. He seldom went out in the evenings and had no romantic interests.

"You're so gentle with the boys," Stacy said one evening.

The boys were finally asleep and they had settled onto the deck, bathing in the light of a full moon and cool breeze.

"Surprised?"

She shook her head quickly. "I adore you for it. I watched you today while you listened to Jesse's story about the sea turtles at the aquarium, while you gave Mike music lessons on the piano, and when you played baseball with Max for an hour. Not once did you exhibit any impatience. You never raise your voice and when they break the rules, you stop them cold with just a look or that emphatic "no" of yours."

"They hate that word."

"You're a very good parent, Brian. I figured you would be after the way you treated me." She patted his arm, looked deep in his eyes, and smiled.

A strange, physical need stirred and Brian shifted in his chair. He wasn't twelve anymore and she definitely wasn't eight. Despite the life she'd led, she still seemed tender and naïve. She looked to him with trust and respect, like a big brother. His brain was willing to meet those standards. His body was reacting in an entirely different manner.

He cleared his throat and plunged into another subject.

"I want you to go back to school. I'll pay the tuition. I did some checking and found out you can start next month."

"I'll go only if you agree to let me pay you back."

He shrugged and looked out at the water. The sweet scent of her drifted over to him on the lazy night breeze and he closed his eyes, inhaling. Remaining fair to her meant adhering to an unspoken agreement of platonic cohabitation. Dating might take his focus off Stacy, but everything about her felt so right, he had no interest in anyone else.

By December, the attraction was nearly unbearable.

Three days before Christmas, Michael flew in to spend the night then fly everyone back to Wyoming in the morning.

At the airport, Michael embraced him then studied his face and smiled. "You're looking better."

"It's getting a little easier."

Michael patted him on the back. "Let's go see my boys"

"I'd better warn you they're helping with dinner."

"What are we having?"

"Lasagna or at least that's what it's supposed to be."

The boys ran for Michael the minute Brian opened the door. Michael knelt and hugged each one. Mike and Jesse both started talking to him at the same time. Max stood next to him content to look on.

Brian interceded after a moment. "All right, guys, give Grandpa some room to breathe."

Michael lifted Jesse up in his arms and rubbed the top of Mike's head. "I promise we'll have plenty of time to talk."

Brian took Stacy's hand and led her forward. "Michael this is an old friend of mine, Stacy Tamboro. Stacy, this is my father, Michael O'Mara."

Michael's left eyebrow lifted in surprise at the word father and he smiled at Brian before turning to Stacy. Brian hadn't given the introduction any thought, it happened naturally. The word father had finally entered his vocabulary.

The glow of lights coming from Michael's house lit up the landscape for miles across the deep white snow. Katie was first out the door and jumped into Brian's arms with a squeal of delight. The house was full of wonderful sounds and smells, friendly faces, and joy. For the first time since Jo died, Brian thought he might get through a Christmas without profound pain.

Red's children, Katie and Emily were making Christmas cookies. Stacy stood next to Max and watched as he punched out cookies shaped like Santa wearing a cowboy hat.

"Here," Beth said, holding out a cookie cutter.

Stacy pushed the metal edges into the soft dough and pulled it back. She stared down at the shape with surprise.

"Grandpa Sam makes everyone their own cookie cutter," Beth said. "Brian told him about your singing snowman."

Stacy looked over at Brian and he smiled. Her eyes filled with tears and she took a deep breath.

Max stood on his toes so he could see the snowman and nodded. "I like it."

The simple statement reminded Brian of his reaction to their snowman on that cold morning so many years ago. Stacy wiped away a tear that slipped down her cheek and shot a look at Brian, then away.

"I guess I'm just one of the kids," she said.

Brian glanced at Beth then back to Stacy. "No, Stacy, it's nothing like that. I wanted you to be part of our family tradition."

"Here's mine," Beth said, holding up a cutter the shape of a bucket.

Stacy laughed, "A bucket?"

"I'm from a little town in Texas named Silverpail. It's where Michael and I met. My older brother Kevin always called it 'Rustbucket.' Michael had Sam make my brother one just like it. Everyone has their own." She turned to Mike. "May I see your cookie cutter for a minute, please?"

Beth held up a cutter the shape of a guitar.

"I'm using Daddy's," Mike said impatiently. "Grandpa Sam's going to make one for me."

With the last batch of cookies cooling, everyone gathered in the living room. Sam told a cowboy Christmas story in his mellow voice. Nellie slowly rocked Jesse on her lap and they fell asleep together.

Brian leaned against the wall near the fireplace surveying the comfortable, happy people and allowed his attention to rest on Stacy. She listened to Sam with the wide-eyed innocence of a child, but that was the only thing childlike about her.

Lately, being close to her nearly drove him crazy. He found himself staring at her lips when she spoke, studying that corn-silk hair in the sun, or sitting out of sight, listening to the sound of her voice as she laughed and talked with his children.

Suddenly, she turned his way and smiled. He put his drink down and slipped away from the group quickly. He went outside to the deck, hoping to tamp down the need running rampant in his body. The door opened behind him and he prayed it wasn't Stacy, the catalyst for his alarm. He was afraid she might have seen the raw desire that sent his heart racing. A hand touched his shoulder and he held his breath, afraid to turn.

"It's too cold out here, Brian," Beth said.

Brian sighed with relief. "I need the fresh air. I'll come back in a minute."

"No, come on, come inside now. We need to talk."

Beth never used that mother-in-charge tone with him and he smiled until she opened the door a little wider, and waved him inside. He followed her up the private staircase to Michael's office and took the glass of warm brandy she handed him. Beth sat next to him on the leather sofa in front of the fireplace.

"So, tell me about Stacy."

He explained about how they met, the snowman, Stacy's parents, and foster homes. He described the night in Baltimore when she managed to get through to him. He explained everything but the sudden charge that sent him running.

"So, basically, you see her as a little sister, is that what you're telling me? She's like Katie or Emily to you?"

Brian gave her a sideways glance and smiled uncomfortably, "Not exactly."

"Good for you." She patted his shoulder. "I was afraid you'd keep pretending."

"I'm not ready for this, Beth."

"You're not ready for what?"

"I'm not ready to feel this way."

She laughed, "Oh, I think you are. You're just afraid to love again."

"It's too late to stop myself from falling in love." He paused, thinking for a minute. "It's just that I brought Stacy to LA to help her. I want her to feel secure and trust me. She thinks of me as a brother."

Beth laughed softly. "Brian, you are a sweet, sensitive man, but you complicate everything just like your father. Don't play the same game with Stacy that he played with me. Don't wait. Don't ignore what you're feeling. Go on and tell her. If my hunch is right, you'll both be very happy."

Michael stepped into the doorway. "Beth?"

Beth turned to the silhouette of her husband, "Right here."

"Oh, good, for a moment, I thought I heard your brother in here giving advice."

Beth shrugged off his sarcasm with a smile. "Sometimes, you O'Mara men need a little advice."

"Brian, the boys are in bed. Jesse and Max are asleep, but Mike wants to talk with you."

"He's always the last one to give in. He'd stay up all night if I let him." He placed his untouched glass of brandy on the table and kissed Beth's cheek. "Thank you. I'm glad you care."

Brian slipped soundlessly into the bedroom. He found Mike looking out the big window by his bed, watching snow fall through the moonlit night. He held the little yellow camera he received for his last birthday in his hands.

Brian sat on the bed next to him, looking out at the falling snow. They didn't speak for a moment. Finally, Mike glanced at him.

"Have you ever seen Santa?" he whispered, looking back outside quickly.

"No."

"Do you think he'd let me take his picture?"

Brian smiled. "Is that what you're waiting for?"

He held up his camera as proof. "I'm ready."

"There's an old myth that says he won't come unless everyone in the house is sleeping."

"I guess that's why there's no picture of the real Santa."

"Guess so."

Mike frowned, thinking, then turned to Brian and handed him the camera. "Okay. I'll go to sleep. Since you stay up so late, would you look out every once in a while for me?" A smile lit his young face. "Maybe we'll get lucky."

"Maybe we will."

Mike got on his knees, hugged Brian, and slipped under the covers, yawning. "Thanks, Daddy. I was kind of tired anyway."

Brian leaned over and kissed him on the forehead. "I love you."

Mike smiled and closed his eyes. "I love you too."

He walked over to Max's bed and kissed him. He pulled the covers over Jesse, knowing Jesse would kick them off again in five minutes, and kissed him too.

He knelt next to Jesse's bed and said a silent prayer of gratitude for these children before going downstairs with Mike's camera.

chapter 23

STACY, MICHAEL, RED and Beth were in the kitchen, sitting around the big table.

"You should have told me you were taking pictures," Red said, fluffing the ends of his long hair, "I would have combed my hair."

Brian laughed and put the camera on the table. He took the chair next to Stacy. "Mike wants me to get a picture of Santa when he comes by. He was watching out the window hoping for a shot, but I talked him into going to sleep."

"We've got a Santa suit," Michael said. "Sam's cousin is coming over tomorrow morning to surprise the kids. One of us could put it on and we could take a few pictures with the Polaroid camera. Think we could fool them?"

"Well, Max will probably figure it out, but he won't tell. I could dress up if one of you would take the pictures."

Red shook his head. "The suit would be too small for you. Sam's cousin is only about five-seven."

"Then I'll do it," Beth said.

Michael grinned at her. "He said five-seven, not four-seven."

Beth stuck her tongue out at him. "Don't be mean on Christmas Eve."

Stacy nudged Brian with her knee. "I'm five-four."

After taking pictures, Brian helped Stacy remove the Santa suit. She slipped off the hat and strands of her silky hair fell over her forehead. Brian brushed them away from her face and a static charge snapped between them. Stacy jumped and looked up at him with her big eyes. Without thinking first, Brian leaned down and kissed her mouth.

A hot blush crept over his face when he pulled back. "Merry Christmas," he whispered.

Stacy caressed his burning cheek. "Wow, what prompted that?"

He smiled shyly and looked away. "Beth gave me permission."

Stacy laughed. "Well, bless her heart."

Later, after Stacy drifted off to bed, Brian sat down at the piano and played softly. Michael joined him for a chat and they talked about the ranch, Brian's house, the kids and Brian casually shared a few stories about the past summer tour.

At eleven-thirty, the phone rang and Michael grabbed it before the first ring was complete. As he listened, he looked to Brian and frowned. He handed over the portable receiver without saying a word.

Brian pressed the receiver to his ear and cringed. "Hello?"

"Honey, it's been so hard to find you."

Recognizing the voice, Brian jumped to his feet. "How dare you call here, Amanda."

"Hey, give me some credit for tenacity. That bitch Theresa wasn't the least bit cooperative, and Sammy, hell, what a waste of time she is."

"Leave me alone."

"Oh, I can't. I need you, Brian. I know we could really have something special again. I mean, my goodness, you're the only man I've ever been with who was strong enough to hold me up while he..."

Brian interrupted quickly, "I'm going to have you arrested for harassment. Do you understand me?"

"Go to hell, you jerk. You can't find me, and, believe me, I know you've tried. Speaking of hell, how is your new housemate, the ultra-darling Stacy? Really superstar, what a cheap piece of work she is," she paused, sighing dramatically. "I suppose someone with her kind of background does have experience and that's probably an important asset to you."

Brian lowered the receiver, pressing it against his chest. He closed his eyes and took a deep breath. With great reluctance, he tried again. "How did you get my father's number?"

"I was just thinking," she began. "Maybe I'll try your Daddy instead. Hoo-rah! Now, that's a good looking son-of-a-bitch. I mean, who cares if he's forty-three? I read this article one time about Melissa Cole, you know the singer he used to date, and she referred to him as the best lay she ever had. "

Brian paced in front of the piano. "What is it you really want?"

"You here, no wait, right, umm, yeah, right there."

Brian dropped the receiver onto a soft chair. He didn't give in to the urge to hang up this time. He was afraid it would just lead to a repeat performance and she would wake everyone in the house.

"Who is it?" Michael asked.

Brian briefly told him the story, leaving out the sexual details and Michael picked up the receiver.

"Amanda, this is Brian's father."

"Hi there Daddy, anybody ever tell you what a smooth voice you have?"

"No, you're the first."

"Are we going to have a nice, civil conversation, Father-stud, or will you get to the point and allow me to return to the harassment of your son?"

"I was hoping to convince you to stop."

"No chance," she laughed. "Unless, you want to trade places with him."

"I think you know this is getting you nowhere."

"Hey! Shut your mouth big Daddy and put that son of yours back on the phone. He's ten times the man you are anyway."

Michael shook his head and laid the phone down on the couch. "She's crazy, Brian."

"No kidding."

Brian picked up the receiver and listened, when he didn't hear anything, he hoped Amanda hung up, but, as if reading his mind, she began again.

"I'm going to go now, sweet-meat. Just wanted to call and wish you Merry Christmas. One more thought before I go, Brian. I've been meaning to ask, did anyone ever question you about the fire? I don't recall hearing about an investigation."

"What are you talking about?"

"The f-i-r-e fire, you know, the one intended to cleanse your life of mistakes. Who knew Theresa would be out with those midgets you call sons?" She cackled, as if she made a great joke. "Of course, you can take satisfaction in knowing your song inspired me. Fallen to Ashes was so appropriate for the two of you." She paused and lowered her voice to a vicious whisper, "I played it while I watched your house burn."

Brian's heart was in his throat. He dropped to the piano bench and made himself ask. "Did you set that fire?"

"Come let me whisper sacred secrets in your ear." She laughed again and the line went dead.

The receiver slipped from Brian's fingers and he covered his face with his hands.

Michael placed a hand on Brian's shoulder. "What in the world did she say?"

Brian found it difficult to speak. "She just told me she killed Jo and the baby."

"Do you think she's telling the truth?"

Brian could only manage a nod. Michael walked away, toward the window and stared out at the night for a few minutes.

"I'll fly you to Pennsylvania the day after tomorrow. We'll see what the police can do."

Brian pushed his bed against an inner wall, slipped into the boys bedroom next door and carried each one back to his bed. After covering them, he lay on the outside edge. The grief he had been able to check lately came back in full force like an angry storm.

Jo's death was his fault. He should be the one in the grave. He should have sensed the truth about Amanda long ago. Jo and their daughter would still be alive if he had paid more attention. The fact that he slept with Amanda sickened him. He was a weak and foolish man.

He stayed awake until after four when he finally fell into a fitful sleep.

At six, the boys woke him and waited impatiently until he stumbled toward the bathroom before they rushed for the door. Michael had assigned them the responsibility of waking everyone in the house on Christmas morning and they were quick about the task.

Stacy was at the big kitchen table, staring out at the dawn when he entered. Obviously, she had been up for hours and he was certain she had been crying.

"I'll get you some coffee," she said and started to the cabinet for a cup, but he stepped in her path.

"What's up?"

"Christmas," she said, glancing at him and flinched. "What's wrong? You look like you've been up all night."

"I got a call last night that was my worst nightmare."

"From who?"

He shook his head, "You first. Tell me what's wrong."

"Brian, I've been thinking. When we get back to LA, maybe I'll get my own place."

He was too surprised not to let his disappointment show. "Is this because of that kiss? I'm sorry, Stacy."

She pressed a forefinger against his lips, silencing him.

"It's time, Brian. I've been in hypernation long enough."

He frowned at her. "Do you mean hibernation?"

"You'll have to excuse me professor," Stacy snapped, turning away. "I've been up all night too."

"I wish I'd known. I could have used your company. "

Stacy poured them both a cup of coffee and took a deep breath. "Brian, I just can't handle another man who isn't on solid ground. I can't fill the void left by Jo's death." She looked him in the eye and shrugged sadly. "I want you to want me."

Mike burst through the swinging kitchen door followed by his brothers. "Dad, did you see Santa?"

"Grandpa spotted him first and got a couple of pictures with his camera," Brian said.

Stacy turned her back, trying to hide fresh tears. Brian pointed to the photographs of Stacy in the Santa suit on the refrigerator door. The boys stared open-mouthed at the photos of Santa near the Christmas tree.

Mike smiled from ear to ear and gave Brian a high-five slap on the hand. "All right, Dad."

chapter 24

CHRISTMAS MORNING WAS a long blur for Brian. He attempted to be a part of things, but knew it was a noticeably poor effort. Waiting was nearly intolerable. He wanted answers about the fire now.

Stacy remained withdrawn most of the morning and her gloom seemed to be gaining momentum. After the presents were open and breakfast was out of the way, he pulled her aside and asked to talk to her privately in his bedroom. He quietly closed the door to the adjoining bedroom where Jesse was taking a nap and asked her to sit down on the bed with him.

"Tell me what's going on," he said. "I don't understand what's wrong."

Stacy examined him closely. She didn't say the words, but he saw her concern for him.

"I'm confused," she said. "I need some space and time to think."

"About what?"

She touched his lips with a fingertip and smiled sadly, "One simple kiss."

He shook his head. "It was hardly simple."

Since Jo's death, he had been in a holding pattern. He lived minute-to-minute without looking right, left or down the road. The kiss was a step forward, but seemed a million years ago now. He wished he could spend the day savoring the magic, instead of enmeshed in a nightmare.

He forced wishful thinking aside and addressed her fear. "Stacy, I wasn't rushing into anything."

"I love having you as my friend and I'm afraid of crossing the line. You know? What if it falls apart? I need your friendship more than I need sex."

He frowned in disbelief. He would never understand women and assigned that fault to his mother.

"Is that what you think the kiss meant?"

"Well, yeah. What did it mean to you?"

He looked away, laughing, and shook his head. "I'm too tired to have this conversation."

"Tell me, Brian."

"I love all the little things you do. The way you walk on the balls of your feet like you're floating across the floor. The way you look at me is so honest. I'm crazy about the sound of your laughter. I find myself daydreaming about the time we will spend together. I love the way you love my children and they love you back. I hoped the kiss would lead to seeing your smile when I open my eyes first thing every morning."

He looked over and discovered tears in her eyes. He had no idea what they meant at this point. Stacy leaned against his chest, closing her eyes. Tears streaked down her cheeks. Brian wrapped both arms around her and held on tight.

"You never said one word before that kiss," she said. "I thought I was just like a kid sister to you, someone you thought you had to take care of. You never let on, Brian. What was I supposed to think?'

"Why would you assume I wanted sex?" He paused then told her the whole truth. "Okay, looking at you drives me a little crazy." He laughed. "Make that a lot crazy. Is desire such a bad thing?"

"No."

"Then give me a break. Will you?"

She tilted her head and kissed his mouth long and slow, offering his heart a new set of plans. He was breathing harder when she sat back. He smiled and wagged a finger.

"Don't do that again. My body can't take it."

It was her turn to smile, "Oh yeah?"

He smiled at her. "Yesterday, I watched you listen to Sam tell that story and it hit me out of the blue I'm not feeling brotherly anymore."

She laughed and kicked her feet out in front of her. "Did this strike like a sudden illness?"

"No," he said, grinning. "It was more like running in the dark and hitting a brick wall with my face."

He leaned against the headboard and stretched his legs out on the bed. Sleep sounded like heaven. Jesse wandered in and Brian lifted him to the bed. Jesse snuggled comfortably against him and fell back to sleep without a word.

Stacy smiled warmly. "Tell me why you were up all night, Brian," she said.

He stroked Jesse's blonde head and explained about Amanda, careful not to say too much in front of the four-year-old.

Stacy shook her head when he finished. "What are you going to do?"

"Michael and I are flying to Pennsylvania in the morning. I'm going to talk to the police and see if they'll do anything." He looked down at Jesse, then back to her, "It's my fault."

She frowned in confusion, "Your fault? How do you figure that? That's like saying Tap beat me because I deserved it."

"It's not the same thing."

"You're wrong. This woman is crazy, just like he was."

Brian sighed and closed his eyes.

Stacy rose and kissed his cheek. "Sleep for a while. I'll take care of the boys."

Finally, he mumbled an apology and succumbed to exhaustion.

After dinner, Michael and Brian sat side-by-side in the family room, acoustic guitars resting on their laps. Katie stood near Michael's shoulder and joined in with a flute. The room glowed softly with candles, the fireplace, and blinking Christmas tree lights and the peaceful atmosphere enabled Brian to momentarily put the ordeal with Amanda aside.

He and Michael played a duet together. Mike stood behind Brian's elbow, watching intently as the fingers of his father and grandfather flew in harmony and rhythm as if they were one.

Katie joined them on some of the Christmas standards then Brian played the twelve-string and sang O Holy Night solo. Without intending to he gave everyone in the room a reminder of who he was outside this family group. Everyone present was familiar with his recorded voice. In Wyoming, he was usually content to leave his work elsewhere. Now everyone including his children sat in rapt attention.

Finished, he looked around at their somber faces and grinned. "What? Was I off key?"

Michael smiled and patted his knee, "Not even close."

Nellie got up from her chair and came over, her blue eyes moist. She caressed his face tenderly. "God only loaned you to us for a while so we can hear what we have to look forward to."

Brian didn't know how to respond to that and settled for a simple thank-you. Mike tugged on his arm impatiently. They had worked on a song for two months and he wanted to play now.

While Brian situated himself at the piano, Mike proudly slipped the strap of his small guitar over his shoulder. Max and Jesse took the chair Brian vacated next to Grandpa Michael.

Mike didn't make any errors. His performance was a little stiffer than at home, but he displayed an evident talent. When it was over, he took a deep bow and threw his arms around his trusted accompanist.

Brian couldn't sleep again that night. He left the boys in their beds and went downstairs around one that morning. He sat in the dark, near the piano, staring at one symbol of his egotism. If he hadn't been so selfish, Jo would be alive.

Michael's voice broke his chain of thought. "Want some company?"

"Sure."

Michael turned on the light over the sheet music and ran his fingertips over the white keys. "Music is an odd mistress. It is such a fine, personal experience yet nothing is more demanding. Wouldn't you agree?"

"I suppose."

"Brian, don't turn this in on yourself. Sometimes the events that have the most impact on your life have nothing to do with you directly. Amanda's obsession may seem to be you, but it's something different. This fixation stems from mental illness. You're the object she's chosen to direct her attention to."

Michael moved closer, looking down at him as he continued, "We'll tell the police what she said and do everything possible to resolve this. Beyond that, this thing is out of your control."

All day a ball of pain had rested in Brian's chest, pulsing, waiting to explode and when Michael reminded him he had so little power that ball burst. A small cry escaped his tight lips and Brian buried his face in his hands.

Michael's strong hands lifted him to his feet and embraced him. "I love you," he whispered. "We'll walk through this together."

chapter 25

THEY WERE FLYING over the Rockies before the sun was up in Pennsylvania. Brian sat in back alone, staring at the dark sky without seeing. The tears were gone now, but grief clung to every thought. A new kind of negative fed on the adherent muck, creating a mutant form of malevolence he had no experience with.

No matter what Michael said, he felt responsible for this nightmare. Chasing a dream had killed his wife and daughter.

An hour into the trip, Michael left the co-pilot in charge and joined him. He poured a cup of coffee from a thermos and watched Brian carefully before speaking.

"What are you thinking?"

Brian shrugged in reply. He didn't want to get involved in a long discussion about right and wrong.

"I talked to her, Brian. I know she's crazy. I won't let you blame yourself for this."

Brian closed his aching eyes and laid his head back against the seat. "Jo warned me a long time ago. I didn't listen."

"Warned you about what?"

"She knew Amanda was dangerous."

"What could you have done to stop her?"

"I could have stayed home with my family."

"You're being ridiculous," Michael said.

Brian sat up quickly, eyeing him with near contempt. "What do you expect me to do, accept this?"

"No, we'll do everything we can, but, after that, I want you to let go. Torturing yourself won't bring Jo back."

"Stop parenting me, Michael," he snapped. "You're way too late for that."

Other than blinking a few times, Michael remained perfectly still for what seemed an eternity. Brian turned and looked at the dawning of this miserable day, choking on his own vicious words. After a few more grueling minutes, Michael moved back to the pilot's chair.

They rented a car at the airport in Philadelphia and maintained a long, quiet ride to the sheriff's office. A fat deputy told Brian the detective who investigated the fire was on Christmas vacation and to come back next week to speak to him. Brian politely explained that he couldn't come back next week.

While Brian again explained what Amanda told him, the deputy scrutinized him with obvious distaste.

When Brian finally mentioned Amanda's name a third time, the deputy halted his assessment and sneered at him. "Are you talking about Amanda Cutler boy?"

Brian short temper flared at the tag 'boy', "Yeah."

The fat man snorted loudly. "Don't you know her father is our mayor?"

Brian stepped closer. "What does that have to do with what I'm telling you?"

Michael put a hand on Brian's shoulder and addressed the deputy. "What's the sheriff's name?"

"Roy Campbell. Why?"

"Because," Michael paused, squinting to read the Deputy's name badge, "Deputy Conrad, I intend to call him."

Michael turned to leave and the deputy got to his feet. "You can't call the sheriff."

"Watch me."

"Well, he ain't home."

"Fine," Michael tossed back. "Then I'll go up the chain of command from there. Come on, Brian, Deputy Conrad obviously has better things to do."

The Deputy hurried his bulky body past Brian, hustling to match Michael's long-legged strides. "I don't know who you think you are, but you ain't coming in here and bluffing your way into nothing, Cowboy Bob."

"I don't bluff," Michael snapped without breaking stride.

Michael walked out the front door and disappeared outside. The deputy looked at Brian then turned and huffed his way to a desk in the small office.

Within fifteen minutes, the deputy got a blistering phone call from the sheriff. The man screamed so loudly, Deputy Conrad had to hold the receiver away from his ear about four inches.

Brian heard the sound out in the hallway where he had been pacing the floor. He leaned against a wall and might have found some satisfaction in the moment, if not engulfed in the muck.

Michael returned and didn't say a word. He stood next to Brian who sensed it was best just to keep his mouth shut right now.

Twenty minutes later, a detective walked through the door and apologized for keeping Michael and his son waiting. He offered to get them coffee. Michael seated himself in the detective's office and accepted the offer.

Brian stayed on his feet as the detective hurried away. He was ready to jump out of his skin. "So, who did you call?"

Michael slid him a peevish look. For the first time since Brian met him, the blue eyes weren't friendly.

"The Governor," Michael said.

"The Governor? Of Pennsylvania?"

Michael nodded and took a deep breath then shifted his weight in the wooden chair. Brian knew it would be best to stay quiet at this point, but couldn't.

"How is it that you know the Governor of Pennsylvania?"

"We were on a few committees together."

"What kind of committees?"

Michael shook his head and shrugged.

Brian's anger bubbled. Obviously, Michael didn't feel like talking. The man and his secrets fired another round at Brian's shredded tolerance.

"Cowboy Bob is always full of surprises," Brian said, turning away.

He walked past the detective's desk to the window and turned his back. He pretended to look out at the day while he checked his displaced anger one more time.

The detective looked through a slender file on the fire and sighed loudly. "Our investigation revealed no suspicion of arson. According to this report, the probable cause was a cigarette. Did your wife smoke, Mr. Burnette?"

"I don't believe this," Brian muttered.

Michael leaned forward. "Detective, this woman bragged to my son about setting this fire. Won't you at least question her?"

The detective's brow creased in feigned regret. "There's little we can do without some kind of proof. Since the house is no longer standing, I'm afraid all I can do is offer my deepest sympathies. I suggest your son get a restraining order to stop the phone calls."

Brian slipped into an old kind of numbness as Michael drove them out of town toward the airport near Philadelphia. Snow slid by the windows in a light dance and daylight was fading fast.

"The committee was about the prevention of child abuse," Michael said quietly about twenty miles down the road.

Brian turned his attention from the once familiar land and frowned at him. "What?"

"I have a personal involvement with a group of safe houses for abused and runaway kids, so they asked me to serve on a council. The second committee was for environmental issues."

Brian shook his head in disbelief. "I really don't know you at all. Why don't you ever talk to me?"

"There are a lot of things in my life I don't talk about."

"I know, believe me."

Michael sighed. "Is there something specific on your mind?"

"Yeah, there is. I've been waiting for the right time. Unfortunately, that perfect moment never presents itself."

"Then do it now."

"All right," Brian nodded. "I'll start with what I know. I know your uncle, the priest, pushed you through school and that after a confrontation between the two of you, he committed suicide and your father blamed you for his death. I also know your father beat the hell out of you and almost killed you in 1967 because Uncle Bob told me."

Michael shifted in his seat and kept his eyes on the road. The snow was coming faster now, covering the roads and blurring the visibility. "Is there a point in there, somewhere?"

"I'm not finished. I know you speak several languages fluently, that you have perfect pitch, and make more money in your retirement per month than most will in a year because other people told me."

He stopped, thinking for a minute. "I guess what I want you to know is that I hate being forced to know you through other people. I want you to trust me."

Brian paused again, swallowing the residual bitterness the words left in his mouth. It wasn't his goal to hurt Michael, yet he couldn't stop. "Damn it, Michael, you give and give to me, but keep me at arm's length. Sometimes, I get the impression you're still atoning for some crazy debt from the past. Am I right?"

"No."

Though the single word was strong, there was a definite catch in Michael's voice. Part of Brian's brain identified too much with that subtle sound of pain, but something foolish made him finish.

"I hate learning the facts from other people. Like that song Angel's Blues. If it weren't for Beth's brother Kevin, I wouldn't know you wrote it."

"Why do you feel you have to know all these little details?"

"Little detail? Didn't you think I would find it pretty damned interesting that a song you wrote won a Grammy?"

"I don't take credit for that song."

"But you wrote it."

"Yes."

"That's just it. You see? Can't you take some pleasure in your accomplishments?"

"I don't consider the song an accomplishment."

"Oh, you are so frustrating! Tell me, why the hell not?"

Michael took a long, slow breath. "Every note reminds me of the twenty-three years I believed I didn't have the right to be happy." He paused for a sip of warm coffee and cleared his throat. "Don't ever think I don't trust you, Brian. My silence isn't a personal affront to you. My thickest scars are the result of my telling the truth as a kid. Silence was my best friend for years. Now, I just can't shake the habit."

Michael stared straight ahead, but Brian didn't need to see his eyes to see the hurt, he had the image memorized. All day, he had misdirected his anger and frustration. He knew exactly why Michael didn't talk about the pain. He always had.

"You know," he said, after a few minutes of heavy silence. "I've been beating you up all day. My only excuse is that I'm not thinking straight right now. I'm really sorry."

Michael nodded, accepting the apology. They drove in silence for a few more miles until Michael spoke again.

"The only person who knows everything is Beth." He looked over at Brian and smiled tiredly. "If I don't talk to her, she makes sure I don't get any sleep."

chapter 26

MICHAEL TOOK BRIAN, Stacy, and the boys back to LA. Brian settled the children in their rooms then went to his studio to check messages and catch up on mail. The first call he returned was Sammy's.

"I got your urgent message. What's up?" He straddled the piano bench in his room and sat, leafing through the mail idly.

"Well, my sweet dumpling, your Sammy got married."

Thinking she was joking, he played along, "Who did you marry?"

"Jason Turnbow."

Brian couldn't suppress a laugh. "The soap star with the tongue?"

"That's the one. I'm officially Mrs. Turnbow."

"Wow, Sammy. Congratulations."

"Thank you. Unfortunately, that's not the urgent part. I have much less pleasant business to discuss."

"What?"

"Amanda Cutler called me on Christmas Eve. She was rather intoxicated, but not so much that she couldn't describe this rainy night in Pennsylvania with a close friend of mine. I'll spare you the graphic details, but she shared a very colorful narration regarding this coupling."

Brian didn't know what to say. Sammy was angry with him and the truth was too embarrassing.

"Would Amanda be the blonde that bartender from the sleazy bar in Pennsylvania described to me that time I found you drunk on your ass in the tree-house?"

"Yes."

"How could you be so stupid Brian?"

He groaned and rubbed his eyes, "Haven't we had this conversation before?"

"The woman is insane!"

"Sammy," he began weakly. "She also called my father's house on Christmas Eve. She told me she set the fire that killed Jo and the baby. I went to Pennsylvania yesterday. They say that without proof there's nothing they can do."

"Brian, she's probably lying just to hurt you. Think about it."

"I want to believe that."

"It's a sick thing to say, but considering that the source is Amanda, lying is a far more plausible explanation. Don't you think?"

"I don't know," Brian sighed and rubbed his temple. "I guess you could be right."

"So, how's Stacy?"

"She's fine."

Sammy cleared her throat. "She dating anyone?"

"Not that I know of. Why do you ask?"

"Well, gee, let me think. Oh yeah, when are you going to make a move?"

"Still worrying about my hormones?"

"Not really, I'm just jerking you around. It's pretty easy to see you two are cute together. Did you pop the question?"

Brian laughed. "No."

"Why not?"

"Do you have marriage fever or something?"

It was Sammy's turn to laugh. "You haven't even slept together, have you?"

"I'm going now Mrs. Turnbow."

"Here's what you do," Sammy continued. "Take her out on a real date."

He sighed and tapped the pedals of the piano with his foot. "I think I can handle this."

"I love you, Brian. Don't hesitate to fall in love again. It's the elixir of the Gods. Mankind's only lasting Utopia."

"'Bye, Sammy," he chuckled. "I love you too."

Brian leafed through his mail absentmindedly, without really focusing. He was thinking of Stacy and what he could, should, or would do, when a letter in his hand drew his attention.

He didn't recognize the handwriting. There was no stamp on the envelope. This letter had been hand-carried to his home. He ripped open the envelope and pulled out a single sheet of paper. The letter, like the envelope, was handwritten.

Hi!

Guess who? Nope, it's not the ghost of Christmas past. This is the voice of your future! I know:

A. You went to Pennsylvania and talked to the police.

B. You can't prove anything.

C. You are obsessing about this, so I think I'll throw a little more fuel on the fire. Oops! Did I say fire?

And I quote...'Brian home from longest tour yet and loves our tree house. Sex was always best in the treetops, but four times is an all time record. I only wish I could store up these moments for when he disappears down the road again. Sometimes, I can't get enough of this man. I want to tie him down and keep him prisoner, so I won't have to share anymore.'

Isn't that touching? Four times? You big stud! Sleep well and remember...Don't smoke in bed. You might drop off to sleep and burn the house down. See you soon.

Love,

A

Brian jumped to his feet and paced the room. That letter had to be from Amanda. She knew where they lived and came to their house and placed that letter in the mailbox personally.

How did Amanda know where he was, whom he saw, where he lived, and the private information about him and Jo? Suddenly, one answer came to him. Amanda was quoting from one of Jo's journals and the only way she could have those was to be in the house in Pennsylvania before the fire.

He threw the door open and ran through the house checking the locks on all the doors and windows. He grabbed the binoculars, ran to the deck and searched up and down the beach for her.

He wanted to break something, destroy something, run into the night and kick the hell out of something. Suddenly, grief bore down on him and he hurried down the hall to the soundproof studio where he leaned against the closed door and slid to his knees. He took deep breaths trying to control the pain, but the tight fist clutching his insides was too demanding. He pressed his forehead against the cool wooden door and let the grief loose.

chapter 27

BRIAN HAD A commitment to a New Years Eve party at the home of his producer in Beverly Hills. Attending show business functions never suited him and this year the idea seemed even more unappealing. He looked across the breakfast table at Stacy on December twenty-ninth and found one reason to force himself out of his self-imposed cocoon.

"Would you like to go to a party on New Year's Eve?"

Stacy put down the morning paper and stared at him blankly, "Party?"

"Would you like to go?"

"I don't have anything to wear to a fancy party."

He shrugged. "You can go shopping."

"I don't think it would be a good idea."

"Why? I'm already committed to this thing. Please tell me you'll make my life easier by going along."

All three boys were listening with undivided attention. Stacy looked at them then rose.

"I think we should talk about this privately."

Brian followed her down the hall to the music room and leaned against the closed the door.

Stacy turned on him. "We can't start dating like this. Have you talked to the boys?"

"I don't need to talk to them. They love you."

"I want you to talk to them first."

"All right, is there anything else?"

"Well, actually there is. Have you thought about what will happen when the press starts poking around in my background? This could hurt your career. I don't exactly fit in with rich and successful people."

"Some people think I'm rich and successful and I think you fit in just fine."

"Stop it!"

The levity he felt a moment ago vanished. "What in the world is the matter with you?"

"Brian for heaven's sake! Right here is what I can share with you." She pointed at the door. "Out there I'm an embarrassment."

"That's ridiculous. You're beautiful, Stacy."

"I'm nobody."

He stared hard and chose his words carefully. "You're the woman I'm falling in love with more every day, that's what matters to me."

"Love, Brian?"

He nodded solemnly, never taking his eyes off her. "I'm sorry, I've been so involved with this other mess I neglected to tell you the most important part."

Stacy's face relaxed into a smile. "Since you put it that way, how can I refuse?"

Brian took her shopping and bought everything she needed, easily spending more money in one day than Stacy spent in an entire lifetime for clothing. She got her hair professionally cut and styled and a consultation on makeup.

On New Year's Eve Brian allowed the boys to stay up past their bedtime just to see her. When she descended the stairs, Brian was on the phone in the living room, but watched her every step.

She had on a tight, red sequined dress, dangling diamond earrings and matching necklace. She smiled and blushed when Mike whistled.

Brian concluded his call and kissed Stacy's cheek. "You take my breath away."

"You don't look bad yourself."

He pulled at the stiff collar of his tuxedo shirt, feeling like one of his children. "Thank you."

He knew she loved his Mercedes coup. Usually, they made any trip in the van, with three rowdy boys behind them and Stacy swore the Mercedes was the epitome of class.

Brian picked up the car phone, punched in a series of numbers then put the receiver to his ear. "John, this is Brian Burnette. It's almost nine. Just calling to say I won't be able to make it. I'll talk to you on Tuesday."

He replaced the receiver and guided the Mercedes into heavier traffic. "So, what do you want to do?"

"Do? I thought we were going to a party."

"I just canceled. Didn't you hear me?"

"I wasn't sure what you were canceling," she said sullenly.

Brian frowned at her. "Did you want to go to that thing?"

"I was all dressed up for it or so I thought. What do you want to do?"

"Let's go somewhere and have dinner then go dancing. I want our first date to be a real date, not a business function."

"It's New Year's Eve. Where can we go on such short notice?"

He glanced her way and grinned.

Stacy smiled back, "You big rat. You never had any intention of going to that party."

"Not true. I merely set up options. The moment I saw you walk down those stairs, I knew I didn't want to share you tonight."

"Careful, my ego is swelling."

"It's about time."

After dinner, he took her dancing in the ballroom of the Beverly Wilt-shire Hotel. She danced so smoothly he felt they were floating and having her so close only made him want her closer.

They were on the dance floor when the old year rolled into the new. Brian looked in her eyes for a long minute then bent down to kiss her lips for the second time. The first kiss at his father's home was tentative, sweet, and soft. This unrestrained statement left them both breathless.

"I hope you thought to get us a room," she said.

Brian grinned widely, "So bold, madam."

She pressed her body closer and he inhaled sharply.

"Please tell me you did."

He stepped back, embarrassed at the way his body was reacting. "Yes, I did."

"Very presumptuous of you," she said, teasing. "Where are we going now?"

Brian rolled his eyes toward the ceiling.

Once they broke down the roles of childhood, their adult relationship found a new personality. Max, Mike, and Jesse accepted the change as the natural order of things. Though Brian and Stacy never slept together at home, the boys stopped getting in Brian's bed.

Sanguine Heart went back to the studio that summer in New York. Brian, Sammy, and Nick had fought to record in LA, but Tara fought back harder. Michael gave Brian the keys to his penthouse apartment in Manhattan.

Brian had seriously considered asking Stacy to marry him, but the band would begin touring again in six months. He decided to put the question on hold until the tour finished. He wanted her to see what life was like when he was really working, so she knew everything.

chapter 28

BRIAN WAS RUNNING late and the last to arrive at the studio. He paused to speak to a few people in the control booth before joining the other band members in the recording studio.

Sammy threw up her hands. "Well, you're finally here. You could have taken a minute to call, Brian."

She stuck her hands on her hips and glared at him. He was only ten minutes late and knew that didn't justify her agitated state. He glanced at Tara and Mary and found smiles.

"Where's Nick?"

"His turn to get coffee," Tara said mildly.

Brian let his heavy leather satchel slip from his shoulder to the floor and looked at the three of them. "What's up?"

"Sammy's hormones," Mary said.

"Jason and I have decided to have a child," Sammy said.

Brian stared for a minute. Sammy was always coming at life from odd angles and sometimes he simply didn't know how to react.

"Congratulations," he said.

He opened the satchel and pulled out some sheet music. After placing the pile on the piano, he found all three women still staring at him.

Tara and Mary giggled, as Nick walked in with a tray of Styrofoam cups filled with coffee. "Good-morning, Brian," he sang, unusually cheerful.

"Morning," Brian returned, looking back to the women. "Does somebody want to tell me what the joke is?"

"Well," Sammy began, then cleared her throat, and forced a smile. "I want you to be the father of my baby."

He continued to stare, completely bewildered then frowned. He opened his mouth to speak, but Sammy held up a hand, stopping him. "Will you hear me out? Please?"

Brian managed a nod. Nick pressed a cup of coffee into his hand and Sammy began pacing.

"You are perfect for this, Brian. I mean, first of all, everyone knows you're potent."

Mary and Tara broke into giggles, interrupting her. Nick announced he had a phone call to make and left again.

Irritated, Sammy raised her voice above the giggling and zeroed in on Brian again. "You are one of my dearest friends. I admire your intellect and temperament. Our child would most certainly be a musical virtuoso before she could talk, not to mention an incredible beauty. Brian, just think of the eyes this kid could have."

"What does Jason have to say about all of this?" He asked, finding his voice at last.

"He's sterile or I wouldn't be asking, damn it," she snapped. She took a deep breath and calmed herself a little. "Look, Jason and I both want kids and I can't wait any longer. I'm already thirty-seven years old."

"Have you talked to your doctor?"

She smiled proudly. "She says I'm in great shape."

"I need to think about this."

"Sure, sure, take all summer. I want you to know you don't have to have sex with me, although I'd prefer that, because I think our child would have a better start on a metaphysical basis, you know?"

Brian couldn't hide his astonishment. Mary and Tara erupted into hysterical laughter.

He glanced at the laughing duo. "Is this some kind of joke?"

"No," Sammy said.

"Sammy," he began gently, "You know I love you, but this makes me uncomfortable."

"Oh, for crying out loud, Brian, all I'm asking you to do is masturbate into a cup."

Tara laughed so hard she fell off the piano bench.

"I'm glad I could be so entertaining, Tara," Sammy shouted then stormed out of the studio.

Brian looked down at Tara and Mary. They were both on the floor and in tears from laughing so hard.

"I think she's serious," he said quietly.

Tara held an empty Styrofoam cup up to him before succumbing to a new wave of laughter just as Nick returned.

Nick shook his head and made a clucking sound with his tongue. "You ladies are a tad insensitive."

Brian found Sammy pacing, smoking, and talking to herself in the lot behind the studio. He came out onto the concrete platform, but didn't dare descend the stairs.

"Go away," she barked. "I've been laughed at enough for one day."

"Why did you ask such a personal question in front of them?"

"I tried calling you last night. The sitter said you and Stacy were at some ball game." Her tone implied what happened inside was his fault.

"I sang the National anthem at the Yankee-Dodger game, remember?"

She waved off his statement. "I guess I should've waited until we could talk in private, but I was just so excited. We made the decision to ask you last night and I wanted to share it with you right away. I've always wanted a child. I waited and waited, because of the music thing, but I can't wait anymore. You understand don't you? I mean, those twins and little Jesse have to be the joy of your life."

Abruptly, she stopped pacing and threw up her hands. "I forgot about Stacy! Do you think she'll mind? It wouldn't be like we're having an affair or anything. This would be strictly business."

"Sammy," he began patiently, "If I do this you and I aren't going to have sex."

Sammy tilted her head and grinned at him. Her cat eyes sparkled. "Thanks for taking me seriously."

Brian held out his hand. "Come on, we're already behind schedule."

Sammy followed him up the stairs to the interior door of the building. "I never noticed before, but they're right about you, you really do have a great ass. Are you sure you won't let me take advantage of your body? I promise to be discrete."

He held the inner door open for her and laughed. "You've never been discrete in your life. You wouldn't know where to begin."

Over the next three months while they worked on the album Sammy, Jason, and even Stacy tried to talk him into it. At the studio, Brian found himself bombarded with a multitude of glass, Styrofoam, plastic, metal, and ceramic cups. Nick gave him a large box of specimen cups with his name printed on each one. Mary presented him with a hand puppet for every day of the week. Tara charted a diet for his "maximum potential." Someone left photographs from X-rated magazines inside his sheet music. There was a generous selection of cigarettes to enjoy after his intimate moment at the clinic.

Brian didn't discuss the subject with anyone, including Stacy after she told him she thought his reservations were silly. In August, with the album finished, Brian went to Sammy and Jason's rented apartment to tell them his decision.

Jason said he understood, but Sammy stared in disbelief.

"Why won't you do this for me?"

"I can't, Sammy. Whenever I see this baby I'll feel connected."

"This wouldn't be your kid."

"I'm sorry. I can't separate things the way you do."

"You are so selfish. I'll never forgive you for this Brian."

"I'm sorry."

In tears, she walked to the door, and threw it open. "Get out."

Two days later, Brian was packing Jesse's clothes for their return to Los Angeles, when Sammy came to see him. Brian took her into the library on the first floor and closed the doors.

Sammy looked around at the walls of books and whistled, "Very impressive. Do you think your father read all of these books?"

Brian shrugged and waited for her to get to the point.

"I'm sorry for throwing you out the other day." She smiled sheepishly. "You had every right to say no. I don't think I'll ever understand how your mind works, but I'll respect your decision. I want you to accept my apology."

He folded his arms over his chest, suspicious of her sudden swing in mood. "How did you get over this so fast?"

"Everything's okay now. Jason's brother's willing to do it and he's got six kids." She smiled and stuck her tongue out at him.

chapter 29

FROM NEW YORK Brian, Stacy, and the boys flew into Jackson and Michael took them the rest of the way to the ranch to see the new house which was finally finished and furnished.

After working all summer on the album, Brian needed to relax and the calmness of Wyoming was the best place to unwind. This would be a short break, but much needed before flying back to LA to begin promoting the album and a long tour.

The boys ran through the house examining every nook and cranny, shouting, laughing and looking at everything in warp speed. Brian followed them upstairs and looked into each of the five bedrooms and the master suite with its private balcony and a bathroom the size of his first apartment. He paused before Mike's bedroom door and found all three boys jumping on the bed.

"Get off there, now."

Each boy jumped from the bed to the floor and took off running again past Michael who was standing in the hall and grinned at their exuberance.

Downstairs, Stacy and Beth were stalled in the kitchen which Brian had little interest in. Brian meandered through the open living room, dining room and kitchen with Michael then they followed the long hall between the kitchen and garage to the back of the house to the secluded music room.

This room was complete with recording capabilities. Three of the wooden walls and ceiling were designed specifically to hold the sound in and acoustically state of the art. One wall was full of brackets to hold his collection of guitars. The back wall was all windows with sliding doors and a deck, providing Brian with the view he fell in love with that day with Beth. A door at the back inside corner allowed access to a staircase that connected to his bedroom upstairs and the family room underneath.

For now, only a concert grand rested in the center of the oblong room. Brian lifted the cover over the keyboard. "Would you mind playing? I'd like to hear the acoustics."

Michael obliged with a little Chopin and Brian walked from one corner to the next, down the center and opened the doors to the deck, resting in the open doorway, letting the music flow over him and out to the valley. Michael's playing cloaked him in sweet, sensuous pleasure.

He stepped out onto the deck and sat on the rail. A gentle wind blew his hair back and sunlight warmed his face. He closed his eyes, reveling in the perfection of this moment, courtesy of the father he couldn't say he loved.

chapter 30

BRIAN SPENT A stressful day in LA doing back-to-back interviews to promote the new album and tour. Though Sammy and Tara were usually right beside him, every interviewer looked to him for a majority of the answers. Without exception, Sammy held him responsible for this bias. Today had been no exception.

He and Sammy argued until Brian stopped responding to her relentless tirade. She was still complaining as he drove away from the last television studio.

It was after eleven and he looked forward to the peace and quiet of home. When he turned into the driveway, the headlights illuminated two police cars and one unmarked Dodge sedan. He expected the worst when he walked through the door.

Stacy was in the living room talking to a detective. Seeing him, she ran to Brian in tears. A knot of fear, the size of his fist, rose in his throat.

"Are you Brian Burnette?" the detective asked, eyeing Brian.

Brian nodded. "Yes, what's going on?"

"It's that woman," Stacy said, looking up at him. "She called all afternoon. She said she was going to get rid of me. Brian, she shot at me."

"We'd need to ask you some questions, Mr. Burnette," the detective said.

"Sure. Let me check on my kids first."

"The children are fine. Your housekeeper is up there with them."

Brian walked Stacy back to the couch, but stayed on his feet. He glanced out the window toward the beach, wondering if Amanda was still there, watching all of this. The detective's voice drew him back.

"I understand you have received threatening phone calls."

Brian nodded, looking back to the police.

"Did you recognize the voice?"

Brian told him a condensed version. He explained the threats and that she said she set fire to the house in Pennsylvania. He showed them the note she sent at the beginning of the year and explained about Jo's journals. When they asked that he explain again and questioned him at length, Brian felt as if he were the one under suspicion.

The detective showed Brian the thirty-eight-caliber slug they had pried from an interior wall and the hole in one of the windows facing the beach.

"Have you considered a security system, Mr. Burnette?" The detective spoke slowly, as if talking to an addle-minded child.

"We have an alarm," Brian explained. He was too stunned right now to address the condescension.

"It wasn't on," the detective explained patiently.

Brian turned quickly to Stacy. "Why wasn't the alarm on?"

"I always turn it on before I go to bed," Stacy said.

"From now on, I want it on all the time."

"Brian, that's crazy. The boys run in and out all day."

"Yeah well new rules, now they stay inside."

"You're being irrational. You can't expect three little boys to live like prisoners."

"I'm not asking your opinion, Stacy." He snapped and turned back to the detective.

Brian finished talking with the police and walked them to the door. Stacy eyed him from across the room as he reset the alarm in the entryway. Finished, he sat down wearily in a chair and stared at the hole in the window.

Stacy sat forward and perched on the edge of the couch. "Why are you angry with me?"

Brian glanced at her, then away again, shaking his head. Her question seemed absurd.

"I love your children," she said. He heard anger and hurt in her voice this time as she continued. "You know I'd protect them with my life."

He leaned forward and put his face in his hands. After a minute, he dropped his hands and looked at her. "Why didn't you take precautions? Don't you understand how serious this is?"

She jumped to her feet. "How dare you accuse me of being careless? I was the one she shot at, damn it!"

"I didn't say you were careless…"

Stacy cut in, raising her voice. "You were a jerk to me in front of those cops. You embarrassed me, Brian. I don't appreciate being talked to like that."

"I'm sorry."

"No you're not. You don't know which end is up."

Brian stared at her, his face flushing crimson. He couldn't sit still anymore today. He leapt to his feet. Stacy flinched and took a few steps back.

He frowned at her, "I'm not going to hurt you."

Stacy's eyes narrowed and she laughed shortly, "You already did."

She turned away, but he grabbed her hand. "Wait. Please, talk to me."

"About what?"

Brian wrapped his arms around her, laying his cheek on the top of her head. Her soft, silky hair, cool against his hot skin.

"I'm sorry," he said her gently. "I shouldn't have talked to you that way. It's just…this makes me crazy."

The phone rang and he grabbed it before the first ring finished.

"Hi, Sweetheart," Amanda said. "I just wanted to let you know that shot was a warning. Don't relax just yet here comes the second stroke."

The line went dead and Brian grabbed Stacy's hand, trying to pull her behind him. She planted her feet in resistance so he scooped her up in his arms, and ran up the stairs.

"Put me down!"

At the top of the stairs, Brian set her on her feet and started toward the bedrooms. "That was Amanda. She has something else planned. Please help me with the boys."

Stacy woke the twins while Brian grabbed Jesse and went to wake Theresa. He herded everyone into his bedroom and picked up the portable phone to call the police. While he talked, he took a forty-four automatic from the top shelf of his closet and loaded it.

Jesse began to cry and crawled onto Theresa's lap. Everyone else stared at Brian in disbelief as he took his frustration out on the police then threw the receiver at the dresser.

Stacy approached him cautiously. "Do you even know how to use a gun?"

"Yes, I've been practicing since January."

"And you honestly believe you can shoot someone?"

He nodded. "If she comes into this house, I'll kill her."

"You should let the police handle this."

Brian had no faith in the police. He glanced at his children then to Stacy and Theresa. "Will you try to calm the boys down?"

"Where are you going?"

"I'm going to wait downstairs. She's not getting up here."

After checking all of the locks, Brian sat on the steps in the foyer. He had a portable phone in his lap and the gun by his side. From that central location, he could ensure Amanda wouldn't get anywhere near the stairs.

An hour later, the phone rang, rattling his frazzled nerves. Stacy picked up the receiver at the same moment he did. Sammy was screaming on the other end.

"Brian! That bitch was here. She was in my house!"

"Oh no," Stacy said.

"I woke up and there she was standing over the bed pointing a gun at my face."

"Are you all right?" Brian asked.

"Yes. She ran when she heard Jason pull into the driveway. This had to happen on a night he was working late. My God! Do you think she knew?"

"Did you call the police?"

"Sure did, but they were no help. Brian she knew about me asking you to father a child. She told me you belong to her. This bitch is seriously sick."

Stacy came down the stairs after they finished talking to Sammy. Brian was still sitting in the foyer, resting his head against the wall.

Stacy sat next to him and wrapped an arm around his shoulder. "Why don't you come to bed?"

"What am I going to do, Stacy? In less than six weeks, I'll be back on the road. I won't be able to work."

"Why don't you move the boys to Wyoming?"

He laughed tiredly. "Michael and Beth would love that." Sighing, he tapped his head against the wall. "I don't know what to do."

"You're tired. Come to bed. We'll figure something out in the morning."

He looked her in the eye and managed a tiny smile. "Does this mean you're not mad at me anymore?"

"No, I still think you were a jerk, but right now, there are more important things to be concerned with."

chapter 31

WITH HOURS OF rehearsal and the tour staring him in the face, Brian hired body-guards for Stacy and the boys. She complained about the intrusiveness, but he couldn't think of another alternative.

He gave the principal at the grade school specific instructions about who had permission to take the boys out of school. Sammy received a picture of Amanda from her brother and Brian gave the police and the principal a copy. He also left instructions that the police should be notified immediately if she came to the school.

He talked to Mike and Max at length about Amanda, whom they had dubbed the "crazy lady," trying not to scare them too much, but hoping to make them understand how careful they must be with strangers.

He left for the tour at the beginning of September with a heavy heart. He called every morning and evening. He talked to the boys, Theresa, and the security guards at length. After one week of this, Stacy grew irritable.

"Brian I've tried to be patient with you, but your paranoia only makes everyone more uncomfortable."

"Better uncomfortable than the alternative," he snapped.

"We're being careful. You have to let go a little or you're going to drive yourself crazy."

It took grit and determination, but he backed off as much as he could.

Stacy's twenty-fifth birthday was in mid-October and he flew home for one quick night to surprise her. She never mentioned her birthday and Brian was certain she thought he'd forgotten. He arrived while she was out running errands and picking up the twins at school.

He watched them pull into the driveway from his bedroom window upstairs. The boys immediately jumped out of the car and Stacy dragged along behind them. She waved to the security guard keeping watch from the upper deck of the house. Brian turned to Jesse who was clutching a homemade card in his little hands.

"Let's go, Buddy."

Stacy was at the refrigerator when Jesse burst into the room and thrust the card at her. Brian waited out of sight, around the corner.

"I made it for your birthday," Jesse said.

Stacy knelt next to him and took the card. Jesse couldn't write yet and the card contained crude drawings of his favorite things. There was the family dog, a bicycle, a heart, purple flowers, stars, and one fish jumping out of the ocean. On the inside, there were portraits of Brian, Max, Mike, Theresa, Stacy, and Jesse. He had placed Stacy next to his father and given her the broadest smile. They looked like a family.

Brian stepped around the corner as she looked up from the card. Her eyes widened in surprise and she fell back to the floor with a thud. The boys laughed and Brian shot them a look that stopped the laughter immediately.

Brian helped her to her feet. "Are you okay?"

"You should have warned me."

He wrapped his arms around her and hugged her gently. "That would have ruined the surprise."

"How long can you stay?"

"I have to catch a plane tomorrow morning. I wanted to wish you happy birthday in person."

Stacy looked into his eyes. "You make me crazy," she whispered.

Brian smiled and held out a ring-sized jewelry case. All three boys crowded around for a peek as she opened the lid. Lying on a bed of black velvet was a pin composed of twenty-eight, one-quarter carat diamonds forming a snowman with a ruby hat, sapphire eyes, and tiny diamond ears.

"Wow!" Max said. "That's some snowman, Dad."

She looked up at Brian, ready to cry. "Thank you."

"You're not disappointed?"

A tiny frown creased her brow. "Disappointed?"

"I thought you might expect something else when you saw the box."

"No," she said, an obvious lie. "I think it's beautiful. Thank you."

She stretched to her tiptoes to kiss his cheek, but Brian stopped her. He dropped to one knee and the boys giggled.

"Please look under the snowman," he said.

She lifted the snowman and its velvet bed with trembling fingers and revealed an engagement ring.

"Will you marry me?" Brian asked softly, then laughed and held up a hand. "Before you ask, I already talked to the boys."

"Yes," she said, unable to hold back the tears.

The boys rushed to hug her and Brian got off his knee, waiting patiently. Finally, Max pulled his brothers back and Brian gave Stacy one sweet kiss.

chapter 32

THE SECOND WEEK of December, Sanguine Heart took a scheduled break until the second week of January. Stacy had school until the twenty-first and Brian took the boys for a two-day visit with Jo's mother, Amelia.

He rented a car at the airport in Philadelphia and drove directly to Amelia's for a visit he still dreaded. Amelia's love for her grandchildren was the only reason he gave in. He deliberately maintained a cordial, but cool distance.

The first day went like all the others since Jo's death. Brian stayed until it became intolerable then gave a little more before retreating to the hotel.

On the second day, he dropped the boys off at Amelia's and met Harlan for breakfast then stopped by his old friend Mark's house for a while before going back to Amelia's.

While Amelia made lunch, Brian stood on the back porch, watching the boys play touch football with their cousins. Overhead, the sky grew darker and there was a sharp bite to the wind. He zipped his coat and allowed his eyes to wander to the old tree house, at the edge of the property. He could see Jo climbing ahead of him and hear the echo of her laughter. He would never forget the way her gray eyes conveyed her love for him that special sunny afternoon they first made love.

Amelia slipped up beside him and followed his gaze. "You know, I thought about tearing that old tree house down," she said. "It sat out there mocking my broken heart. Then I remember Kenny's pride when it was finished and the joy my daughter found there with you and I can't get rid of it."

Surprised, Brian glanced at her quickly, blushing at the thought of her knowing what he and Jo did up there.

She laughed at his expression. "Yes, I knew. It was hard to miss, you two practically glowed." She squeezed his shoulder. "My daughter was lucky to be loved so completely."

"Are you saying you finally approve of me?"

"Brian, my experience with the kids Dad left me incredibly bitter and I'm ashamed I took some of that out on you." She paused to watch the kids playing and laughing then patted Brian's hand. "You're doing a wonderful job with the boys."

"Thank you," he managed.

They stood in silence watching the children, sipping their coffee for a few minutes.

Amelia sighed and turned back to the kitchen, "Come inside and share a quiet lunch with me before we feed the children."

Sitting at the kitchen table with a fresh cup of coffee and a slice of chocolate cake in front of him, Brian fought another wave of melancholy. It was always this way when he visited this town, but especially this house. Though he tried to prepare himself for the torture, nothing could prevent the onslaught. Jo was everywhere. The memories would leave him raw and exhausted.

Amelia watched his face carefully. "Jesse says you're getting married again."

"In February."

"She sounds wonderful."

"I see Jesse's doing a lot of talking." He had no appetite and pushed the cake away.

"I want you to be happy. You've been alone too long."

He sat back in the chair and managed a smile. "I'm never alone."

"You know what I mean." She smiled back. "I'd like to meet her some time."

The phone rang and Amelia reached for it. Brian rose and peeked out the window at the kids.

"Brian, it's your mother."

He took the receiver from her. He couldn't imagine why Jean would call, unless something happened to Harlan.

"Hello Brian, this is Jean, your mother."

"Amelia told me."

"I know you're probably on a tight schedule and all, but I was wondering if you would agree to meet me. I only need a few minutes. It's very important."

"Is Harlan all right?"

"This isn't about Harlan. This is about you and me." She took a deep breath and her tone shifted to a softness he'd never heard when she spoke to him. "Please?"

"Just a minute," he turned to Amelia. "Can I leave the boys here a little longer?"

"Of course."

Jean said she would meet him at a restaurant downtown in one hour. Brian replaced the receiver with a growing headache. He really hated coming to this town.

chapter 33

B<small>RIAN STARED OUT</small> at the dark sky and pouring rain. He absentmindedly tapped the edge of his water glass with the tip of a forefinger, growing more restless every second. He glanced at his watch for the third time and decided to give her five more minutes.

"Sorry I'm so late," Jean said, as if on cue.

Startled, he swung around and stared at her. The last time he saw her was when she delivered those Christmas presents to the boys. She looked older, but oddly she appeared softer. His mother was actually pretty again.

"I thought you might have changed your mind," He said getting to his feet awkwardly.

"Harlan insisted on buying a Seville. Of course, I'm the one who's stuck driving the thing. It's quite a job to parallel park such a beast."

They stood there for an uncomfortable moment, physically close yet an enormous distance loomed between them. Brian couldn't recall her giving him one hug and there was never a time when he believed she would welcome any act of affection from him. He opted for pulling out her chair and waiting until she sat before sitting himself. He took the seat opposite her and caught her staring at him.

Jean quickly picked up the menu, as the waiter approached. "Have you ordered?"

"I ate at Amelia's."

"I'm not really hungry either. I'll just have coffee."

"Two coffees," Brian said to the waiter.

He wanted to examine the new Jean in front of him, but didn't want to be obvious. When she lit a cigarette, he sat back reflexively. Sometimes, like today, he still wanted to smoke. Of course, his mother read his reaction wrong.

"Would you excuse my smoking, please? I'm just so nervous."

Brian grinned. "That's new."

Jean's gaze flicked over him then away. "Of course, you're referring to my days of drunken bravado. I gave that up when I got serious about changing my life. Once I got sober, I realized how much work I faced."

"Have you had a revelation, Mom?"

Jean stared at him for a minute as if she were digesting his obvious anger then nodded as if conceding a point. "You have every right to hate me. I was a lousy mother and I know I hurt you."

"But it's time to let bygones be bygones, is that it?"

"I don't expect that much," she tossed back. "I'm trying to be realistic."

The waiter returned with the coffee and Brian asked Jean for a cigarette. He lit it, inhaled and screwed up his face in distaste and put it out. He had forgotten she smoked menthol.

"If only you didn't look so much like him," Jean murmured.

"I'll never understand why you don't let go," he snapped.

"Do you want to know the truth about Michael and me?"

"Yeah," he exhaled, finally looking directly at her. "Tell me why I exist."

"In 1966, after I dropped out of college, I moved to New York mostly to get away from the warmth of my loving family. I stayed with some friends, got a job in a music store, and eventually had enough money to get a place of my own."

"In the building Max Burnette owned," Brian said.

Jean grimaced at the reminder, "Right. The day I moved in was the day I met Michael for the first time. I looked right into eyes so beautiful I forgot where I was. You know whenever I see his picture, in the papers or magazines, they still don't look real to me, they are such an incredible blue. Did you know that singer Melissa Cole wrote Angel's Blues about his eyes? They dated way back when he was a model in New York. I saw her in an interview on television once and she said she named it that because his eyes haunted her. Boy, do I understand that problem."

Brian interrupted irritably. "Could you skip the discourse about Mike's eyes? I really don't have that long."

Unmistakable anger flashed in her eyes, but she nodded. "Excuse me."

She stared out the window for a few minutes as if seeing something out there in the driving rain. She began again, her voice was soft, almost a whisper, as if she was talking to herself. "Michael was a beautiful boy and he had this sensitive, vulnerable quality. I wanted to control him completely."

Turning her attention away from the window, she paused for a sip of coffee, before continuing. "I didn't expect to fall in love. He might have been just a sixteen-year-old kid, but no man ever hurt me the way he did. When he said good-bye, I thought I was going to die of heartache."

She took a small sip of her coffee and cleared her throat. "Good old Max just had to tell him I was pregnant the day I was leaving New York and Michael showed up at my apartment. He wanted to know if I intended to get an abortion." She paused for a little smile. "After all, he was a Catholic at heart. He offered to give up college and raise you by himself. He asked me for an address so he could stay in touch with you. Not once did he suggest he was interested in me and that made me even angrier.

"I told him he wasn't old enough to make any of the decisions and that it would be a cold day in hell when I'd let him see you. I smoked a joint in front of him as a parting shot, got in a cab to go to the airport and left him standing in the pouring rain."

Her gaze flicked over Brian quickly then away. "When I look back on that day, I'm so ashamed. I said some terrible things to punish him for breaking my heart." She paused again and Brian glimpsed her inner struggle. When she spoke her voice was lower, full of emotion. "He was just a kid and his life had been nothing but misery, yet all I could think of was my pain."

Again, the altar boy picture of Michael popped to mind and Brian reached a long overdue decision. He too had been punishing Michael for far too long. Over the course of the holiday, he was going to apologize and say the overdue words Michael had a right to hear, words like father and love.

Jean's voice drew him back. "My parents wanted me to give you up for adoption. My brother suggested an abortion. I decided those choices weren't something I could live with." She looked at him directly. "The first time I held you, all I saw was the result of my need for a sixteen-year-old boy. I wanted to run as far away as I could, but something wouldn't let me completely leave you."

Jean paused again, took another sip of her coffee and cleared her throat. "It didn't take long before it became apparent you had his face, and, oh God, those damned eyes. Brian, every time I looked at you, all I saw was Michael staring back..."

"So, that's it? You hate me because I look like him?" He hadn't attempted to keep the edge out of his voice and she flinched.

"I never hated you Brian. It was only my self-pity talking. Nobody ever loved poor little Jean." She sighed dramatically. "And when he came looking for you, I ran to punish him, but in the end I hurt you the most."

"What do you mean when he came looking for me?"

She blinked a few times as if confused. "I thought you knew..."

"Knew what, Mom?"

"Michael hired a detective to find us and had an agreement with Max..."

Brian's spirits fell, this was old news. "Max told me about their agreement."

"I bet you didn't know that when Max showed up on our doorstep he had no intention of telling Michael he found us, did you?"

"When did Max ever show up?"

"In Cleveland, you were twelve."

"I never saw him in Cleveland."

"That's because Max and I went on a bender together that lasted almost two weeks. I guess you don't remember my being gone for all that time."

He certainly remembered more than one extended period without her, but let that point go for now. "How do you know he had no intention of telling Mike?"

"All Max wanted was for us to get back together."

"Us, as in you and him?"

"I was always able to manipulate Max," she admitted softly. "I knew how to derail any plans he had for taking you away."

She sighed and took a sip of her coffee. "Max was always jealous of my feelings for Michael and wanted to hurt him as much as I did. Following our little tryst, Max had to get back to Brooklyn and after I promised to join him there, he swore he would never tell Michael he found you."

"Mike is actually a pretty nice guy, Mom. I think you two gave him a pretty raw deal."

She nodded shortly. "I've done many things I'm ashamed of, a few include him."

"But why hold on all these years? Why not let your feelings for him go."

She crushed her cigarette in the ashtray. "Michael haunted me because I needed the excuse."

"And now?"

She smiled, but her eyes filled with tears. "I'm just here to tell you how proud I am of you. I'm amazed at your strength. Life's been so cruel, but you keep right on putting one foot in front of the other."

He shrugged. "I never had a choice. If I hadn't kept moving life would have rolled right over me a long time ago."

"I asked you to meet me today because I wanted to look you in the eye and tell you how sorry I am for all the years I hurt you."

He raised his eyes, meeting her direct gaze for a moment before dropping his focus back to the table.

"Harlan always told me you had a generous, forgiving heart. He encouraged me to talk to you, but I was so afraid."

Brian shook his head. Harlan was the one with the forgiving heart, not him. He had used all his generosity up years ago. She was too late.

"Afraid of what, Mom? What did you have to lose?"

"I was afraid of your anger, of being rejected. Now, I realize I have to make amends, at least attempt them. I owe you that much. If you choose to never forgive me, well, I'll have to learn to live with that decision."

Suddenly, remembering the time, Brian glanced at his watch. He had to collect the boys from Amelia's and get to Philadelphia to meet Michael.

Jean visibly bristled. "Am I keeping you?"

"I have to pick up the boys and catch a plane in Philly by five-thirty."

"I guess you don't have much time to spare then do you?"

"No."

"Maybe you should go. With this rain and all, you'll have to drive slower."

"Mom," he began then sighed at length. "I understand about mistakes, I've certainly made my share, but the truth is I don't want to examine all that again. You did it. I lived through it. Now, it's just the past. I want to leave it there."

"What about me? Do you want to leave me there too?"

He thought about that for a minute. It wasn't his nature to be cruel, but she was asking so much.

He sighed loudly. "You have to give me more time. One afternoon of apologies just doesn't seem adequate."

She laughed shortly, "You're tough."

He looked her in the eye. "It's an acquired trait."

She sat back suddenly as if he had slapped her. The tears in her eyes tapped further into his anger. Jean pushed her chair back and started to get to her feet, but he stopped her with a cold look.

"You owe me some patience," he said.

"Why Brian? It's obvious I waited too long. I've made my apology, if you don't want to accept it that's your right, but I won't grovel."

"I'm not asking you to grovel. I'm glad you apologized. I hope you meant it."

Her eyes narrowed in anger. Finally, she looked more like the mother he remembered.

"Are you testing me?"

It was time to go before this escalated further. Brian stood and held a large envelope out to her. "Those are pictures of my sons. I forgot to give them to Harlan this morning."

Jean took the envelope, but her eyes never left his face. For the first time, Brian noticed the haunted look no longer existed. She finally saw him.

"You don't have his eyes anymore," she whispered.

He sighed loudly, turning for his coat. "I've got to go."

"Let me finish. Please?"

Summoning patience she didn't deserve, Brian turned back. Jean was moving toward him and he tensed.

"I never meant the color, you know. It was the need, the pain, and the condemnation. He couldn't stop expressing it with his eyes and neither can you. That's what I meant. I saw everything I did that was wrong right there in your big blue eyes and it tortured me. "

He was sick of her self-serving dialogue, "And now?"

"Now, I see a man. I see your gentleness and capacity for love. You're so strong." She reached up and touched his face.

The simple act left him teary-eyed and confused. He was beyond this. He was too old to care. The gentle touch sliced through scars an inch thick and hit him where he was most vulnerable. He still wanted her to love him.

Jean smiled and looked down at the envelope. "May I look at these?"

"Of course," he managed.

Jean opened the envelope with a shaky hand and pulled out a studio shot of all three boys. She slipped on a pair of half-glasses and smiled broadly. "I expected Jesse's hair to turn dark like Mike and Max's. I see it's still blond."

"He looks like you," Brian admitted softly.

Jean looked at him, over the top of her glasses, and smiled. "Now that's irony."

"Yeah," Brian laughed and some of the tension in his chest loosened and he breathed easier.

Suddenly, without warning, she embraced him. Brian nearly jumped back in surprise.

"I love you," she said, holding on.

Before he could react, she broke the embrace and hurried toward the door. Brian tossed money on the table and followed her. He caught her just outside the door and pulled on her coat sleeve.

"Mom, please wait."

Jean turned but did not look up and Brian knew she was crying. He wrapped his arms around her, proving Harlan right after all.

chapter 34

BRIAN TOOK THE seat next to Michael in the cockpit while the co-pilot watched a movie in back with the kids.

"I saw my mother today," Brian said casually.

Michael tossed him a questioning look, but said nothing.

"She apologized," Brian said, watching Michael carefully. "She even told me she loved me."

"Is she still drinking?"

"I don't think so. She looked better than I've seen her in years."

"Be careful," Michael said tightly.

Brian grinned broadly. "Are you giving me unsolicited advice?"

Michael's face relaxed into a little smile and Brian felt this was a good time to begin making some amends of his own. He looked out his window and dropped the first bomb. "I'm glad you haven't given up trying to parent me."

Michael laughed. "You haven't made it easy. I feel like I'm reinventing the wheel every time I see you."

"That must be exhausting."

Michael patted his shoulder. "Not when there's light at the end of the tunnel."

It was late when they reached the ranch and Michael took them directly to Brian's house. After putting the boys to bed, Brian slipped on a T-shirt and shorts then worked out for an hour. He was walking past the music room just after midnight when a sound from the dark room caught his attention. He started to turn just as a blast of pain shot through the back of his head.

His face bounced off the floor, waking him. Hands gripped his ankles, dragging him face down across the wooden floor of the music room. He twisted to the right and discovered his hands were bound at the wrists. He felt the blackness descending again and desperately tried to cling to consciousness, but lost.

A strong smell woke him and ammonia burned his nose. He opened his eyes to a blinding headache. He was seated on the floor and his wrists were now secured above his head to one of the empty brackets for a guitar.

Amanda stood over him wielding a shiny, four-inch switchblade and a wide, crazy grin.

"Welcome back." She sat down on his outstretched legs and planted a kiss on his mouth, "Ready to party?"

"Amanda..." he began weakly.

"Shh, you don't get to talk, until I let you. Be a good boy, Brian. Don't make me hurt you more than I have to."

She placed the cold blade of the knife against his inner thigh and slowly moved it upward. The razor edge sliced through the cotton shorts with a quick zip, leaving a cut that began to trickle blood. Amanda pulled the shorts away, leaving his lower body naked and started on his T-shirt.

"You have such a great body. I'm glad you take the time to stay in shape. You even sweat sexy."

Brian trembled violently and Amanda laughed and kissed his lips again.

"I don't make you nervous, do I?"

Amanda continued talking as she cut his shirt and the knife nicked his skin repeatedly. However, the pain in his head was so intense he couldn't think about such minor irritations.

"You better not make a sound, Brian. I don't want you to wake those brats of yours. I don't want them interfering. They might get hurt and it's not time for that yet."

"Please Amanda, don't hurt the boys. I'll do anything you want."

She made a tight fist and punched him between the eyes. "It's too late to bargain! All you had to do was give me just a little of your time. You're always too busy for me though. Now, you're mine and there will be no bargaining. Do you hear me, Brian?"

She placed the tip of the knife at the end of his nose. "I'm going to get your babies in here and I'm going to blow their brains out one by one. You get to watch. So, the longer you maintain some self-control and let me play, the longer your kiddies get to live. Got it?"

She held the knife as if it was a pencil and carved an "A" into the muscle of his forearm. Blood ran down, over his elbow, dripping to the floor. Brian gritted his teeth, determined not to make a sound.

"You're a fast learner. Aren't you? Guess you don't want to jeopardize those little bastards so soon."

She removed the last of his shirt and imbedded the knife in the wooden floor beside his leg before pulling a gun from the waistband of her jeans. She ran the cold barrel of the gun up his thigh and pushed it into his stomach.

"Before I gag you, I want you to sing for me, Brian. Tell me with your million dollar voice how much you love me."

Perspiration rolled down the side of his face, into his eyes, stinging them.

"Sammy says you sing best under pressure." She slid the gun down, between his legs and smiled. "How's this?"

She leaned forward pressing her mouth on his while she slid the gun up his abdomen and over his chest. She put her tongue in his mouth and the barrel of the gun under his chin then cocked it. Pulling back slightly, only inches from his face, she smiled broadly.

"You're shaking, Brian. Are you excited? Does S & M turn you on? "

Mike's silhouette appeared in the doorway, "Daddy?"

Amanda stood quickly and raised her arm and Brian realized she intended to shoot.

"Run, Mike!" he screamed. He kicked her leg up and knocked her off balance as she pulled the trigger.

Mike turned toward the hallway, but the loud pop of the gun startled him and he tripped. The face-first slide brought him eye level with a bloody baseball bat. Brian felt a small thud in his side and the world turned black.

chapter 35

"DAMN IT, WAKE up!"

Amanda shook him roughly and Brian opened his eyes. Remembering where he was, he panicked and looked around the room for Mike. The bat was still lying there, but Mike was nowhere in sight.

"Looking for your nimble prodigy? Don't worry, he got away, for now. I'll find him when the time is right."

While he was out, she had stuffed a gag in his mouth and tied it tightly around the back of his head. His right side hurt so badly he figured she must have stabbed him. The darkness pulled at him, enticing him back to the peace of unconsciousness.

"I really didn't think it would come to this," Amanda said. "After all, I'm not a violent person. If you'd just stop these stupid little games, you know I hate playing games."

Amanda was a blur in front of him, pacing back and forth, gesturing at him with a gun. She paused to light a cigarette and squatted down, blowing smoke in his face.

"You tell me with your music that you want me to come to you. When I do, you act like we're strangers. It hurts me Brian and frankly it's time you learned that if I can't have you no one will."

She straddled his legs and ran the barrel of the gun up one of his bare arms. "Maybe I'll just blow off some of your precious fingers. Or, maybe I'll cut your tongue out and wear it around my neck on a chain." She paused, laughing at the thought. "That would put an end to your lovely career, wouldn't it?"

She slid the gun down his neck, over his chest, then down his stomach to his crotch again. "This is such a turn on. I think maybe I'll see how you respond to a little stimulation."

She took a long drag on her cigarette then rolled the fire up his neck. Brian groaned weakly, not so much from the burn, but her knee was pressing into his torso. The pain was staggering.

"Be quiet!" Amanda slapped him. "Do you want me to shoot you? Are you really that stupid?"

Her mood shifted quickly. She smiled and cocked the gun again. "Let's play a game. I'll just put this here." She pressed the gun barrel into Brian's abdomen. Leaning forward, she sank her teeth into the flesh of his upper chest until she drew blood. Brian put his head back and inhaled through his nose, determined to remain silent as long as possible.

Pleased, Amanda sat back. "There. You see? You can do it. Let's just see what else I can find to nibble on."

She bit him three more times, but when she bit into his inner thigh Brian couldn't take any more. He screamed into the gag and she raised the knife for a new lesson. "You haven't heard a damned word I've said to you Brian. I'm afraid you're going to have to forfeit a body part this time."

"Put the knife down, Amanda," Michael said, stepping in from the hallway with a flashlight pointed at them.

Amanda swung toward his voice dragging the knife across the muscle of Brian's upper thigh. "Don't come near us."

Michael moved closer. "Get on your feet and back away."

Amanda dropped the knife and picked up the gun. Michael moved even closer until he saw she pointed the barrel of the gun at Brian's heart.

"I'm not leaving without him."

"Yes, you are," Sam said from the doorway.

Brian's vision was hazy and double images floated in front of his eyes, but it appeared Sam was aiming a rifle at Amanda's back.

She smiled at Sam. "You won't shoot me old man. If you do, it will go through to him."

"I'll put a bullet in your crazy head if you don't get away right now."

Amanda rose and swung around pointing the gun at Sam. Michael rushed forward and grabbed at her arm, but just caught her sleeve. Amanda staggered out of her heavy coat and dropped the gun before dashing for the door at the back of the room.

Michael immediately knelt beside Brian. He untied the gag and pulled the wadded material from Brian's mouth. He removed his own coat and placed it over Brian's lower body then took off his shirt and used it to wipe the blood running into Brian's left eye. He raised the flashlight and gasped at the bloody mess.

Sam crept to the back door, locked it then hurried to turn on the lights and took out his pocket knife and cut the bonds on Brian's wrists.

Michael carefully lowered Brian's cold arms and rubbed them. Brian was still perspiring yet trembled violently as if he was freezing. Sam removed his parka and covered Brian's bloody upper body carefully. Seeing a flash of light outside, Sam walked over to the windows and peered out at the night.

"The police are here," he said. "I'll go tell them she's out there somewhere then I better call Red, she may be headed towards his place."

Michael glanced up from his position near Brian, "Did they bring an ambulance?"

"Yes," Sam said and hurried toward the door. Michael turned back to Brian.

"Are the boys all right?" Brian asked weakly.

"They're safe with Beth."

"Thank you." Brian closed his eyes. "My side is on fire."

Michael pulled back Sam's parka and gasped. "My God," he murmured. He ran to the doorway and called down the hall to Sam. "Tell them he was shot!"

chapter 36

MICHAEL'S QUIET VOICE infiltrated the drugged sleep. Brian opened his eyes and Michael leaned over the hospital bed, smiling tiredly.

"Good afternoon."

Brian didn't speak. He closed then reopened his eyes slowly, trying to focus his vision and his mind. He had no idea where he was. Suddenly, the image of Mike standing in a doorway and the sound of a gunshot rolled over him and some machine began beeping loudly.

"Is Mike okay?" he asked hoarsely.

"He's fine."

"Good." Brian squinted around at the machines connected to his body. "What's the heart monitor for?"

"You went into renal failure in the helicopter and your heart stopped."

His brain was still foggy from the drugs, but he made himself focus, "Renal failure?"

"Amanda shot you, Brian. You lost a lot of blood. They had to remove your right kidney."

During surgery, an inhalation tube had been inserted into his windpipe, leaving his throat raw and speaking was difficult, but he had to know if Amanda was still lurking around the corner.

"Did they catch her?"

"Red found her about a mile from your house about the time they were taking you away in the helicopter. He tried to convince her to come with him and give herself up, but she went berserk and jumped in Miller's ravine. This morning they spotted her lying in a crevice and right now they're organizing a party to go down and bring her body out."

He stared at Michael, trying to absorb all that had happened. "I don't remember much."

Michael smiled sadly. "That's okay. Go back to sleep. We'll talk later."

Stacy kissed his forehead gently, as if he was fragile and woke him later. He tried to smile, but it didn't quite work.

"We've all been so scared," Stacy said, her eyes tearing.

"You should try it from this end," he joked weakly.

"Brian, the boys need to see you, especially Mike."

"No, I don't want them to see me like this. Make them be patient, at least until they remove some of this hardware."

"They're scared Brian, especially Mike. He saw the gun. He heard her shoot you. They cried for you so hard Nellie and Sam brought them here."

"Damn it." He sighed heavily, closing his eyes.

"Let me bring them in. Talk for just a minute. It would help them so much. Please?"

In order to accommodate the various machines attached to his body the hospital bed was in its highest position. Mike and Max shared a step stool in order to see him. Stacy put Jesse on a chair and stood behind him with a hand on his little shoulder. Max calmly took in the tubes, wires, and machines. Jesse looked from Brian to his brothers to check their reaction. His lower lip quivered and he was on the verge of tears when he looked up to Stacy for reassurance. Mike reached out and touched Brian's shoulder.

"Does it hurt, Daddy?"

Even with the pain medication drip, every inch of his body hurt so much he wanted to scream. "No, not much," he said.

"When are you coming home?" Max asked, finally looking at Brian's battered face. Brian saw he was just as frightened as his brothers, but Max was always the most pragmatic.

"Soon I hope."

Brian talked to them for five minutes, making every effort to alleviate their fears. He told them how proud he was of their courage and lay back exhausted as Stacy led them away.

Sammy leaned over the rail, gently pushing the errant lock of hair from his forehead and waking him. She forced a smile.

"So, give me the scoop, are you gonna make it?"

"I'm trying, Sammy."

"Are you in a lot of pain?"

"It comes and goes."

"Come on tell me, I'll be discrete."

"I've fallen for that line before." He laughed a little then gasped as a pain shot from his lower abdomen and up his spine.

"Oh, Brian," Sammy was immediately in tears. She bent over and kissed his forehead. "I love you so much. Please, please be strong. You've got to get through this. I can't make it without you."

Tara arrived that afternoon. While she and Sammy quietly talked in the corner, Nick walked in. He approached Brian's bed cautiously. His disheveled appearance was nearly as alarming as Michael's was.

"I came as soon as I heard, Brian. I'm so sorry."

Brian didn't speak. His throat hurt too much and the drugs made him sleepy.

Nick glanced at the machines and Sammy. "How's he doing?"

"He's developed a pretty serious infection, probably from all the bites."

"If I'd just put it all together none of this would have happened," Nick said, running a hand through his wild hair. "I knew there was something weird about her."

"Are you saying you knew Amanda?"

"She told me her name was Pam," he said weakly.

"Pam!" Sammy exclaimed, "The sex goddess of your dreams?"

Nick nodded miserably and focused on Brian. "She got the phone numbers and addresses from my organizer. I caught her snooping once, but she made a joke about looking for the phone numbers of my other girlfriends. I didn't have a reason not to believe her. She used to ask me questions about Brian, but I didn't pay much attention. People are always asking me about him."

"This isn't your fault," Brian interjected quietly.

"I saw the story on the news and when they showed her picture I felt like dying. Thank God, she didn't hurt the boys."

That evening, his temperature spiked to 102 and the next day was a blur. He woke a few times, but was either hallucinating or suffering to the point it drained all his energy.

He talked to Jo, as if she was in the room, and asked about the boys repeatedly. When Stacy stood next to his bed he pleaded with her not to cry and promised to get another hat for the snowman. He begged Michael to make them do something about the pain.

In a brief moment of coherency, he refused pain medication and asked to see Michael and Beth separately. He didn't want to speak of the fear eating at him, but realized there was a chance he might not walk out of the hospital.

Michael approached his bed and Brian saw his exhaustion. Beth told him earlier that Michael hadn't left the hospital except to shower and change clothes. He slept just down the hall in the waiting room.

Those eloquent eyes conveyed a father's love and sorrow without restraint. A flood of emotion for this man overwhelmed Brian. For a moment, he was incapable of speaking.

After thanking God for this moment of lucidity, he plunged ahead. "I wanted to tell you how much you mean to me." He began carefully. "Michael, you're the father I always wanted. I never told you because it was so hard for me to let go of the anger."

Michael touched the fingertips of Brian's hand and just listened, the way he always did.

"I've known for quite a while that I loved you, but the words always got stuck in my throat. I'm sorry. I wish I could have made that first step. I cheated us both."

Tears glistened in his father's eyes, seeing them, Brian's chest constricted in pain. He forced himself to finish.

"Thanks for not giving up on me. I want you to know I love you."

Michael leaned over and kissed Brian's hot forehead then touched his cheek gently. "I wasn't sure you'd ever forgive me."

The spot on his forehead where Michael bestowed that soothing touch seemed to be the only place in his body that didn't wish to torture him. Brian closed his eyes to keep tears from slipping out. "This hurts so much, Dad. I don't know how much more I can stand."

Michael turned to leave. "I'll tell them you need that pain medication now."

"No," Brian managed. "I have to talk to Beth."

Beth entered the darkened hospital room and touched his hand lightly. He opened his eyes, slowly focused on her, and Beth smiled at him.

"You summoned me?" she said, putting her hand on his forehead.

"I need a favor."

"Anything."

"If I don't make it through this would you guys please take the boys? Don't let anyone else raise them. I put all this in my will, but I want you to move quickly."

"Of course."

"And Stacy needs a family. Don't let her run away."

"Baby, you don't have to ask for these things. Your father and I'll always do what we can for you."

Brian shifted his weight carefully. Still, pain shot up his back. He clenched his teeth against the agony and his breathing became rapid.

Beth squeezed his hand and looked away. "When was the last time you had something for the pain?"

"I wanted to be clear headed when I talked to you and Dad."

Beth took a moment to digest hearing him say the word for the first time. "Your father believes you just told him good-bye. Convince me you're not giving in to this thing. I want to go out there and tell him he's wrong."

Brian shook his head in response and allowed his heavy eyelids to close. He needed to escape the prison of pain his body had become. Darkness beckoned and the pull was powerful.

"Listen to me, Brian," Beth cried urgently. "You can't give up. Think of your boys."

Brian squeezed her hand weakly. "I'm ready for the Demerol now."

Someone called his name. The bare room was cold and he didn't want to get out of the warm bed. Still, the voice was insistent. He pushed the covers away and put his feet on the floor. Glaring light poured in through the dirty windows and the voice called from that direction. Looking out and down, he saw Stacy standing knee deep in snow. She was a child again. She smiled and held up a red cap.

"Look what Daddy gave me."

Her father stood next to her, working on the ear of a snowman. He smiled at Brian and waved, indicating Brian should join them.

Brian reached for the doorknob and his hand seemed very small. He looked down at his body and realized he too was a child again. He started downstairs, but the door to the apartment across the hall was open, so he paused to look inside. The television was on and Stacy's father was there, just like old times.

Then he was outside and snow chilled his bare feet. Brian carefully stepped around the red stains. Stacy was no longer a child and much taller than him. She placed the red hat on his head, pulling it down over his ears.

Brian reached out and touched one ear of the snowman. The smooth, icy curve immediately melted at his touch.

"Come closer to the fire," a voice whispered.

He swung around and faced Jo. He started to explain about Stacy before Jo got jealous, but she took his hand and the heat of her touch distracted him.

The fire she spoke of came from their house in Pennsylvania. The heat was intense and he stepped back in fear, but Jo gripped his hand firmly, pulling him toward the flames.

"You need the warmth, Brian."

Someone pulled him into their arms and the embrace was so comforting Brian started to cry.

"Mama's here," Jean said.

He jumped back in surprise.

His mother smiled at him and stroked his cheek affectionately. "I hear you're letting this one roll over you. You have to keep putting one foot in front of the other, son. I thought you knew that."

"I can't. I'm too tired. The pain never stops, Mom."

"Nonsense, use your anger."

"I'm not angry anymore."

"You're abandoning your sons," Jo said, standing to his right.

"I don't want to leave them," he cried.

"Fight, Brian," Jo said, turning away, walking into the flames.

"Jo don't go in there!"

He struggled out of his mother's arms and ran into the inferno. Sammy appeared out of nowhere and shoved him hard.

"Go back," she said. "There's nothing here except heartache and ashes."

Brian turned, but didn't know the way back. He was so hot and the pain was worse than ever.

Michael's voice called his name. The sound floated down from above. Brian looked up through the flames but all he could see were his father's blue eyes, floating like an oasis in the red heat.

"Help me," Brian said.

"All you had to do was ask."

Strong, loving hands reached through the fire, lifting him above the flames, up and up, until it was cool and safe. The refuge looked like the long deck adjacent to Brian's music room in Wyoming yet there was no house.

A very young Michael smiled at him. He didn't appear to be much older than he was in that sad picture on his parent's mantel. He patted Brian on the back.

"Your mother's wrong. You're never alone."

"I think Amelia said that."

Michael turned quickly, "Listen!"

Music moved through the long canyon toward them until it rolled over them like the waves of a lazy sea. Michael smiled, closed his eyes and threw open his arms.

Brian listened carefully. The song sounded familiar, but he couldn't place it. "What's this song?"

The young Michael looked at him and grinned as if it were a silly question. "That's the song of the snowman."

"Snowmen can't sing," Brian informed him gently.

Michael rolled his eyes. "I guess they don't have ears either."

Brian laughed and Michael joined him. Together, they opened their arms, welcoming the lazy waves of music and sang in perfect harmony as the sun peeked over the Tetons.

"Brian?"

Someone's cool hand touched his forehead and he realized he had been dreaming. He opened his eyes and immediately saw Stacy. It was her hand on his forehead. Beth and Michael stood at the end of the bed.

Stacy smiled and her eyes twinkled, "Merry Christmas."

"It's Christmas?"

Beth walked up on the other side of the bed and kissed his cheek. "Yeah, Rip Van Winkle, you've been out for two days. By the way, what was so funny?"

"Funny?"

Beth grinned. "You were laughing in your sleep."

Brian looked back to Stacy. Right now, only she would understand. "I just heard the song of the snowman."

Stacy's eyes filled with tears.

The reaction stung Brian. "I thought it would make you happy."

"It's not that," she sobbed. "I've missed you so much."

"Well," he grinned, "I'm back."

Beth leaned over the side of the bed and put her lips close to his ear, so only he would hear what she had to say.

"Thank you."

Brian looked beyond the women to Michael. The memory of strong hands pulling him from the confusion and pain was still fresh. The image of Michael as a boy, standing with his arms outstretched, embracing joy, was a lesson forever imprinted on his heart. Brian understood the man much better now.

Michael smiled slowly and those special eyes filled with a new kind of light. The light told Brian all he needed to know. There was no need for words. They were in harmony.